THE LIAR'S DICTIONARY

Also by Eley Williams

Attrib. and Other Stories

THE LIAR'S DICTIONARY

Eley Williams

WILLIAM HEINEMANN: LONDON

1 3 5 7 9 10 8 6 4 2

William Heinemann
20 Vauxhall Bridge Road
London SW1V 2SA

William Heinemann is part of the Penguin Random House group of companies
whose addresses can be found at global.penguinrandomhouse.com.

Penguin
Random House
UK

First published in Great Britain by William Heinemann in 2020

www.penguin.co.uk

A CIP catalogue record for this book is available from the British Library.

ISBN 9781785152047

Typeset in 11/16pt Bembo Std by Jouve (UK), Milton Keynes
Printed and bound in Great Britain by Clays Ltd, Elcograf S.p.A.

Penguin Random House is committed to a
sustainable future for our business, our readers
and our planet. This book is made from Forest
Stewardship Council® certified paper.

for Nell, too marvellous for words

novel (n.), a small tale, generally of love

from Samuel Johnson's *Dictionary of the*
English Language (1755)

jungftak (n.), a Persian bird, the male of which had only one wing, on the right side, and the female only one wing, on the left side; instead of the missing wings, the male had a hook of bone, and the female an eyelet of bone, and it was by uniting hook and eye that they were enabled to fly – each, when alone, had to remain on the ground

from *Webster's Twentieth Century Dictionary*
of the English Language (1943)

Preface

Let us imagine you possess a perfect personal dictionary. A, the, whatever. Not a *not-imperfect* dictionary but the best dictionary that could ever exist for you.

Let's specify: this should be printed rather than digital. Dictionaries as practical objects. You could hold a volume of it out of someone else's reach, wave it around or use it to chivvy a wayward moth out of a kitchen. As I say, dictionaries as practical. It might have a meaningful heft in the hand with lightly scuffed corners: trustworthy enough to be consulted and not too hot to handle. It would have a silk bookmark perhaps, and page numbers, so that it's not jealous of other fancy books on the shelf. The perfect preface would know why dictionaries have page numbers. The dictionary's title would be stamped in gold across the spine. Its paper would have a pleasing creaminess and weight, with a typeface implying elegance, an undeniably suave firmness or firm suaveness. A typeface that would be played by Jeremy Brett or Romaine Brooks – a typeface with cheekbones. Leather covers come to mind if one imagines a perfect dictionary, and if you were to flick your perfect dictionary's cover with a thumbnail it would make a satisfying *fnuck-fnuck* sound.

I admit that I have a less-than-great attention span so my

perfect personal dictionary would be concise and only contain words that either I don't yet know or ones that I frequently forget. My concise, infinite-as-ignorance dictionary would be something of a paradox and possibly printed on a Möbius strip. My impossible perfect dictionary.

Let us dip into a preface and push it open with our thumbs as if we are splitting some kind of ripe fruit. (Opening a book is never anything like that though really, is it, and this simile is a bad one.) My *perfect* dictionary would open at a particular page because of the silk bookmark already lodged there.

Two thousand five hundred silkworms are required to produce a pound of raw silk.

What is the first word one reads at random on this page?

[I have been sidetracked. Some words have a talent for will-o'-the-wispishly leading you from a path that you had set for yourself, deeper and deeper into the parentheses and footnotes, the beckoning SEE ALSO suggestions.]

Exactly how many dictionary covers could one make by peeling a single cow?

Who reads the prefaces to dictionaries, anyway?

fnuck-fnuck-fnuck

To consider a dictionary to be 'perfect' requires a reflection upon the aims of such a book. *Book* is a shorthand here.

The perfect dictionary should not be playful for its own sake, for fear of alienating the reader and undermining its usefulness.

That a perfect dictionary should be *right* is obvious. It should contain neither spelling nor printing errors, for example, and should not make groundless claims. It should not display any bias in its definitions except those made as the result of meticulous and rigorous research. But already this is far too theoretical – we can be more basic than that: it is crucial that the book covers open, at least, and that the ink is legible upon its pages. Whether a dictionary should *register* or *fix* the language is often toted as a qualifier. *Register*, as if words are like so many delinquent children herded together and counted in a room; *fixed*, as if only a certain number of children are allowed access to the room, and then the room is filled with cement.

The perfect preface should not require so many mixed metaphors.

The preface of a dictionary, often overlooked as one pushes one's thumbs into the fruit filled with silkworms and slaughtered cows, sets out the aims of the dictionary and its scope. It is often overlooked because by the time a dictionary is in use its need is obvious.

A dictionary's preface can act like an introduction to someone you have no interest in meeting. The preface is an introduction to the *work*, not the people. You do not need to know the gender of the lexicographers who worked away at it. Certainly not their appearance, their favourite sports team nor favoured newspaper, for example. On the day they defined *crinkling* (n.) as a dialect word for a small type of apple, the fact that their shoes were too tight should be of absolutely no matter to you.

That they were hungover and had the beginnings of a cold when they defined this word will not matter, nor that unbeknownst to them an infected hair follicle under their chin caused by ungainly and too-hasty shaving is poised to cause severe medical repercussions for them two months down the line, at one point causing them to fear that they are going to lose their whole lower jaw. You do not need to know that they dreamed of giving it all up and going to live in a remote cottage on the Cornish coast. The only useful thing a preface can say about its lexicographers is that they are qualified to wax unlyrically about what a certain type of silly small apple is called, for example.

The perfect dictionary *reader* is perhaps a more interesting subject for a dictionary's preface. One generally *consults* a dictionary, as opposed to resting it upon lecterned knees and reading it cover to cover. This is not always the case, and there are those who make it their business to read full, huge works of reference purely in order that they can say that the feat has been achieved. If one rummages through the bletted fruit of history or an encyclopaedic biographic dictionary of dictionary readers, one might discover such a person, Fath-Ali Shah Qajar, and a short biography dedicated to the same. Upon becoming the [SEE ALSO:—] Shah of Persia in 1797, Fath-Ali Shah Qajar was gifted a third edition of one very famous encyclopaedia. After reading all of its eighteen volumes, the Shah extended his royal title to include 'Most Formidable Lord and Master of the *Encyclopædia Britannica*'. What a preface! A small picture of the Shah accompanying an article about his life might be a steel-plate engraving and show him seated, wearing silk robes with fruit piled high next to him. There is a war-elephant in the background of the portrait. So much fruit, so many silkworms, so much implied offstage trumpeting.

If you put your eyes far too close to an engraving all is little dots and dashes, like a fingerprint unspooled.

Perhaps you have encountered someone who browses a dictionary not as a reader but as a grazing animal, and spends hours nose-deep in the grass and forbs of its pages, buried in its meadow while losing sight of the sun. I recommend it. Browsing is good for you. You can grow giddy with the words' shapes and sounds, their *corymbs*, their *umbels* and their *panicles*. These readers are unearthers, thrilled with their gleaning. The high of surprise at discovering a new word's delicacy or the strength of its roots is a pretty potent one. Let's find some now. (Prefaces to dictionaries as faintly patronising in tone.) For example, maybe you know these ones already: *psithurism* means the rustling of leaves; part of a bee's thigh is called a *corbicula*, from the Latin word for basket.

For some, of course, the thrill of browsing a dictionary comes from the fact that arcane or obscure words are discovered and can be brought back, cud-like, and used expressly to impress others in conversation. I admit that I shook out *psithurism* from the understory of the dictionary there to delight you, but the gesture might be seen as calculated. Get me and my big words; *phwoar*, hear me roar, obliquely, in the forest; let me tell you about the silent *p* that you doubtless missed, etc., etc., and that *psithurism* is likely to come via the Greek ψίθυρος, whispering, slanderous. *How fascinating!* says this type of dictionary-reader. *I am fascinating because I know the meaning of this word.* When used like this, the dictionary becomes fodder for a reader, verbage-verdage. We all know one of these people, whose conversation is no more than expectorate word-dropping. This reader will disturb your nap in the café window just to comment upon the day's *anemotropism*. He will admit to *leucocholy* just in order to use the word in his apology as you drop your napkin and reel back, pushing your chair away. He will pursue you through hedgerows just to alert you to the *smeuse* of your flight.

Of course, this dictionary reader also celebrates the beauty of a word, its lustre and power, but for him the value of its sillage is turned to silage.

He would use *crinkling* as a noun correctly, with a flourish. (Preface as over explanation, as metabombast.)

There is no perfect reader of a dictionary.

The perfect dictionary would know the difference between, say, a 'prologue' and a 'preface'. Dictionary as: *so, what happens?*

Dictionary as about clarity but also honesty.

If one *is* wont to index these things, another category of reader, submits to the digressiveness of a dictionary, whereby an eyeline is cast from word to word in sweeping jags within from page to page. No regard for the formalities of left-to-right reading, theirs is a reading style that loops and chicanes across columns and pages, and reading is something led by curiosity, or snagged by serendipity.

Should a preface pose more questions than it answers? Should a preface just pose?

A dictionary as an unreliable narrator.

But haven't we all had private moments of pleasure when reading a dictionary? Just dipping, *come on in, the water's lovely* type of pleasure, submerging only if something takes hold of your toe and will not unbite. Private pleasures not to be displayed in public by café windows.

A sense of pleasure or satisfaction with a dictionary is possible. It might arise when finding confirmation of a word's guessed spelling (i.e. *i* before *e*), or upon retrieving from it a word that had momentarily come loose from the tip of your tongue. The pleasure of *reading* rather than *using* a dictionary might come when amongst its pages you find a word that is new to you and neatly sums up a sensation, quality or experience that had hitherto gone nameless: a moment of solidarity and recognition – *someone else must have had the same sensation as me – I am not alone!* Pleasure may come with the sheer glee at the textures of an unfamiliar word, its new taste between your teeth. *Glume. Forb.* The anatomy of a word strimmed clean or porched in your teeth.

★

In some even quite modern dictionaries, if you look up the word *giraffe* it ends its entry with [SEE: *cameleopard*]. If you look up *cameleopard* it says [SEE: *giraffe*]. This is the dictionary's ecosystem.

From childhood we're taught that a dictionary begins, roughly, with an *aardvark* and ends, roughly, with a *zebra* and the rest is a rough game of lexical tug-of-war between the two, *cameleopards* and *giraffes* playing umpire.

I think the perfect dictionary would not be written in the first person because it should make objective claims. It probably should not refer to a second-person 'you' because this might feel like bullying. A preface should be sure of itself. Dictionaries as tied to longing, tied to trust, tied to jouissance and surrender – but all this seems a little too fruity and affected. Better, surely, that both lexicographer and user should be unseen or unregarded. More overlookable than a well-known word that does not need defining.

The perfect preface would know when to shut—

Dictionaries as unsafe, heady things. It is safer in many ways to treat your memory as an encyclopaedia, and keep your dictionary mobile in your mouth. Words passing from mouth to mouth, as baby birds take food from the mother.

How many similes can you fit in a preface? How garbled can a preface be? The perfect book should grab the reader and the perfect dictionary should be easily grasped.

The green leather of a perfect dictionary might have lines that look just like the back of your hand. If you were to dig your nails into its surface the crescent shapes would remain. Don't tell me why anyone might ever be gripping a dictionary quite so hard.

This book is queasy with knowledge. To name a thing is to know a thing. There's power there. *Can you Adam and Eve it?* Words are snappable and constantly distending and roiling, silkworms trapped somewhere between the molars. Dictionaries as the Ur-mixed metaphor.

A preface as all talk and no trousers.

The perfect dictionary is the fruit of the labour of silkworms and cattle spinning yarns. Words as cud. Each definition as eulogy, each account an informed hunch.

The perfect dictionary has the right words and the worst words in the right order. In the perfect dictionary, it is all correct and true. Incorrect definitions are as pointless as an unclear simile, as useless as a garbled preface or an imprecise narrator.

There is no such thing as the perfect dictionary.

Not every word is beautiful or remarkable, and neither is its every user or creator.

Finding the right word can be a private joy.

A preface can be shorthand for *take my word for it*.

A preface can be shorthand for *look it up*.

'Look it up.'

'Look up from it.'

look up

A is for *artful* (adj.)

David spoke at me for three minutes without realising I had a whole egg in my mouth.

I had adopted my usual stance to eat my lunch – hunched over in the stationa/ery cupboard between the printer cartridges and stacked columns of parcel tape. Noon. It can be a fine thing to snuffle your lunch and often the highlight of a working day. Many's the time I've stood in Swansby House's cupboard beneath its skylight lapping soup straight from the carton or chase-licking individual grains of leftover rice from a stained piece of Tupperware. This kind of lunch will taste all the better when eaten unobserved.

I popped a hard-boiled egg into my mouth and chewed, reading a dozen words for *envelope* printed in different languages down the side of some supply boxes. To pass the time I tried memorising each term. *Boríték* remains the only Hungarian I know apart from Biró and Rubik, named after their inventors – the penman and the human puzzle. I chose a second hard-boiled egg and put it in my mouth.

There was the usual degree of snaffling, face-in-trough rootling when the door opened and editor-in-chief David Swansby sidestepped into the cupboard.

It was only etiquette that gave David this title, really. He came from a great line of Swansby editors-in-chief. I was his only employee.

I stared, egg-bound, as he slipped through the door and pressed it shut behind him.

'Ah, Mallory,' David said. 'Glad I've caught you. Might I have a word?'

He was a handsome seventy-year-old with a spry demonstrative way of using his hands which was not suited to such a small cupboard. I've heard people say that dog owners often look like their pets, or the pets look like their owners. In many ways David Swansby looked like his handwriting: ludicrously tall, neat, squared-off at the edges. Like my handwriting, I was aware that I often looked as though I needed to be tidied away, or ironed, possibly autoclaved. By the time afternoon tugged itself around the clock, both handwriting and I degrade into a big rumpled bundle. I'm being coy in my choice of words: *rumpled*, like *shabby* and *well-worn*, places emphasis on cosiness and affability – I mean that I looked like a mess by the end of the day. Creases seemed to find me and made tally charts against my clothes and my skin as I counted down the hours until home time. This didn't matter too much at Swansby House.

David Swansby was not a physically threatening presence and it would be unfair to say I was cornered by him in the cupboard. The room was not big enough for two people, however, and a corner *was* involved and certainly in that moment I was directly relevant to that noun becoming a verb.

I waited for my boss to tell me what he needed but he insisted on small talk. He mentioned something mild about the weather and recent sporting triumphs and dismays, then mentioned the weather again, and when he had got that out of the way I began to panic, mouth eggfulsome: surely now he must be expecting me to offer some response or to vouchsafe or confess or at the very least contribute a thought of my own? I considered what would happen if I tried to swallow the egg whole or chew it and speak around it, act as if this was normal behaviour. Or should I calmly spit it, gleaming and tooth-notched, into my hand and ask David to spit out what it was he wanted, as if it was the most casual thing in the world?

David twiddled the handle of a label dispenser on a shelf near his eye. He straightened it a touch. This is editorial behaviour, I thought. He glanced up at the skylight.

'I can't get over this light,' he said. 'Can you? So clear.'

I mumbled.

'Just look at that.' He switched his gaze from the skylight to his shoes in their weak pool of sunlight.

For my part, appreciative noises.

'*Apricide*,' David said. He pronounced it with fervour. People who work with words like to do this: enunciate with admiring flourishes as if a connoisseur and to show that *here* was someone who knew the value of a good word, the terroir of its etymology and the rarity of its vintage. Then he frowned, paused. He did not correct himself, but unfortunately I remembered this word from Vol. I of *Swansby's New Encyclopaedic Dictionary*. David meant *apricity* (n.), the warmness of the sun in winter. *Apricide* (n.) means the ceremonial slaughter of pigs.

You might spot a volume of *Swansby's New Encyclopaedic Dictionary* mouldering somewhere as a prop book on a gastropub mantelpiece or occasionally see one being passed from church fete bookstall to charity shop to hamster-bedding manufacturer in your local area. Not the first nor the best and certainly not the most famous dictionary of the English language, *Swansby's* has always been a poor shadow of its competitors as a work of reference – from the first printed edition in 1930 to today it has nowhere near the success nor rigorousness of *Britannica* and the *Oxford English Dictionary*. Those sleek dark blue hearses. *Swansby's* is also far less successful than *Collins* or *Chambers*, *Merriam-Webster's* or *Macmillan*. It only really has a place in the public imagination because *Swansby's* is incomplete.

I don't know whether people are endeared to an *almost*-complete dictionary because everyone enjoys a folly, or because of the Schadenfreude that accompanies any failed great endeavour. With *Swansby's*, decades' worth of work was completely undermined and rendered inconsequential by an ultimate inability to deliver a too-optimistic promise.

If you asked David Swansby about the nature of *Swansby's* as an incomplete project and therefore a failure, he would draw up to his full height of circa two hundred foot and tell you he would defer to Auden's quotation: that a piece of art is never finished, it is just abandoned. David would then check himself, escape to a bookshelf and come back ten minutes later and say of course that particular quotation belonged to Jean Cocteau. Another ten minutes would pass and David Swansby would seek you out and would clarify that line was actually first and best said by Paul Valéry.

David Swansby was a man who liked to quote and did so often. He was at pains to show he cared about quoting correctly. He would also not think twice about gently upbraiding people who misuse the verb *quote* in place of the noun *quotation* to which I would say, *pick your battles*, but I was only an intern.

I nodded once more. The egg in my mouth was Jupiter, the egg was my whole head.

Maybe the nation is fond of *Swansby's New Encyclopaedic Dictionary* because it holds artistic or philosophical allure as an unfinished project. Not in the way David wanted to style it – *Swansby's* is not the textual equivalent of Schubert's Symphony No. 8, Leonardo da Vinci's *Adoration of the Magi* or Gaudí's Sagrada Família. You could certainly admire the work that went into it. The *Swansby's New Encyclopaedic Dictionary* spans nine volumes and contains a total of 222,471,313 letters and numbers. For anybody who has the time or patience for mathematics, that is approximately 161 miles of type between the dictionary's thick green leather-bound covers. I did *not* have the patience for mathematics, but on this internship I certainly had the time. When I was starting my role at Swansby House, my grandfather told me that the most important quality of a dictionary is that it could fit in your pocket: that would probably cover all the important words anyway, he said, and would be slim enough to go with you wherever you went without distorting good tailoring. I wasn't sure that he understood what was involved in an internship ('Did you say *internment?*' he hollered down the phone, to no real response. He tried again: '*Interment?*') but he seemed pleased for me. Never mind a bullet – the nine volumes of *Swansby's New Encyclopaedic Dictionary* (1930) first edition could probably stop a tank in its tracks.

In the nineteenth century, Swansby House in London employed over a hundred lexicographers, all beavering away in the vast premises. Each worker, famously, was gifted a regulation Swansby House leather attaché case, a regulation Swansby House dip ink pen and Swansby House headed notepaper. God knows who bankrolled this operation, but they certainly appreciated uniform brand identity. The prevailing myth is that these lexicographers were coralled fresh from university, recruited for well-funded positions to bring about *the* British encyclopaedic dictionary. I thought about them occasionally, these young bucks probably younger than me, plucked from their studies and put to work on language in this same building over a century ago. They were under pressure to bring out the first edition before the *Oxford English* managed it, because what are well-defined words and researched articles if they are not the earliest to be acknowledged as great? David Swansby's great-grandfather presided over the operation from the mid 1850s. He had the forename *Gerolf*, which always struck me as worth another round of spellchecking. His heavily bearded, patrician portrait hangs in the downstairs lobby of the building. The word *be-whiskered* was made for such a face. Gerolf Swansby looked like his breath would be sweet. Not bad breath, just not good. Don't ask me why I would think that or could possibly guess just by looking at a portrait. Some things just are possible to know to be true for no good reason.

I had been on this internship for three years. On my first day, I was given a run-down of the company's history on my tour of the building. I was shown the portraits of its initial sub-editors and funders who had vied to keep the business going both before and after the wars. It all began with Prof. Gerolf Swansby, a wealthy man who seemed to attract unctuous funding for his lexicographical enterprise. By the late nineteenth century, he had accumulated enough for building works to commence at an address overlooking St James's Park. The property was built for purpose, and for its time was state-of-the-art, designed by architect Basil Slade and fitted with features such as a telephone, electric lift and synchronome master clock which used electrical impulses to ensure that all clocks in the building kept uniform time. Prof. Gerolf Swansby named the building after himself. The 'state-of-the-art' lift was designed in order to go down to the basements of the building which housed huge metal steam presses, bought and installed from the outset by David Swansby's be-whiskered great-grandfather to sit in readiness for the dictionary to be completed *A–Z* and go to print. From the beginning, the enterprise haemorrhaged money.

Before a single edition of the *Dictionary* was printed, before they had even reached the words beginning with Z, work came to an abrupt halt. All this early, costly industry on *Swansby's Encyclopaedic Dictionary* was interrupted when its lexicographers were called up and killed en masse in the First World War. Every day I walked past a stone memorial to these young men on the side of Swansby House, their names chiselled alphabetically into its marble index.

The unfinished dictionary, its grand hopes for a newly ordered world truncated, potential never fully realised, was considered an appropriate memorial to a generation cut short.

I get that. It makes me feel deeply uncomfortable, for various reasons, but I get it. The dictionary exists in an incomplete published form as a sad, hollow, joyless joke.

The original presses were melted down to make munitions for the World War. On my tour of the premises, I just nodded at this detail. My mind was solely on the fact that I would finally be making a living wage.

David and I worked in shabby offices on the second floor of Swansby House. Given its prime location close to St James's Park and Whitehall and its wonderful period details and space, the lower floors and large hall of the building were leased out as venues for launches and conferences and weddings. It was all kept pretty plush and impressive for visitors, and David employed various freelance events managers to add marquees and banners and floristry according to various clients' various tastes. The uppermost storey was not open for events – while downstairs was kept spick and span, its brass fittings polished daily and dust kept at bay, the abandoned higher floors above our offices were untouched and unused. I imagined there must be enough dustsheets up there to keep a village of ghosts in silhouettes, with cobwebs hanging from the rafters as thick as candyfloss. Occasionally I heard the scuttle of rats or squirrels or unthinkable somethings running above my office ceiling. Sometimes this caused plaster to drift down onto my desk. I did not mention it to David. He never mentioned it to me.

The rooms we used were sandwiched between the prospectus-ready, glossy and celebratory eventeering of down-stairs and these ghost-rat, deserted upper floors. Our offices had been reupholstered in a drab, blank, modern fashion: my room was the first one that any lost visitor might come across if they made their way up the stairs. It was next door to a dingy photocopying room, then there was the stationery cupboard, and finally David Swansby's office at the end of the passage. It was the largest, but still felt cramped with books, filing cabinets and document folders.

These rooms were all that was left of the vast *Swansby* scope and ambition. I counted myself lucky that I had an office of my own, however tiny. The sole employee in such a large, for-midable house. I should have felt glad to have the run of a place, even one that was state-of-the-art and now slipping into disrepair.

You may know the expression *weasel words* – deliberately ambiguous statements used in order to mislead, performing a little bait and switch of language. I think about weasel words whenever I hear the phrase *state-of-the-art*. It begs the question of which art and what state. For example, 'my office has state-of-the-art air-conditioning' as a phrase does not specify that *disrepair* is technically a 'state' and that the *art* in question might refer to 'weird humming from a box above your head that drips rigid yellow sap into the printer every two weeks'.

The idiom *weasel words* apparently comes from the folklore that weasels are able to slurp the contents of an egg while leaving the shell intact. *Teaching your weasel how to suck eggs. Weasel words* are empty, hollow, meaningless claims. My reference and CV for this internship contained some weasel words concerning focus and attention to detail, as well as a misspelling of *passionate*.

It was my job to answer phone calls that came every day. They were all from one person, and all threatened to blow the building up.

I suspected the calls were the reason *for* my internship: it was not as though Swansby's had any money to spare to lavish on 'experience-hungry' (citation needed) twenty-somethings. My last job had paid £1.50 less per hour and involved standing by a conveyor belt and turning un-iced gingerbread men by 30 degrees. I did not mention this fact in my interview with David nor on my CV – at least being at Swansby's meant no more dreams of faceless, brittle bodies.

To stop me going mad, I passed the time between calls by reading the dictionary, skipping through an open volume on my worktop. *Diplome* (n.), I read, 'a document issued by some greater esteemed authority'; *diplopia* (n.), 'an affection of vision whereupon objects are seen in double'; *diplopia* (n.), 'an affection of vision whereupon objects are seen in double'; *diplostemonous* (adj., Botany), 'having the stamens in two series, or twice as many stamens as petals'.

Use those three words in a sentence now, I thought. And then the phone would ring again.

'Good morning, Swansby House, how may I help you?'

'I hope you burn in hell.'

The nature of my duties had not been mentioned in my interview. I can appreciate why. On my first day in the office, answering the phone with no idea what was to come, I cleared my throat and said brightly, too brightly, 'Good morning, Swansby House, Mallory speaking, how may I help you?'

I remember that the voice newly lodged on my shoulder sighed. In discussion later, David and I decided that its speech was disguised by some mechanical device or app so it sounded like a cartoon robot. I did not know that at the time. It was a tinny noise, like something unhinging.

'Sorry?' I said. Looking back, I don't know whether it was instinct or first-day nerves. 'I didn't catch that, could I ask you to repeat—'

'I want you all dead,' said the voice. Then they hung up.

On some days the voice sounded male, other times female, sometimes like a cartoon lamb. You might think that answering these calls would become commonplace after the first couple of weeks, as formulaic as sneezing or opening the morning post, but it was not long before I found this was my routine every morning: the moment the phone began to ring, my body cycled through all the physical shorthands for involuntary terror. Blood drained from my face and curdled thick in whomping knots along my temples and in my ears. My legs became weak and my vision became narrower, more focused. If you were to look at me the most obvious effect was that every morning as I reached for the phone, gooseflesh and goosepimples and goosebumps stippled all across the length of my arm.

In our close-quarter cupboard that lunchtime, David kept his eyes on some shelving. 'The call?' he said. 'Did I hear it come through at ten o'clock?'

I nodded.

David unfolded an arm and, awkwardly, hugged me.

I muttered thanks into his shoulder. He stood back and re-realigned the label dispenser on the shelf.

'Come along to my office once you've finished with your –' he glanced at the now-empty Tupperware in my hands, apparently noticing it for the first time – 'lunchbox.'

And then the editor-in-chief left the intern-on-guard to her cupboard and the *apricity* and the skylight. I stood there for a full second then looked up *Heimlich manoeuvre* on my phone as I ate my remaining hard-boiled egg. It took four attempts to spell *manoeuvre* correctly, and in the end I let Autocorrect have its way with me.

B is for *bluff* (v.)

Peter Winceworth experienced an epiphany midway through his fourth elocution lesson: the best chance he had of conquering his headache would be folding both legs under his chin and rolling straight into Dr Rochfort-Smith's blazing hearth.

'"A roseate blush with soft suffusion divulged her gentle mind's confusion."'

The doctor repeated his quotation. He did not notice his patient's second longing glance towards the fireplace.

If the testimonials in the papers were to be believed (*With Just A Little Application, You Too Can Achieve Perfect Diction!*), Dr Rochfort-Smith was in great demand in London. His visitors' book boasted numerous politicians, members of the clergy and most recently the lead ventriloquist at the Tivoli – the overbiting and the spluttersome, the stuttering and the hoarse, the great and the good of the garbling. Winceworth wondered whether his fellow patients also fumbled when they handed their hats to the doctor's housekeeper in the hallway. Surely they did not all make such painfully self-conscious small talk in the corridors before their appointments and apologise quite so profusely for letting the cold January air of the Chelsea street seep inside? *They* probably sat *forward* in their chairs, excited to finally have fullness coaxed from their lungs

22

and have their lips twitched into nimbleness. Winceworth doubted few of the doctor's other patients slumped quite so abjectly. They would not try and repeat tongue twisters while yesterday's whisky still coated their throats and a headache kicked them squarely in the pons.

Pons was a word Winceworth had learned the previous day. He was not sure that he completely understood what it meant – the person who said the word tapped the back of their neck and then their forehead as they said it, as if to provide some context for its use – but the shape and sound of the word lodged in his mind like a tune one can't stop humming.

His relationship with the word *pons* and with words generally had soured since first learning of its existence. A case of passing familiarity quickly breeding contempt. Earlier that morning, Winceworth awoke still dressed in last night's evening clothes with the word *pons* ricocheting between his ears. It had been an acquaintance's birthday and they had turned a thirsty age, and the party had careered from genteel to festive to sodden very quickly. *Pons pons pons.* Eventually finding his face in his dressing-room mirror, Winceworth conducted a clumsy, horrified and fadingly drunk levée. He removed his bow tie from about his forehead and clawed pillow feathers that were buttery with hair pomade from his chin. It was only once he had pried his feet from his dress shoes that he remembered his scheduled appointment. With fresh socks applied and a search for his umbrella abandoned, Winceworth was out of the door and flapping towards Chelsea.

★

Dr Rochfort-Smith studied his client's face. Winceworth cleared his throat to gain purchase on his thoughts and in order to be heard above the songbird, a small but pernicious feature of the doctor's rooms. The issue was not just that the bird whistled throughout his weekly hour of treatment. Mere *whistling* would have been a boon. *Whistling* might have saved the situation. This bird made a point of catching Winceworth's eye across the room once he was settled in his chair then with something approaching real malice, visibly breathing in, and doing the ornithological equivalent of letting it rip.

Politicians, members of the clergy and the lead ventriloquist at the Tivoli might share Winceworth's temptation to toss the birdcage and its occupant out of Dr Rochfort-Smith's window.

The doctor repeated his phrase. ' "A roseate blush—" '

Winceworth was unsure of the type of songbird. He researched potential candidates after his first consultation in an attempt to better know his enemy. Winceworth was employed by an encyclopaedic dictionary and was well-placed to know who to ask and which books to trust on the matter. Identifying this bird from memory and through spite became an obsession for a week, conducted to the detriment of any actual work he was meant to be doing. He pored over zoological catalogues and pawed through illustrated guides but for all he was able to glean about various small birds' feeding habits, migratory patterns, taxonomies, use of ants to clean their feathers, use and misuse in mythology and folklore, prominence on menus and milliners' manifests, &c., &c., its species remained a mystery. Basically, it was a sparrow with access to theatrical costumiers. No encyclopaedic dictionary will tell you this, but Winceworth would want it to be known that if ever a songbird was designed to glare, Dr Rochfort-Smith's specimen was that bird. If ever a bird was designed to spit, this was the species that would relish such an advantage. It always had an air of biding its time.

'"A roseate blush with soft suffusion",' Dr Rochfort-Smith said, '"divulged her gentle mind's confusion."'

The songbird was an absurd orange colour. Much of Dr Rochfort-Smith's consulting room was orange, to the extent that Winceworth might compile a list:

Dr Rochfort-Smith's Consulting Room
(the orange complexities thereof):

amber, apricot, auburn, aurelian, brass, cantaloupe, carrot, cinnabar, citric, coccinate, copper, coral, embered, flammid, fulvous, gilt, ginger, Glenlivet-dear-god, hennaed, hessonite, honeyed, laharacish, marigold, marmaladled, mimolette, ochraceous, orang-utan, oriele, paprikash, pumpkin, rubedinous, ruddy, rufulous, russet, rusty, saffron, sandy, sanguine, spessartite, tangerine, tawny, tigrine, Titian, topazine, vermilion, Votyak, xanthosiderite—

Orange wall-hangings, orange satin throws, the array of bright orange walnut sapwood pieces of furniture, the orange songbird. In contrast to all this, Rochfort-Smith always wore a particularly lichenous cut of tweed. Perhaps it was the headache, but in this fourth elocution session Winceworth thought this suit clashed against the room's decor with a new and particular energetic violence.

When Winceworth had first entered the room, the bird trialled some chirrups and then progressed to a trilling burr. As the clock hiccupped something about the passage of time and Dr Rochfort-Smith began his solemn incantation about *soft suffusion*, the bird decided its talents would be better spent in the percussive arts rather than just simple *arietta* and began slamming its body against the wire of its cage.

The doctor inclined his head and waited. Winceworth closed his eyes, marshalled his resolve, and repeated the phrase back to the room. Every syllable took the effort of a poorly thought-through lie.

'"A ro—"'

CLANG, went the birdcage.

'"—with—"'

  CLANG

'"—divulged?—"'

   tingINGting

    TING TING-TLINGting

     tingTLINGtlllingling

The slamming, the screeching, yesterday's whisky excesses: the headache bit across the length of Winceworth's skull and rocked him back, defeated, into the recesses of his chair.

Winceworth's lisp was the official reason for his time with Dr Rochfort-Smith. He had not booked these sessions and was quite opposed to the idea of them for the very good reason that his lisp was completely manufactured. Since childhood and throughout his youth and certainly for the five years that he had been working at the *Swansby's New Encyclopaedic Dictionary*, Peter Winceworth had concocted, affected and perfected a fake speech impediment.

He was not sure that he had developed the lisp for any reason other than sheer boredom. There was perhaps a childish, childlike idea that it made him endearing, and from an early age the act of altering his speech in this way made people respond to him with a greater gentleness. As far as he knew, which is as far as he cared, the deceit hurt nobody. Simple pleasures, small comforts.

Occasionally in private Winceworth repeated his name in his shaving mirror just to check that the lisping habit had not become ingrained.

' "Roseate"!' urged the doctor.

' "Roseate",' Winceworth said. His tongue flicked the back of his teeth.

While Winceworth's mother found his boyhood lisp endearing, his father found it ridiculous. This made child–Winceworth even more resolved to keep up the pretence. A great-uncle on the paternal side had spoken in a similar way and family legend revolved around this forebear's sudden shyness when *The Times* swapped the long, medial ∫ form to *s* on its pages so that his gruff declarations of 'finfulneff!' and 'forrowful!' over the breakfast table could no longer be excused as simply too-quick reading. In truth, this family legend was made up by Winceworth to scatter into conversations when pauses were too awkward for him to bear. Winceworth lied easily when there was no clear harm in doing so. Once his school years were completed, with accusations and repercussions of perceived effeminacy duly weathered on the sports pitches and in detention, Winceworth considered leaving the lisp behind him with the chalkboards and the textbooks. Out of habit, however, and perhaps nervousness, he accidentally let slip a *nethethary* during an interview for a minor proofreading role at *Swansby's New Encyclopaedic Dictionary*.

The editor's eyes had softened with an unmistakable sympathy. The lisp persisted and Winceworth gained meaningful employment.

The lisp became a more pressing issue when Winceworth's job at *Swansby's* focused on the letter *S*. Day in, day out he shuffled powder-blue index cards covered with *S*-led words across his desk, headwords and lemmas all sibilance and precise hissing. The same editor who had been so well disposed to Winceworth's non-impediment at the time of interview summoned him from his desk and explained, gently, that rather than a Christmas bonus this year Winceworth would be enrolled on a series of classes with one of the premier elocutionists in Europe.

'As we enter the *Ryptage–Significant* volume,' Prof. Gerolf Swansby had said, placing a hand on Winceworth's shoulder. He was close enough for Winceworth to detect his breath – a strange mix of citrus zest and Fribourg & Treyer's finest tobacco. 'I thought it might be a good time to address the matter – you know, as you go on working as an ambassador for our great *Swansby's New Encyclopaedic Dictionary*.'

'Ambassador, sir?'

Swansby replied after a pause, trying to look kind. 'Exactly.' The hand on Winceworth's shoulder tightened a degree.

The lisp was so much a part of Winceworth's identity and presence at *Swansby's* that this offer was difficult to refute or dismiss. Sessions with Dr Rochfort-Smith were duly scheduled at considerable cost to the company's pocketbooks, and so it was that January's Winceworth sat back in an orange armchair, battling a headache and feigning a lisp to a doctor for the fourth week in a row.

Dr Rochfort-Smith's methods of tutelage proved curious but not wholly unenjoyable. This was due in part to the added cat-and-mouse element, Winceworth having to hide his perfectly standard diction and evade detection. Their last appointment featured pebbles inserted into his mouth while he read passages from Dr Rochfort-Smith's Coverdale translation of the Bible. Another involved a kind of puppet show whereby the active musculature of a speaking mouth was demonstrated using a silk, larger-than-life-size model of the human tongue. Winceworth was informed that this tongue had been made by the absent Mrs Rochfort-Smith. Although surely a woman of many talents, at the time it occurred to Winceworth that tongue manufacture was perhaps not one of her greatest. Some of the silk's stitching was too obvious and a few wisps of stuffing escaped in sad papillae at its seams.

With the bundle safely clamped between the jaws of a pair of vulcanised rubber dentures, Winceworth had watched for a good half-hour as Dr Rochfort-Smith revealed the ways by which one's enunciation might be improved.

Presumably primed and ready for its next exhibition, today the tongue was hanging unwaggingly from its nail by the door.

Dr Rochfort-Smith held a tuning fork in both of his hands. 'Your pitch,' the doctor said, 'is adequate and tone assured. But, I wonder: "roseate", once more?'

Maybe the doctor was fully aware the lisp was false: *If you waste my time, I shall peep-twang my way through yours.* This was Winceworth's only rational explanation for the tuning forks. It was doubtful that their resonance could be heard over the songbird, anyway. He had no idea how Dr Rochfort-Smith stood this sound – for his part, Winceworth's headache set about trying to wring liquid or pluck a particular note from his optic nerve. Blood thudded in his ears, *pons pons pons*, and Dr Rochfort-Smith suddenly had either far too many teeth or too small a mouth. A squint might clarify things, Winceworth thought. A thorough, concerted winching of the eyes might portion the world into tolerable slices. He did not want to appear rude. Gently does it, steady, the Buffs – he need only lower his brows by a fraction and bend his forehead into the subtlest of corrugations so that his squint would pass as mere attentiveness.

Dr Rochfort-Smith's tuning forks struck again and Winceworth's face buckled.

★

There really should be a specific word associated with the effects of drinking an excess of alcohol. The headaches, the seething sense of paranoia – language seemed the poorer for not having one. Winceworth decided he would bring this up with one of his editors.

Whisky was the cause of his morning's horrors, and on this point Winceworth was sure, but the preceding night's wines, eaux de vie and spirits no doubt contributed. Some of the blame must also lie in not having eaten sufficiently prior to the birthday party. Winceworth remembered buying some chestnuts from a barrow. He could not swear that he had dined on anything more than this and on reflection he suspected that the chestnuts may have been boiled to look plumper before roasting. Bad chestnuts, enough drink to fell a buffalo – Winceworth had returned this paltry meal onto the frost-glazed early-morning pavement somewhere near the Royal Opera House. Memories coalesced and glistened with new brightness. A lady had dropped her lorgnette into the mess and, profuse with brandied bliss, Winceworth had scooped up the eyeglasses in order to return them. The lady had reeled away from him, aghast.

Winceworth rediscovered this lorgnette still nestled in his coat pocket as he hurried from bed to Dr Rochfort-Smith's rooms. One of the lenses had a small asterisk shatter across it.

Winceworth dipped his hand into his trouser pocket while Dr Rochfort-Smith spoke. There he experienced one of the most exotic disappointments possible – his fingers closed, firmly, around an uneaten slice of birthday cake.

'Are you all right, Mr Winceworth?'

The patient coughed. 'It is rather – ah, only that it is rather warm today, I think,' he said.

'I do not think so,' said the doctor, looking at his fire.

'A trifle close, perhaps,' Winceworth said. He made sure to emphasise the false wasp-wing buzz of the lisp. He added an extra heartfelt *sorry* too to compound the effect and across the room the songbird looked disgusted.

Dr Rochfort-Smith made a scribble in an orange note-book. 'Never lose heart, Mr Winceworth. You are in good company – after all, Moses lisped, God lisped.'

'Is that right?'

'Yes!' Dr Rochfort-Smith spread his arms. 'And it would be remiss not to pass on my congratulations: there have been some definite improvements in your diction these few weeks.'

Winceworth dabbed his upper lip with a sleeve. He noticed there was cake icing on his thumb and he folded his hands into his lap. On his way to the doctor's rooms he had mistakenly walked through a spiderweb – that horrible feeling of being snagged, caught by an unseen force, had stayed with him all morning. 'That is heartening to hear, thank you.'

'And now,' Rochfort-Smith went on, bringing the tuning forks back down to his knees, 'with your chin slightly relaxed: "'Zounds!' shouted Ezra as he seized the amazed Zeno's ears."'

It was never entirely clear to Winceworth whether these phrases were standard tests or just borne of Dr Rochfort-Smith's own invention. After their first meeting Winceworth had been sent home with instructions to repeat *Silly Susan sitting on the seashore stringing seashells and seaweeds, softly singing or listening in silence to the sirens' songs*. From chit-chat during the session Winceworth gleaned that 'Susan' was the absent Mrs Rochfort-Smith's name. Her sepia portrait hung above the doctor's fireplace like a crinolined gnat in amber, memorialised as if she were dead. Dr Rochfort-Smith described the absent Susan as suffering from some mysterious, debilitating illness for a good many years, currently sequestered to a sanatorium in the Alps for the sake of her health. A number of her letters littered the doctor's desk, detailing the tonic of Alpine air and new-fangled *Müesli* breakfasts. Poor Susan with the sirens. Winceworth had not felt entirely comfortable invoking the doctor's ailing wife in such a winsome setting as a sibilant fantasy beach, whether *softly singing or listening in silence to the sirens' songs*. After the fortieth repetition, he found that he could inject a real impassioned emphasis on the word *silly*.

Winceworth became ever more certain that rather than reporting the de*th*eption to *Thwansby's* or upbraiding his patient on the waste of his valuable time, Dr Rochfort-Smith had devised ridiculous vocal exercises to see how far his patient would be prepared to carry on the charade. Winceworth was sure that the blasted songbird definitely knew he was lying, possibly by using the same instincts animals are said to use when sensing ghosts or storms before they hit.

This new abuse of *amazed Zeno* and his *ears*, however, was impossible to attempt without laughing. Winceworth's face, head nor stomach lining could not manage that today. He hazarded for a distraction.

'Did you – sorry, did you say *God* lisped?' he asked.

Clearly anticipating the question, the doctor leapt to his desk. 'I refer you to the Coverdale! I have marked the very place in Isaiah, Chapter twenty-eight, I think—'

Winceworth tried to crumble some of last night's rediscovered birthday cake into the fabric under the cushion of his seat. The songbird noticed and began banging the bars of the cage.

'Yes, and, elsewhere, Moses, did you know,' continued the doctor, 'yes, Moses, too! All to be found in Exodus.' Dr Rochfort-Smith closed his eyes. '"But Moses said unto the Lord: 'Oh, my Lord, I am a man that is not eloquent, from yesterday and heretofore and since the time that thou hast spoken unto thy servant: for I have a slow speech, and a slow tongue.'"'

'I had no idea I was in such elect company,' Winceworth said once he was sure the doctor had finished.

The Coverdale shut and the doctor's face grew sorrowful. 'It was through hissing that sin entered into this world –' Winceworth stopped crumbling the birthday cake and stiffened in his chair – 'and it is perhaps more beneficial to consider your affliction as nothing more than a reminder of this.'

CLANG, went the birdcage.

The doctor brought his hands together sharply. 'It is

nothing that cannot be remedied, however. So, now, if you would: " 'Zounds!' shouted Ezra—" '

Winceworth had managed some dialogue, some repetition, and he had not been sick onto his own shoes: he should be proud, he remembered thinking as the blood drained from his head and his eyes swam.

'And so must end our penultimate session,' the doctor said. He dusted his hands on his knees.

'No more tongues and pebbles? No more *Zeno*?' Winceworth dragged the heel of his hand through his hair.

'I will see how many more *Zeno*s can join our final encounter next week.'

Dr Rochfort-Smith's next client was already waiting in the corridor, a young girl of about seven years whose mother wittered *hello!*s and *good morning!*s. The girl shrank from Dr Rochfort-Smith's attempted swipe at a headpat. Winceworth recognised her from previous weeks when, curious, he had queried the child's reason for visiting the practice. Apparently the girl suffered some kind of idioglossia and entirely refused to speak in anyone's presence. She could read and write to an exceptional standard but was entirely mute when in company. Dr Rochfort-Smith explained that her parents overheard her speaking a language of her own devising when she was alone. When asked whether there had been any progress during his tutelage, the doctor would not be explicit but said they had established through the use of paper, pen and orange crayons that the girl believed she was speaking to an imaginary tiger.

This tiger accompanied the girl everywhere and was called Mr Grumps.

That morning, both patients locked eyes as they passed on the threshold of Dr Rochfort-Smith's door. Presumably Mr Grumps was in the corridor even as the girl and her mother were ushered into the doctor's rooms. Winceworth pictured Mr Grumps regarding the songbird in the doctor's study with invisible, ravenous zeal. Winceworth shot the girl a small conspiratorial smile.

The child regarded him with puzzled politeness. Then her face darkened and she released a clear, snarling growl.

Pons pons pons

Peter Winceworth collected his hat and made his way rather quickly down the stairs and into the street.

C is for *crypsis* (n.)

My task for the day was to look over David Swansby's efforts at digitising the text of *Swansby's New Encyclopaedic Dictionary*. It was his dream to honour the family name and the scope and vision of his forefather editors by updating the unfinished dictionary and putting it all online for free. He spoke of this as a noble project, for the betterment of humanity, and as a way of securing the Swansby legacy as something accomplished and celebrated rather than a noble damp squib.

Privately, I looked up the entry for *hubris* (n.).

In order that he might achieve his vision, much of Swansby's meagre finances were being ploughed into the digitisation of the dictionary and updating its definitions. The first, last and only physical edition of the incomplete *Swansby's* had come out in the 1930s using the huge archive of abandoned notes and proofs made in the previous decades, so this was no small task. In our discussions, David made it very clear that he would not be adding *new* words to this archive, as this did not seem in keeping with the Swansby spirit: rather, he wanted to make sure that the words that had been defined were updated for a current audience.

When I learned this, I couldn't help but point out that there were online dictionaries already, online encyclopaedias updated every second by experts and hobbyists. I showed him on my phone. There was no competition. David looked bored and a little hurt that I did not share his vision.

'But to have Swansby join that list,' he said as I reeled off the names of various sites. 'To finally put *Swansby's Encyclopaedic Dictionary* to rest!'

I did not understand the logic of this, but not understanding the logic of it paid the bills. Each time I passed the portrait of Prof. Gerolf Swansby on the downstairs floor, I looked up an article on my phone about whether eccentricity is genetic.

Each day David Swansby disappeared into his office to spend hours typing up every individual entry from his family dictionary, updating each definition as best he could. If I'm candid, I think one of the main reasons for the delay in digitising the dictionary and the reason my 'internship' had lasted over three years stemmed from David's discovery of online chess. Not only that, he had found a site where you could 'play' as if you are taking part in famous, historical chess matches: some program had mined archival data and provided the original moves made during specific games by a player, so you could pitch your wits against the ghost of that player and see whether you would have fared any better in opposition. David had spent over eight months locked in a game first played in 1926. In the online game, he was playing Harold James Ruthven Murray (1868–1955), a prominent chess historian of the early twentieth century. You may know him as a chess historian. You may also know him as one of the eleven children of the first editor of the *Oxford English Dictionary*.

Every time I passed David's office and heard him slamming his hands on his laptop and swearing at the screen, I could not help but think that there was something of an old rivalry between *Swansby's* and the *Oxford English* that he was trying to put to bed. I don't know whether he ever won. I'm sure he would have told me.

I tried to explain the digitising of the dictionary to Pip one evening back in our flat. Most of the notes for the dictionary are from the last years of the nineteenth century, and the words that appear or do not appear amongst its pages reflect the times. I looked around our kitchen for an example. Say, for instance, *teabag*. In 1899, no one was yet using the word, so it wouldn't appear in the body of the dictionary.

'Verb or noun?' Pip asked. Rude. I made a face.

Teabag had yet to bob up amongst the draft pages or sketched-out columns in 1899. A teabag had yet to be invented. If you trust other dictionaries published during that time, as of 1899 one could not *cartwheel* as a verb either because that meaning was not yet established, nor could one travel up an *escalator*. In 1899 you're still a year away from *blokeish*, *come-hither* and *dorm* making an appearance in any English dictionary's pages. The modern use of *hangover* and *morning-after* as having anything to do with alcohol only cropped up in 1919, so they never made Swansby's war-decimated pages. Language went on regardless, of course. God knows what happened at the office party to require that update.

The more I thought about it at work, the more I liked the close-but-unreachable sound of 1900 and its neologisms, the words that entered mouths and ears and inkwells that year. *Teabag, come-hither, razzmatazz.* 1900 sounds like a lot more fun than 1899 and its note-taking lexicographers.

In 1899, elephants were being slaughtered in huge numbers to keep up with the demand for high-quality billiard balls, with no more than four balls being made from a single tusk. I found these facts listed under *Ivory, trade of* in Vol. V when I skipped forward a little out of sheer boredom on my first day reading the dictionary. Then the phone rang, and it was with thoughts of slaughtered elephants that I perched the receiver between my chin and ear and answered the call.

Updating the meanings of entries in an encyclopaedia or dictionary or encyclopaedic dictionary is of course no new concept. I spent most of my time reading about it, between panic attacks on the phone and eating my lunch in the cupboard. Biographies need updating, countries are renamed or disappear completely. *Swansby's* was in good company in this regard, and part of a long lineage of reference books attempting to keep up with the times: Abraham Rees's *Proposals* were published in an attempt to revise Chambers' *Cyclopædia* (1728), and Rees emphasised in his sermons prior to publication that it was his intention to 'exclude obsolete science, to retrench superfluous matter'. As new progress is made in science, new coinages and advances in understanding constantly render previous column inches of articles superfluous, if not meaningless. For example, copies of the nineteenth-century *National Encyclopaedia* include entries for the word *malaria* where the disease is still described in terms of transmission by some strange noumenal ether that lurks over swamps, *mala aria*, bad air: the facts are broadly true, and etymologically valid, but ignorant of mosquitoes' role in malaria's vector control. David was always quick to point out that the *OED* left *appendicitis* (n.) out of its earliest editions, an omission that was roundly criticised in 1902 when Edward VII's coronation was delayed thanks to this particular affliction and the word's use became widespread in the media.

A conventional dictionary is often determined by lexicographers' particular intellectual milieu and potentially their personal bias. I'm sure David Swansby comforted himself with the thought that a perfect encyclopaedic dictionary, free from all error and completely relevant in every particular, is impossible because any compiler or compiling body lacks complete objective oversight. No man is an island, no dictionary a fixed star, or something something something. Of course, the decision to *remove* words in order that more 'relevant' words in a dictionary might take their place can be controversial. Recent editorial proposals to replace, for example, the words *catkin* and *conker* with *cut and paste* and *broadband* in an edition of the *Oxford Junior Dictionary* gained national coverage and much outraged comment. *Swansby's* received far less blowback following its online updates, chiefly because hardly anyone noticed.

Hardly anyone.

The phone rang again.

No further words were to be added to the *Dictionary*, although many of the current words required an update. The verb *refresh*, for example, needed some tweaking since its 1899 iteration where 'refreshing mobile stream' meant something quite different. Similarly, the words *tag*, *viral* and *friend* have changed quite a bit since the first time they popped up. Another word was *marriage*.

The 1899 definition of *marriage* began (emphasis my own [How often do you get to truly say that?]):

marriage (n.), referring to both the act and ceremony by which the relationship of ***husband and wife*** is constituted and the blissful physical, legal and moral union between ***man and woman*** in complete community, ready for the establishment of a family

For the new digital edition, this had been updated by David to:

marriage (n.), referring to both the act and ceremony by which a person's relationship to another might be constituted, and the physical and legal union between those ***persons***

For whatever reason, it was this change that caused some ruckus in the press. It was also the cause of the phone calls.

As well as answering the calls, it was my job to check the spelling and punctuation of David's updated words. This was laborious because David hated technology that wasn't online chess. Also, he had scrimped on buying office equipment. To use a computer in Swansby House was to hate the sight of an hourglass. The one on my computer's loading screen was silent, monochrome and smaller than a fingernail, six black pixels in its top bulb and ten in the lower. I wondered how many months of people's lives had been spent staring at this pinch-waisted little graphic. It made me think of the different tidemarks on the keyboard I inherited. Not quite grey, not quite black, not quite brown. Of what: skin? Grime? The transitive verb *slough* came to mind. The noun *sebum*. The record of previous hands resting on this very same piece of plastic. Some of them might have died and this little scuff mark could be the only trace of them left on this earth. The keyboard made me feel a little sick.

This loading hourglass, though. A further pair of pixels was suspended in the centre of the graphic to imply that sand was falling – as one watched the screen, this hourglass would swivel on its axis as if tipped and re-tipped by an unseen moderator's fingers. Everybody knows this. Why bother explaining hourglasses to myself? Proximity to encyclopaedic dictionaries made me a bore. *Prolix*ity, *pedantry, ploddiplodplod*. I'm sure that I was not alone in my dread of the hourglass. Having worked alongside the arrow and manicule forms of the computer's cursor, it is a shock to have it suddenly transformed into a tool dedicated to some other project, a project that is not only apparently out of one's control but that takes priority. With the operating system too busy to accept input from the keyboard or mouse one is stuck there until the computer has come to terms with itself, the spinning hourglass your unwanted company for the duration.

The phone on my desk gave another sharp ring.

Perhaps the hourglass caused so much anxiety because as a graphic it offered no hint of eventual relief. Yes, it confirmed, you are rotting where you sit! This is all pointless! It was all for naught! Why did you learn all those piano scales, why did you memorise song lyrics, why did you ever care about pronouncing *pronunciation* correctly? The constant trickling of sand from one obconical end to the other gave no indication that any specific amount of time was being counted down. I mean, really, the hourglass was the perfect icon for frustrated flux rather than a sense of progress, an image of a fixed, inescapable 'presentness' rather than promising any future. A clock face devoid of hands, perhaps, would have the same uncanny effect. Why was I thinking like this? *Flux* and *uncanny*. What was in my hard-boiled eggs? Who did I think I was—?

The phone gave another ring.

The iconography of the hourglass hinted at a particular progression: that all natural things tend towards death. This was not good for office morale. Waiting for the computer-screen hourglass to empty and refill and empty again generated a feeling not just of futility but also of mortality. I understood why it was a favoured prop whenever 'Father Time' or 'Death' are figured as personae in Western culture, and if Disney's *Alice in Wonderland*'s White Rabbit had been described as crying, 'I'm late, I'm late, I'm late!' while clutching an hourglass rather than a pocket watch, he would have been a far more morbid (I Googled this on my phone) *leporine sigil*. Shouldering for room with skulls, burned-down candles and rotten fruit, hourglasses are also one of the recurring tropes of *vanitas* pieces, those works of art that illustrate the world's physical transience. Crumpled tulips, dry parchment. Trading upon this saturnine thrill of *memento mori* set-pieces, pirate ships of the seventeenth and eighteenth century bore hourglasses upon their flags alongside the more famous skull insignias. Hourglass iconography is also prevalent on a number of gravestones, often supplemented with mottoes such as *Tempus fugit* ('Time flies') or *Ruit hora* ('The hour is flying away').

The work computer was old and slow: the previous week I had to face a couple of turns of the hourglass while checking the words *obconical* and *saturnine* in the dictionary by my elbow.

My desk phone gave a fourth ring, which was usually as long as I could bear.

Hourglass imagery is not always coincident with a sense of hopelessness, however. In fact, thinking about it, sometimes it exists as a symbol for a certain necessity to seize the hour: perhaps for this reason hourglasses feature on many heraldic crests. I've looked it up. Of course I have. In one of its more savoury definitions, the online UrbanDictionary.com lists the verb *hourglassing* in reference to 'when a computer is "thinking" and is currently unresponsive. Not exactly frozen, *hourglassing* gives a potentially false sense of action on the part of the computer.' Many families unite in baying, unfestive horror during games of Charades or Pictionary as the final grains of sand fall through the necks of supplied hourglasses. Hourglasses of this size are also called *egg-timers*. Although this is probably a practical description of its use amongst, say, the soft-boiling breakfast community, I do think that *egg-timer* lacks the poetry of the other possible synonym *clepsammia*. The lexicographer Noah Webster listed this word in his 1828 dictionary – its etymological roots are the Greek words for *sand* and *theft*, the idea being that as each grain slips through the hourglass's waist another moment is being taken away. *Clepsammia* certainly has a pleasing clicking sibilance to it, and as a word evokes a slick trickling of the contents from bulb to bulb as well as the flipping-over of its body. Unlike *Webster's*, *Swansby's New Encyclopaedic Dictionary* overlooked the word *clepsammia* in its published incomplete 1930 edition. It does, however, provide the word *hour-glass* as a hyphenated noun. With its symmetry and little dashed isthmus between the two words, 'hour-glass' on the page is like the object itself, lying on its side or balanced mid-spin.

The phone kept ringing, boring into my skull.

Of course, the hourglass is not the only symbol that accompanies hapless computer users (me) and their periods of waiting. There's Apple products' spinning orb known affectionately as the 'Spinning Beach Ball of Death' or the 'Marble of Doom'. My old BlackBerry occasionally presented me with a graphic of a squared-off clock, its hands rotating uncontrollably. BlackBerry-time, Apple-time, egg-time. My laptop at home was far newer than my office computer and ran on a far more up-to-date operating system. Bereft of hourglasses, my waiting was instead accompanied by its replacement, its inheritor: a glowing ring, a tiny green ouroboros graphic forever eating its own tail. The same irritation existed, the feeling of being trapped in a state of suspension rather than progress being made, but stripped of the more esoteric timekeeping device. This glowing circle felt somehow more clinical and inhumane, its cultural implications less to do with pirates and Father Time and more HAL 9000 from *2001: A Space Odyssey* or the KITT vehicle's front-scanning bar in *Knight Rider*. Armed with the iconography of *vanitas*, maybe other operating systems in the future will adopt symbols of futility such as skulls or rotting flowers. Perhaps a small pixelated Sisyphus could be forced to clamber up my scrollbar. As it stands and stood, the charm of the hourglass was gone and I missed it. *Tempus* won't stop *fugit*, sure, but at least we once had the chance to watch it play out in style.

The word *hourglass* lost any meaning for me beyond frantic rage.

The phone made another petulant ring. I sighed and picked up the receiver, smiling fixedly at the stain on the wall opposite my desk.

'Hello, Swansby's Press,' I said, 'how may I help you?'

'Burn in hell, Mallory,' said the synthetically distorted voice on the other end of the line.

'Yes,' I said, and gave the stain a thumbs-up. 'Yes, you're through to the right department. How may I help you?'

There was the sound of breathing. Digitised breath shuttlecocked down the phone line.

'Twice in one day,' I said. I'm not sure why.

'There's a bomb in the building,' the voice said. Then they rang off and the hourglass on my screen flipped one final time.

D is for *dissembling* (adj.)

Winceworth had an unqueer desire to delay the inevitability of his working day for as long as possible. Usually there was a gaggle of lexicographers outside Swansby House in a similar frame of mind, procrastinattering about the weather or the state of nearby St James's Park lawns while counting their cigarettes and fiddling with glove fastenings. A game of etiquette usually developed amongst this fluctuating group with each member desperate to prolong their time beyond the confines of the office. The rules of the game were unspoken and certainly the sport was never explicitly acknowledged as a way of dawdling on company time. It involved tilting the brim of one's hat up on the forehead and voicing admiration for the streaky-bacon brickwork of Swansby House. The more architectural terms you were able to use in order to express your admiration, the more points you gained. The game was over when you ran out of things to say or the silence became too awkward. At that point, the working day began.

Winceworth's working day was starting at a later than conventional hour and there were no fellow idlers to join on the front step. He tipped his chin above the lapel of his coat to look up at the building and list terms over the chaos of his headache. *Streaky-bacon brickwork* probably wouldn't sit right with an expert in the field so that was already a duff start. Was it *Queen Anne*, the building style? Is that what he had been told on one such milling, loafing morning or had he misheard and *queenan* was an architectural term for Swansby House's shape, design, material? He had just nodded along at the time, accepting it as writ. Language is something you accept or trust rather than necessarily want to test out. *Queenan* wouldn't be the most unlikely-seeming architectural term he had come across, certainly – current work on the S volume of *New Encyclopaedic Dictionary* recently necessitated research into *scutcheon*, *squinch*, *systyle*, each one rolling around his mouth with unfamiliar textures and sloshes. Every word seems a nonsense until you need it or know more about it. Winceworth's eyes drifted from the queenan steps and rashered walls up to the windows of the first floor, the quoins of the second floor, the oriel windows in the storeys beyond that and thence to the pediments and chimneys, the stupid blank January sky, the blotch of a starling or a pigeon on the wrought-iron weathervane, &c., &c., &c.

Time to help attempt a pointless census of language. Winceworth could not put it off any longer. He straightened his tie and braced his shoulders against the broad wooden door.

Ingrained behaviours are asserted unconsciously. Some are entirely automatic and shared from person to person, such as the impulse to pull a hand away from the steam of a breakfast kettle or a forehead perspiring in order to keep a body cool. Sometimes these responses are cultivated rather than spontaneous. They begin as autonomous performances then grow ritualised through habit until they are embedded in the culture of day-to-day action. For example, Winceworth could not imagine crossing the stone step threshold of Swansby House without his false lisp falling like a portcullis down across his tongue. He didn't even have to think about it.

He had worked at *Swansby's New Encyclopaedic Dictionary* long enough to acquire a kind of muscle memory. He steered his body from the front door to the coat rack then up to his desk in the central Scrivenery hall on the first floor, knowing the precise momentum at which to swing an arm to most efficiently catch and release the stair-rail. Winceworth's were not the only feet on the stairs and the *pons pons pons* of soft paws on stone steps joined his pace – one of the many cats that Prof. Gerolf Swansby allowed to roam the press and keep mice away from paper documents accompanied him up to the Scrivenery hall. This mouser was big and yellow and Winceworth reached down to scratch behind its ear. It turned its face away with a chirp. Maybe it too had a headache. Cat headaches were probably sleeker affairs.

On the walk from Dr Rochfort-Smith's rooms to Swansby House Winceworth had returned to vexing over why no word had been coined for the specific type of headache he was suffering. The bitter meanness of its fillip, the sludgy electric sense of guilt coupled with its existence as physical retribution for time spent in one's cups. A certain lack of memory, as if pain was crowding it out. You drink too much and this headache was the result – the world was surely in the market for such an affliction to bear a name? And if no word did exist, could it be named after him as an autoeponym?

Stricken by a ghastly case of the Winceworths. I am sorry I cannot come into work today, I've a Winceworth like you wouldn't believe. This could be his legacy, the way his name might yet echo down the generations. He made a mental chit to see whether the word already existed in slang or dialect words – perhaps something bracing and earthy from Dorset with gruff fricatives and flat, thudding vowels.

The squeak of soles on parquetry met Winceworth and cat as they reached the corridor adjacent to the Scrivenery. *Decorum*, in architecture, is the suitability of a building, and the several parts and ornaments thereof, to its station and occasion. Swansby House's central, circular, shelf-lined Scrivenery was a bright, vast room with high windows and whitewashed stuccoed dome. A bookish bullring with the acoustics of a basilica. Even on a dull January day, sunshine lanced down upon the Swansby workers below, light curdling the dust in the air whenever it rose from disturbed old papers. There must have been at least fifty desks in the room, all regularly spaced and facing the entrance. Light glinted from the flat blades of paper knives in flashed blurs.

The majority of the sounds of the Scrivenery were dedicated to paper – the sibilance of documents slid across desktop, the slightly more stuttered shuffling of leaves arranged into order or the *khuhhkunk-ffppp* of a book removed from its purchase on the shelves lining the large airy room. It is a lexicographer's impulse to categorise these things. All this was a welcome, cathedral-like calm compared to the orange oriole nightmare of Dr Rochfort-Smith's office, let alone the braying scheme and flux of Birdcage Walk and London's many other streets. The general noise was low; the peeling back of pages, the plopping of cats from desk to floor and the occasional sniff or sneeze were the highlights as lexicographers moved quietly from their desks to the ranked pigeonholes of index cards set into the walls of the domed Scrivenery hall. These pigeon-holes were arranged alphabetically in huge towering labelled wooden shelves all around the perimeter of the room.

Pigeonholes – depending on whether it was a good or bad day at *Swansby's New Encyclopaedic Dictionary*, informally this manner of shelving was referred to by the lexicographers as either *the dovecote* or *the cloacae*. Winceworth's desk was amongst the *S* words.

He slunk into his seat with his head still a-clanging. Notions of *slinking* seemed to characterise even his most fluid gestures. Just as the lisp descended over his tongue as he entered the building, so too his shoulders shot unnaturally high once sat at his desk. Winceworth intuitively moved to pick up his Swansby standard-issue pen. It was not in its usual place. He looked at his hands as though trying to remember what possible use they could be.

Conversation in the Scrivenery took place in muttered tones. All was conducted at the level of *murmur*, *grumble* or *croon* apart from rare moments of particular inspiration or when grievous error and frustration were realised. Generally this was frowned upon but, after all, even the most slapdash of lexicographers is only human and Winceworth was certainly guilty of such eruptions. Misspellings and grammatical up-slips snagged his eyeline and produced a physical reaction. A sprightly *tsk* usually released some of the tension. Perhaps all readers experience this feeling – a well-crafted sentence runs through the reading mind as a rope runs through hands but when that sentence contains errors or distracting ambiguities, eccentric syntax or bleurghs of vocabulary or grammar, its progress is stalled or coarsened. Compare the textured skeins of these two examples:

The quick brown fox jumped over the lazy dog.
The jumx quickfoot browned oevr the, dogly laze.

Surely a *tsk* might be excused in the latter case.

The colleague occupying the desk next to Winceworth was not a *tsk*er. Whenever Bielefeld encountered an error or disruption on a page, a kind of whinnying, sniffing gag tore from his throat. It was quite distressing and often made Winceworth start. Bielefeld's eyes would widen, his hands would draw up on either side of his neatly whiskered cheeks and a small, high, vocalised peal would ring through the air. The noise was animal in nature but also not unlike the sound of a finger being pulled across a wine glass. It made cats and lexicographers turn their heads. The moment would then pass and calm returned to his face as Bielefeld scored a line through the error or retraced his steps on the page, carrying on as if nothing had happened.

The peace in Swansby's Press was rent by these squawks

quite regularly and nobody other than Winceworth seemed to mind.

Shoutsnorting colleague Bielefeld was already scribbling away at the desk on Winceworth's left. Bielefeld was shaped like a carafe. On Winceworth's right sat Appleton, shaped like a cafetière. All three exchanged the normal noises of pleasantry.

Winceworth's desk was littered with yesterday's blue index cards and scrunched pieces of paper, ready for work even if he was not. He wished he had thought to clear his desk. Clear desk, clear mind. There must be a word for that, too – when your environment is arranged so as to inspire calm and rational industry. It would be indulgent to come up with such a word. But – if he did – perhaps a sprinkling of classical Latin, the cool of its marble statuary in its vowels and cadences. Yes, maybe bring in something of *quiescent, quiescens*, present participle of *quiescere*, 'to come to rest, to be quiet'. As he ordered his space, he considered the composition of a new word as if he was concocting a recipe. Could borrow from *quiescens*-stock, then, but add to it the steadying influence of 'elbow-room' or 'ease' implied by something like Old French *eise, aise* cognate with Provençal *ais*, Italian *agio*, 'relieve from burdened or laborious duties' then stir in, what? – something foraged from an Alpine stroll along to the cooling tributaries of *fresh* through *fersh*, 'unsalted; pure; sweet; eager' via Old English *fersc*, 'of water', itself transposed from Proto-Germanic *friskaz*. A neat enlivening spritz of etymology to this new word. So: his desk might be *freasquiscent* and ready for work?

A hand patted Winceworth's shoulder and he fully jumped in his chair.

'Quite the party last night, hah!'

Winceworth looked from the hand to the face peering at him. While working at Swansby's, he had made a conscious effort not to make a taxonomy of his fellow workers. Even a private cataloguing (Bielefeld: carafe; Appleton: cafetière) seemed unfair, dehumanising even, but so many figures just slipped into set types. Without wanting to stereotype or acknowledge cliché, therefore, Winceworth knew that the person blinking breezily down at him was an Anglo-Saxon scholar. This specific species within the Swansby's stable of lexicographers all seemed to be half-composed of clouds. White clouds on top of their heads and white clouds on their chins – their eyes were cloudy and their breath was somehow warmer and heavier than anyone else's when they leaned in too close to speak. They always *did* lean in too close as if nudged forward by an unseen crosswind, and seemed to take up a lot of room whenever they moved, always choosing to walk in the centre of a corridor or channel between desks rather than stepping to one side. It was a gentle filling of space, not an aggressive one. The Anglo-Saxon scholars wafted rather than surged or marched.

They spoke softly with lumpy, lilting vowels. This one was no exception.

'The party,' Winceworth repeated. 'Last night? Yes, quite a party, that party.'

The cloud nodded, smiled, puffed away.

★

The content and extent of Winceworth's conversations within the domed hall generally fell into certain patterns. For example, the puff-bearded genius behind *Swansby's New Encyclopaedic Dictionary*, Prof. Gerolf Swansby, always said, 'Good morning, Winceworth!' when he passed Winceworth's desk before lunch. Always the same intonation and word order. There was a boy, Edmund, employed to distribute packets of letters and documents. Whenever he came by, his wicker barrow wheedling a note beneath the breath of its wheel, Edmund's cry of 'There's your lot!' always prompted a 'Let's see what we have here then!' The same inflection each time, the same pitch and register and volume.

On the rare occasion that a colleague approached Winceworth's desk to comment on the weather or the cricket score or some minor matter of politics, they never seemed to come to him with queries. No one ever spoke to him expecting to receive a certain, specific answer.

Winceworth wondered how *they* all stereotyped *him*. A piece of the furniture. A lisping feature of *decorum*.

Edmund the barrow boy was approaching now, and sure enough—

'There's your lot!' came the call as papers and letters smacked onto Winceworth's desk. He jumped again, despite himself, at the impact.

'Ah! Let's see—' The words sprang automatically to his lips. His eyes moved to the back of the departing cloud. 'See what—' he continued, and his voice had a distinct waver to it, still faintly whiskied from the night before.

The boy was already moving on to the next desk and reaching into the basket for Appleton's papers.

'There's your lot!' said the boy to Appleton.

'Thank you ever so much,' Winceworth mouthed to no one in particular.

'Thank you ever so much!' said the lexicographer, taking up the papers.

The system for the day was simple: Winceworth received various words, and sources for their definitions, from the public each day, which he would sift and assess and annotate. When he was ready to draft a final definition for a word, he would write it with his regulation Swansby pen on one of the powder-blue index cards stacked in front of him. These cards would be collected by Edmund at the end of every day and he would slot them in the alphabeticised pigeonholes lining the Scrivenery. There, the words were ready to be added to the *Dictionary* proofs.

Appleton caught his eye. 'Did you make it home last night, Winceworth? You look a little grey about the gills.'

'Yes. Yes, wasn't it?' Winceworth said. As expected, Appleton completely ignored him.

'Must say, my head was quite the belfry first thing. Who knew selling *rhubarb jam* would keep Frasham's family in quite such a fine line of cognacs?'

'Wasn't it,' said Winceworth again. And then, once more, grist for the mill, 'Yes?'

'Still,' said Appleton. He dug his paper knife into the envelopes strewn across his desk. 'Good to meet the happy couple at last.'

Winceworth blinked. A memory of the previous evening surfaced.

Bielefeld chipped in, 'Frasham mentioned her in his letters back, had he not?'

Appleton's head angled towards Frasham's empty desk, the only one on the Scrivenery floor apparently free from paper and index cards. Instead it was feathered along the fringes with pinned photographs and mementoes sent back from his travels.

'No, he didn't,' Winceworth said. 'Not once.'

'And so good to have Terence back in the country, too, where we can keep an eye on him,' said Appleton.

'Entirely awful,' Winceworth said.

'Been too long, far too long; wondering about him and his silent Glossop shadow trudging across God knows where doing God knows what.'

'Aubergine,' Winceworth contributed.

Appleton's expression didn't flicker. 'But yesterday was far too busy to get a proper word with him; I shall have to grab him by the sleeve the next time he dares shows his face around the door. Did you see him with the balalaika: what a thing! Wonderful man. But!' Appleton stretched and wiggled his shoulders. 'To the task in hand!' He met Winceworth's gaze again. Winceworth smiled blankly. 'Did you say anything, just then?'

'No?'

'Just so,' said Appleton. He had the courtesy to frown.

Khuhhkunk-ffppp. The sound of a book removed from a nearby shelf.

'Quite the looker, wasn't she?' came Bielefeld's voice from Winceworth's other side.

'What's that?' said Appleton, and he bent forward so that he could see across Winceworth's desk. In this posture Winceworth could not help but notice that Appleton's eye was very close to a number of pencils arranged in a pewter cup in front of him.

'The fiancée: what's-her-name,' Bielefeld urged. 'Did you manage to speak to her?'

'I did not,' said Appleton.

'I did not,' grieved Bielefeld.

'I did,' said Winceworth but nobody paid him any mind. He was still staring at the pencils and their proximity to Appleton's eye. One pencil in particular was just a matter of millimetres away.

'I did not have the pleasure of speaking with her either. Very haughty, I thought.' A rare female voice came from a desk behind them – one of the twin Cottingham sisters who worked at the dictionary. Winceworth knew that one of the sisters was an expert on Norse philology, the other an authority on the Goidelic branch of the Celtic languages and they were identical but for the fact that one had entirely black hair and the other's hair was entirely white. This was not a natural quirk, but one achieved through various dyes and oils, applied in order that some sense of individuality might be established. Indeed, the darker Miss Cottingham had once, unbidden, explained at length that she was convinced a commixture of rum and castor oil should be rubbed into the roots of one's hair at night to promote growth and a healthy gloss. Perhaps because of this regime, the collar of her chemise was often stained as if with rust.

Winceworth had a theory – either nobody on the *Swansby* staff knew the twins' individual Christian names or they did not care. During his five years at Swansby House, he had not once been introduced to either of the twins separately and he had not been confident enough to enquire. In his head he called them the Condiments whenever he had cause to speak to them, one being pepper-headed, the other salt.

There was a vile limerick about them scratched into the tiles in the bathrooms in the Scrivenery, the rhyme scheme of which used the word *Ossianic* with particular inventiveness.

Bielefeld and Appleton swivelled in their seats at the voice of the Cottingham, craning their necks. Half an inch closer and this action would have had Appleton's eye out, Winceworth thought. He daydreamed a little. He imagined the eye plucked out and flicked directly into post boy Edmund's wicker basket as he snaked between their desks.

'Does she even speak English?' Bielefeld pressed, and the Cottingham twin with the white hair came over to their desks, shrugging.

'Who can say?'

'Who can get a word in edgeways with Frasham?' Appleton supplied, and all but Winceworth laughed a light, frank and tender laugh.

'Hah hah hah,' said Winceworth, very slowly and deliberately half a second after their titters had finished. Another Anglo-Saxon cloud scurried between their desks and Bielefeld pretended to be busy with some small chits on his *freasquiscent* desk. He put them in a pile, disordered them, then put them in a line again, miming an approximation of work.

'*I* heard that she is *related* to the *Tsar* somehow,' the Miss Cottingham continued.

Winceworth turned in his seat as Bielefeld and Appleton both said, 'No!' and 'No?'

'Not a daughter or a niece or anything,' said the Condiment. 'But perched somewhere in that family tree.'

'You are pulling my leg,' Appleton said.

'If the tree's big enough, I'm probably related to the Tsar too,' scoffed Bielefeld.

'And the Préfet of Timbuctoo,' agreed Miss Cottingham, and they all laughed again.

'But, you know, I really wouldn't be surprised,' said Bielefeld. 'Frasham seems to move in all types of circles. A tsarina in our midst, imagine.'

'I think Frasham mentioned she was from Irkutsk?' the gossiping Appleton went on.

'Yes, I've just been updating our entry for *Irkutsk*,' Bielefeld said. 'I thought it might come in handy if I was permitted to talk with her.' Winceworth waited for the inevitable one-up-manship of trivia that Swansby researchers could never bear to not perform. 'Did you know its coat of arms shows a beaver-like animal holding a sable-fox skin? Due to a mis-translation of the word *babr*, which in the local dialect meant a Siberian tiger! *Babr* became *bobr*, meaning beaver. Quite extraordinary.'

Stifling a yawn, Winceworth thought about his morning and tigerish imaginary Mr Grumps while Bielefeld and Appleton twirled back to their desks with eyebrows raised in appreciative silence. Winceworth picked up the topmost envelope in front of him and shook its letter free. He scanned the page. Its lettering was in a looping, brown ink with lots of underlining.

> *. . . enclosed, as <u>directed</u>, evidence of a number of words beginning with <u>the letter S</u> . . . One particularly arresting example from a recipe given to me by the Very Reverend . . . Although quite <u>why</u> the sultanas would be complemented by <u>two</u>-day-old rind in such a way remains entirely . . .*

'You know Frasham's father was friends with Coleridge?' came a hiss from the other Miss Cottingham behind them. Winceworth, Bielefeld and Appleton whirled in their seats once more, orbiting with the intractable tug of gossip.

'You are pulling my other leg,' said Appleton.

'Well, *there's a thing*!'

Looking Appleton directly in the face, Winceworth said, 'You look just like a cafetière; I've often thought so.' Again this went completely unnoticed.

'Or was it Wordsworth?' said Pepper-Cottingham. 'One of the two. No, I'm sure it was Coleridge.'

'I've just been writing up one of his – where is it—?' Bielefeld flapped his papers along his desk, scrabbling and adding a frantic new pace of rustle to the Scrivenery's hall. 'Yes! Here! One of Coleridge's first coinages—' Bielefeld held up one of his blue index cards, face flushed with triumph. '*Soul-mate*, noun!' His cry caused a flush of *Shhh!s* to ripple across the room. Correspondingly, the group's voices sank. ' "You must have a Soul-mate as well as a House- or a Yoke-mate," ' he quoted. 'You see: there! First used in Coleridge's letters.' Bielefeld had the smile of a Master of the Hunt, Winceworth observed.

'I caught an early use of *supersensuous* in one of his articles just yesterday,' said Salt-Cottingham. A competitive edge crept into her voice.

'How wonderful.' Appleton paused, then added with the flourish of an Ace across baize, 'Of course, it was in Coleridge's papers that I netted – now, what was it – ah, yes, *astrognosy* and *mysticism* some months ago. And I was rather pleased to catch his deployment of *romanticise* over the summer.'

'Don't forget *narcissism*,' Winceworth said. 'Noun.'

Three faces turned to him.

'I'm sorry, Winceworth,' Miss Cottingham said, 'did you say something?'

'Only—' Appleton looked at his pewter cup of pencils, then at the ceiling, then at Miss Cottingham and Bielefeld for camaraderie before settling back on Winceworth. 'Well, you know, the old lisp, *ah!* It's sometimes difficult to—'

'I've often said,' Bielefeld spoke up, 'that if Coleridge's maxim holds true, and poets are the unacknowledged *legislators* of the world, lexicographers are doubly so, hidden in plain sight.'

'Oh, very good!' Appleton said, and Miss Cottingham gave an abrupt clap of her hands.

'That was – that was *Shelley*, I think—' Winceworth said, but at that point one of the innumerable Scrivenery cats jumped up onto his desk.

'Oops!' said Appleton.

'To what do we owe the pleasure!' said Bielefeld.

'Steady there!' said Miss Cottingham.

The cat looked at Winceworth, right into the heart of him. He extended a hand. Without breaking eye contact, the cat reversed a couple of steps, paused and then, protractedly and calmly, coughed something hairy and pelleted and faintly damp over Winceworth's paperwork and into his lap.

Appleton and Bielefeld's chairs squealed against the floor in their haste to push away and *Shhhhh!*s filled the air of the Scrivenery once more.

E is for *esquivalience* (n.)

I had not received any training regarding specific bomb threats. I had not received any particular training at all, so I stared at the phone receiver for a good minute. I picked up my mobile and texted Pip in the café where she worked, *I'm sorry this might be it, I love you, goodbye, x*. I switched off my computer without saving, I watched the ivy outside my window bounce and waggle in a light breeze, then I smashed my fist into the red *BREAK GLASS TO ACTIVATE* fire alarm just by my desk. I did this with all the zeal of an employee who has fantasised about doing so since their first day on the job.

It was then I learned that the fire alarms in the building were not functional, the result of another cost-cutting decision. Unsure what to do next, I remembered that there was a laminated Health and Safety sheet of guidelines in the stationery cupboard, spotted with damp beneath the plastic. It had little pared-down ideograms of men falling over triangles and red *POW!* explosion shapes over pictures of bent knees. I walked to the cupboard, picked this sheet up and held it tight to my chest. I knocked on David's door. He sat stooped over his computer, typing with his two index fingers.

'Did he call again?' he asked, not looking up.

I explained the situation, miming hitting the fire alarm with particular vigour, and he rolled his eyes.

'I think that means we should –' I consulted the Health and Safety poster for the right wording – 'vacate the premises?'

'Lest we evacuate ourselves,' David said, and he looked pleased. I smiled because it seemed expected of me.

'Should I take the cat, do you think?' he went on, looking vaguely around his feet under his desk, then, 'No, no, not a priority, come along—' and we made our way down the stairs past the central hall, beneath the portrait of smiling Prof. Gerolf Swansby and out into the street, our shoes skittering against the stone one-hundred-and-twenty-years-of-bustle-polished steps.

'Have you rung emergency services?' David asked as we descended. I nodded, then behind my back thumbed the numbers into my phone.

The police came quickly and appeared to take the bomb threat seriously. Swansby House was so close to Buckingham Palace that they had all the right gear and were presumably ready to spring into onto unto action. One of the officers wore camouflage *and* a high-vis tabard, which seemed perhaps a mixed approach. Special officers with a whole index of particular equipment barrelled through the building's doors, presumably in order to sweep the building. This was a phrase I had heard on crime dramas. We watched from the sidelines, a little overwhelmed. I mean, I was overwhelmed: David seemed more concerned that the officers not scratch the paintwork on the doors.

'A good thing the building was not booked today,' David said, a little absently, as we watched them swarm in. 'Just the two of us rattling around – imagine if there had been a wedding.'

We were told to wait. I described the disguised voice on the phone as best I could, as well as the frequency of the calls. An officer took down all these details and asked if I was all right, and wrote down my answer to that too. She asked my name and checked the correct spelling, 'Like the mountaineer?'

David listened intently to my response and I wondered whether he harboured theories about my first name, its provenance or meaning. He seemed like the kind of person to have opinions about names. If I was descended from someone called Gerolf, I would too. In the past I've been asked whether I was named after the vain, uppity character who doesn't kiss Michael J. Fox in the TV series *Family Ties* (1982–89). I've been asked whether I was named after the psychotic wife who *does* kiss Woody Harrelson in *Natural Born Killers* (1994). People's minds run, misspellingly, to those Enid Blyton books with their Towers and jolly hockey sticks (1946–51) or further back to writers of Arthurian legend. Handsome male lieutenant lost on mountainside (1924) was a new one, however. What these people must think of my parents, I don't know.

Some books say that *Mallory* comes from the Old French, meaning *the unlucky one*.

If that's the case: what I think of my parents, I don't know.

When David spoke to the officer, he waved his hands and arms around a lot as if that might hurry the conversation and process along. 'Just some nut,' he said, spreading his considerable wingspan. 'Completely crackers. A fruitcake. One sandwich short of a picnic.'

'Those aren't the appropriate words to use,' the police officer said.

'No, quite right. Barking?'

Telling us that his colleagues might be in there for some time, another officer went to get us unseasonal ice creams from a kiosk in St James's Park. He bought David a 99 Flake, a Calippo for himself, and a choc-ice for me. I tried not to think how he had profiled us as a group to choose these ice creams. He handed them out and we all leaned against an advertising hoarding, the flashing blue of the police car's lights making David's ice cream bruise an occasional neon. Some tourists took pictures of us standing looking up at Swansby House with our arms crossed.

A voice from across the road.

'Mallory?'

Here's a thing – you carve out a code and mode for yourself at work. The job is not demanding and some of us, many of us, choose to switch off parts of our character, all of our character, just to get through the day. But then the pattern of the day shifts because of a threat on your life, say, and let's say that across the street, there, *right there, suddenly*, it's the person you love most in the world. But they appear just *so*. They might as well have risen from a manhole or a Vegas platform or been pulled from a hat, descended from on high fretted with golden fire, etc. You know their voice better than your own name, you want that voice to be the first thing you hear in the morning and the last thing at night, you want to know them long enough that you have heard every word in their accent and with every possible inflection. You fall in love every time you see them, you fall in love with the idea of falling in love purely because they exist, and they define what good can be in a day for you. They define *good* to you.

Love's a lot of wonderful nonsense like that, isn't it? Poppycock, codswallop, folderol, balderdash, piffle, hugger-mugger, fiddlesticks, silly slush, tosh, horsefeathers, etc. All of that, and all at once. Other things like *fear* are more concise but in its own way *love* gets straight to the point.

'Mallory!' Pip shouted. She tried to run across the street, but an officer stopped her before she could reach us. 'You're OK? Are you OK?'

'I'm fine,' I said. 'What are you doing here?'

'Your text, you complete—' She bit back her sentence. 'I'm – I'm sorry it's taken me so long—'

David sank his teeth into his ice cream and regarded the two of us politely. The Calippo'd police officer had an arm on Pip's shoulder so that the two of us were separated. This was dreadful but also, somehow, a good thing because my idiot mind was already trying to conjure a context for Pip's familiarity. *This is a friend. This is my cousin. This person just guessed my name right off the bat, what's that about, what are the chances—*

'Excuse me,' the police officer was saying. Pip stood back. 'Do you know this young lady?'

Pip looked at me, then at David Swansby.

'We're flatmates,' she said.

I nodded.

Before she got ready for work that morning, Pip had pointed at various bits of me for no reason whatsoever and listed their names. '*Lunule*,' she said at my fingertips. She moved along, '*Purlicue*,' then she listed across and up the bed until, '*Glabella*,' was said between my eyes. Then a pause. '*Thingamabob*.'

'*Philtrum*,' I said.

'Yes,' she said, 'that one.'

'All present and correct.'

'The whole kit and caboodle,' she said and we carried on carrying on.

I believe you don't always have to explain everything to everyone. Pip disagrees, or rather expresses it differently. I was not out at work. She did not call this cowardice on my part. I probably would.

I remember at school the test of a good dictionary would be whether it included specific parts of anatomy or swear words. Four-letter words. Usually these were the only dog-eared pages in the whole thing – if I had applied that standard to Swansby's drafts I could have learned that *dick* was another word for a workman's apron and that *jizz* might be defined as 'the total combination of characteristics that serve to identify a particular species of bird or plant'. A waste of an education. The thrill of seeing a *bad* word there was palpable – at school, you could stick your nose between *cunopic* and *cup* or between *penintime* and *penitence* and find there, nestling in the columns, something you'd grown up knowing was obscene or to be blushed at or spoken only in hushed tones. You felt the lexicographer had been depraved, and imagined them typing the word up with faux po-faced ribaldry, or smuggling the terms into the pages purely for your classroom titillation in public and charged thrill in private.

This use of the school dictionary was a kind of panning for immature gross-out gold, and had us plunging right in. It was only alone in the form room once everyone had gone home that I dared to look up other words. I told myself it was curiosity spurring me on. I didn't realise that a dictionary might be like reading a map or looking in a mirror.

butch (v. transitive), to slaughter (an animal), to kill for market. *Also*: to cut up, to hack

dyke (n.), senses relating to a ditch or hollowed-out section

gay (v. intransitive), to be merry, cheerful, or light-hearted. Obsolete

lesbian rule (n.), a flexible (usually lead) ruler which can be bent to fit what is being measured

Figurative, pertaining to something, esp. a legal principle, which adapts to fit the circumstances

queer (adj.), strange, odd, peculiar, eccentric. *Also*: of questionable character; suspicious, dubious. Of coins or banknotes: counterfeit, forged

queer (v. intransitive), to ask, enquire; to question. To put out of order; to spoil. *Also*: to spoil the reputation or

chances of (a person); to put (a person) out of favour
(with another)

Even at school I remember wondering about closets, whether
there was a subtle difference between *someone* being in the
closet and a *skeleton* being in the closet. I checked the dictionary for clarification, but found none. I turned the pages, hot
with a growing sense of shame.

Pip was out at the café where she worked. Of course she was –
she was out to her family, she was out at work, out and about,
out-and-out out. I suspected she emerged from the womb with
little badges on her lapel reading *Lavender Menace* and *10% is
not Enough! Recruit! Recruit! Recruit!*

'David Swansby wouldn't bat an eyelid if you told him,' she
once said to me. She had brought the topic up. 'And if he *does*
bat an eyelid, you can tell him where to get off.'

She was right, of course. And wrong, of course.

'Where to get off,' I repeated.

'Or,' she said, 'you could tell him that your big bad butch
will come and sort him out.' She tuff-pranced across the bedroom, growling.

'You can be brave enough for the both of us,' I said. I meant
it as a joke but it sounded melodramatic, or maudlin. Pip
didn't say anything.

It wasn't that I didn't want to be out, I told myself. I
admired people who were, I envied them, I thought them
brave and wonderful. I just didn't have the words in the way

they all seemed to. It was the most prosaic, unflaming, snuffed, tamped-down kind of fear. I watched a documentary once about abattoirs and I remember there was an on-camera discussion about the biological effects suffered by livestock prior to slaughter. Apparently the taste of the meat can be altered by the build-up of lactic acid and adrenaline if the animals are distressed. The phrase *fear degrades the meat and its flavour* flashed up in the subtitles. I stopped watching documentaries about abattoirs.

Offhand, while washing the dishes, I told Pip about the phone calls coming in at work. She had surprised me by bursting into tears and bringing me in close.

Outside Swansby House and surrounded by police, a pigeon took this moment to scrump ice-cream-cone crumbs from around my boss's ankles.

'Ah!' said David. 'Mallory's flatmate, I think she's mentioned you.'

'Is that right?' Pip said.

'A pleasure, a pleasure.' David shook her hand and immediately I resented their closeness and wanted to divert them away from one another. They were two circles on a Venn diagram that should not have intersected or bounced up against another. London was surely big enough that this should never happen.

'Bit of a ruckus here,' David continued shyly to Pip's concerned upturned face. 'Bit of nothing.'

'Can it be both? Ruckus and a bit of nothing?' Pip turned to me. 'Your text—'

'It's nothing,' I said.

'It looks like something,' she said, gesturing at the police van and officers.

'Just a silly hoax. They're just making sure everything is safe. The fire alarms didn't go off, so I had to—'

'You could have been torched where you sat!' Pip looked David up and down. Given his height, this took some time. 'That's incredibly illegal!'

'It can't be incredibly one or the other,' David said. He couldn't help himself. 'Something's either illegal or not illegal.'

Mansplain (v.) was unlikely to ever enter any version of the *Swansby's Encyclopaedic Dictionary*.

'I guess that makes *you* incredible,' Pip said, and she reared up as really only she can do, but David was not concentrating, he was inspecting something at his feet—

A man, apparently unmoved by the presence of police officers and blithely attempting to keep to the pavement and enjoy their normal route unimpeded, strayed between us. I had to commute every day through Westminster, and some people there just refused to recognise that not every path was available to them. In this instance, this person also had a small dog. Horrified that a bomb threat was distracting any possible attention from it, this passer-by's dog chose that moment to slowly and theatrically defecate at my boss's feet.

'Ah!' said David.

'Oh!' said Pip.

'I'm so sorry,' said the passer-by. 'She's never done this before.'

The ice-cream police officer asked his companion, 'Isn't that against a by-law?'

'Not if it's picked up,' David said.

Pip patted her pockets, making a pantomime of looking for a carrier bag.

I put the whole choc-ice into my mouth, bent down and used the cheap plastic wrapper to scoop the day's simpler mess into my hand. I thought, maybe this is what I was put on earth to do. I was never going to be brave or proud but I know about timings and small interventions.

'Chivalry,' Pip said. I straightened for everyone.

The ice cream hurt my teeth.

'Are we done here?' David said to the police officer. She spoke into a radio.

No rest for the wicked, said the dog's face, and she tugged at her leash, pleased by her efforts to communicate efficiently and without formality.

'Nice meeting you,' said Pip. I'm not sure to whom she addressed this. She took the choc-ice wrapper from my hand and left the scene without looking back.

F is for *fabrication* (n.)

Winceworth opened his regulation Swansby House leather attaché case, making sure no one was looking over his work. For some years now, just to pass the time and for his own amusement, he had been making up some words and definitions. He sketched these idle thoughts on borrowed notepaper whenever the mood took him: sometimes inspired by interactions with his colleagues in the Scrivenery – *bielefoldian* (n.), an annoying fellow; *titpalcat* (n.), a welcome distraction. Sometimes he just improvised little fictions in the style of an encylopaedic entry. To this end, he made up some fourteenth-century dignitaries from Constantinople and a small religious sect living in the volcanic Japanese Alps. More often than not, however, these false entries allowed him to plug a lexical gap, create a word for a sensation or a reality where no other word in current circulation seemed to fit the bill. This ranged from waxing poetical about a disappointing meal – *susposset* (n.), the suspicion that chalk has been added to ice cream to bulk out the serving – to ruminations concerning everyday events – *coofugual* (v.), the waking of pigeons; *relectoblivious* (adj.), accidentally rereading a phrase or line due to lack of focus or desire to finish; *larch* (v.), to allot time to daydreaming.

Winceworth flexed his hands. He meant no harm by this, he told himself, and he was allowed these small private amusements. He considered the much-discussed, absent Frasham and gnawed the end of his rediscovered Swansby pen. It was cheap and hollow, and infrequently he was worried he would chew right through it. Winceworth selected a new blank index card and wrote

frashopric (n.), the office or position of a dullard, acquired by money.

Terence Clovis Frasham was one of the few people for whom Winceworth's lisp presented an opportunity for cruelty. He was quite the darling of Swansby's, not because he was a particularly talented lexicographer nor a very hard worker. He was, however, both exceedingly rich through some family jam-making business. Just as usefully, he also had a real flair for attracting and massaging the egos of exceedingly rich friends. Every so often, whenever Prof. Gerolf's coffers ran low, Frasham was able to amass some glinting and bulging soirée and press his associates and acquaintances for donations, and magically money appeared. This genius for accruing funds for the dictionary meant that whenever Frasham *did* make an appearance at Swansby House, he was fêted as a princeling and benefactor.

Occasionally Winceworth saw invitations to these fundraising events – dances or regattas depending on the season – but never felt moved to attend. He had nothing to offer, after all, and was sure that some fault would be found with his attire or that he would make some embarrassing slip of etiquette. *Terenth Clovith Fthrathm*. According to the invitation slipped onto his desk the previous month, Frasham had been accepted to the 1,500 Mile Society on the occasion of his twenty-seventh birthday and would Peter Winceworth like to join him in celebrating this achievement?

There were many reasons to drink heavily in the presence of Terence Clovis Frasham. He was handsome, popular and had the posture of a professional tennis player. Tennis was a sport, along with fencing and long-distance swimming, for which Frasham had received Blues whilst at university. Winceworth, by contrast, if one was in the business of contrasts, had the posture of a middle-ranking chess player. Frasham also possessed that particularly resentful quality of being a complete braggart while also seeming simply charming. He had entered the employ of *Swansby's New Encyclopaedic Dictionary* at the same time as Winceworth and both were of similar ages.

According to the party invitation, Frasham qualified for entry to the 1,500 Mile Society having successfully returned from Siberia. This jaunt had been funded by Swansby House in order that the etymology of the words *shaman*, *struse* and (obtusely or abstrusely) the correct spelling of *tsar* might be researched for the *S* volume. Winceworth was still not quite sure how Frasham had talked Prof. Gerolf Swansby into this since Frasham did not speak, nor was qualified to translate, a word of Russian as far as anyone knew. *Spurious* (adj.), from Latin *spurius* 'illegitimate', from *spurius* (n.) meaning 'illegitimate child', from the Etruscan *spural* meaning 'public'. According to one of the letters Frasham sent back to the offices, pursuing the etymology of *starlet* (n.) necessitated a funded audience with various members of Russian aristocracy.

Given the parallels between their lives thus far, the fact Frasham was sent to the steppes of Asia whilst Peter Winceworth was funded to undergo Dr Rochfort-Smith's attentions in Chelsea seemed fair. Then Frasham's photographs started arriving back at Swansby House. As London passed through smog-fumey summer and autumn, with horses slaughtered in the street to make way for automobiles and the city filleted for the Underground railways, the photographs sent by Frasham caused grown men and women at the *Dictionary* to coo with envy and excitement. Here was one featuring Frasham on camelback, another with him wreathed in silks looking over Lake Baikal and taking tea with a diplomat. A particularly dramatic shot of Frasham mock-wrestling a walrus was greeted with something bordering hysteria by members of Swansby House's staff and was immediately pinned above his empty desk, shrine-like.

In the corner of the photograph one could just make out Glossop, the other Swansby House employee sent on the trip. While his companion was tall and strapping, Ronald Glossop was unprepossessing. Perhaps it was testament to Frasham being quite so particularly good-looking but standing next to him – and Glossop *was* invariably somewhere close to Frasham whether in the Westminster offices or on the coast of the Bering Sea, forever scampering at the latter's elbow with pen and paper – it was difficult to remember any real defining features for the man. Winceworth could not even recollect what his voice was like or even if he had ever heard him speak. One thing he could recall of Glossop was the lime-green handkerchief carried in his waistcoat's jetted pocket – it was a bright enough colour that everyone grew used to catching sight of it flashing like St Elmo's fire across the wide central hall of the Scrivenery. Glossop was very much treated as Frasham's assistant, although they actually held the same role at Swansby House and Glossop's faculty for languages and philology was far more advanced. Winceworth suspected Glossop did most of the actual lexicographical work during their year-long Siberian trip together as well as any heavy lifting (other than for theatrical effect, cf. walruses).

In the walrus photograph Glossop stood almost out of frame. He was in the background, blurred and obscure, using a hatchet to saw a flipper from one of the put-upon walrus's floe-mates.

Frasham's photographs were accompanied by letters, often elaborate with metaphor and regularly ill-spelt. The progress of Frasham's etymological investigations was never really emphasised.

At their desks in Swansby House, Bielefeld once noticed Winceworth glancing with particular dolefulness at the walrus photograph and said in passing, cheerfully, 'The valour of the field versus the elbow-grease of the desk!'

Winceworth smiled in answer and gripped his Swansby House pen too hard. He looked down to find his notes on *solecism* (n.) spattered with ink.

G is for *ghost* (v.)

Once the police let us back into the building, guaranteeing that the call was just a hoax or prank, David and I returned to our second floor. David twiddled with something in a box of electrics under the stairs, assuring me that the fire alarm would work in the future. I left him to it. After about an hour David rang the internal phone line – making me jump circa 400 feet in the air – and requested that I come into his office.

I knew it couldn't be because he had met Pip. That was a mad idea. Wrong wrong wrong, and yet there the idea lay, flat and flattening, at the base of my throat.

David rose from his seat as I knocked and entered, starting a little as if shocked. Unfortunately, David's sudden move- ment set off a chain of reactions that caused a *flurry* to intensify into a *chaos*. While some seventy-year-olds grow stooped with every passing year, David Swansby had unfurled: he was the tallest man I had ever met. This quick unwinding of his body from sitting to standing knocked a cup of coffee skidding and rolling across his desk. This startled the office cat, who ran headlong into the printer which spontaneously powered up and began shrieking something like the word 'Paroxysm!' over and over and over and over and over again. The spilt coffee scribbled a fresh, hot, organic 'WELL, WHOOPS!' flourish across the length of the editorial desk; I could tell the coffee was fresh because it steamed even as it spread across the paperwork and filing.

A few minutes later, when calm was restored, the cat Sphinxed on the armrest of a chair with its eyes closed. I gave its spine a nudge with my knuckles. Its body rumbled something about solidarity against my hand.

'Sit sit sit,' David said.

'Thank you.' I noticed the game of online chess open on David's computer screen.

'Tits Tits Tits,' said David Swansby.

I had first met Tits during the interview for my current role. He was a rangy, yellow-eyed duffer-moggy with a coat the colour of old toast. His presence as co-interviewer ('Ignore the cat at your feet! Please, do sit down!') was not unwelcome: this explained the shallow ceramic bowl on the desk in front of me, placed next to the *Swansby's New Encyclopaedic Dictionary*-branded mug and the block of Post-It notes. At first I had thought that the bowl might be an ashtray, and if not an ashtray then a horrible version of a hotel reception's Mint Imperials, half-filled with little dusty brown pellets. Not quite powder, nowhere near meat: *kibble* is the name, isn't it, for that kind of catfood. I've only ever heard that word thanks to American sitcoms. Satisfyingly apt combination of sounds and letters, and carries the overtones of *kitten* + *nibble* + *rubble*, as well as the vague sense of onomatopoeia as it is shaken out of the bag.

Halfway through the interview for the internship I noticed this shallow ceramic bowl had TITS written on it. David – then just Mr Swansby for the interview's sake – followed my line of sight.

'Short for Titivillus,' he said. He came around the desk and began talking to the cat. 'Isn't it, Tits? Tits Tits Tits.' He reached for Tits's ears and gave them a scratch. My job-hungry brain kicked in and I recognised the cat had been transformed into a conduit for diplomacy so I put my hand onto a tuft above its cat-shoulder. As Mr Swansby worked his thumb around to Tits's jaw, finding the sweet spots there that make cats smile, I focused on its withers. If that's the right word. Maybe this was all unconnected, but Tits purred at our teamwork and I got the job.

As David mopped up the coffee with what appeared to be a spare pair of socks, I felt I needed to say something mild, to dissipate the mood. God knows why I always feel driven to do this.

'You know, you never fully explained the cat's name,' I said.

'Strictly speaking,' David said, not looking up, 'all the cats at Swansby's have been called that, ever since the very first mouser kept down in the printing press. Rats make nests out of the discarded galley papers, you know. Dynasty stuff. Eighteen Tits. Would you like some tea? Coffee? Water?'

'No, thank you.' I rubbed a thumb down Tits's nose.

'I thought *Titivillus* was a bit too long for collars so I short-ened it to the inevitable,' David said. 'That was funny for the first year but then – well, I always forget how it must look. Bowls all around the building with TITS written on them, me shouting "Tits!" out of windows. I'm so used to the name by now that I hardly notice.' David busied himself with a kettle and a small cafetière.

'Titivillus,' I said again, to check the pronunciation. 'Is that an emperor? Empress?'

'A demon – I think Milton mentions him, possibly not.' David waved at the lower half of his wall-to-ceiling bookshelves, presumably indicating an *M* section. I was not prepared for the editor of an encyclopaedic dictionary to admit ignorance so candidly while also asserting how well-read he was. 'Certainly crops up in mystery plays: used to be blamed for introducing errors into written works. Slip-ups, typos, that kind of thing. There's also something in *The Pickwick Papers* about "tits" being a word for calling cats. "Puss, puss, puss – tit, tit, tit." Along those lines.'

Tits's purring intensified against my hand. David hit the cafetière plunger with the stance of someone detonating a mountainside.

'He's a boy, by the way,' David said.

'Got it,' I said. 'Hello,' I added, to the cat.

'But all that's something completely by-the-by,' said David. 'I want to ask you about whether you are any good at keeping secrets.'

I blinked.

'This will all be rather quick and informal. In fact,' David said, checking his tone, 'I'd rather that what I'm about to say doesn't go beyond these walls.'

It occurred to me that I might be fired. From a cannon, in a kiln, from a job, fretted, fretting, flaming. I began to make calculations about rent and overdrafts as David cleared his throat. I realised I had been making these calculations in the back of my mind every day since I started this job. There should be a specific word for that: the sluice of adrenaline that comes when you are able to pinpoint the reason for exhaustion. Precarity and teetering and grocery lists with question marks and budgeting apps and crying in the shower and adding water to pasta sauce and—

'First of all, I want to emphasise that I am deeply aggrieved by today's events,' David said. 'Thank you for taking time out of your day, and I am so incredibly sorry for any upset caused.'

I waited.

'I need to talk to you about *mountweazels*.'

'*Mountweazels*,' I repeated.

'There are mistakes. In the dictionary,' David said. There seemed to be a sob edging the softness of his voice. I stared at him. He assumed a defensive tone. 'Well. Not *mistakes*. Not-quite mistakes. They're words that are meant to be there but not meant to be there.'

'*Mountweazels*,' I repeated again.

'Other dictionaries have them! Most!' David Swansby said. 'They're made-up words.'

'All words are made up,' I said.

'That is true,' David Swansby replied, 'and also not a useful contribution.'

'Fake words?' I said.

'That might be one way to put it.'

David rearranged the pencils and notepads on his desk as he went on. The speech felt rehearsed, thesis-like. He explained that factually incorrect words can crop up in any work of reference. While they do undermine any overall sense of a dictionary's objective authority, these entries will not necessarily be considered 'fiction', however. It was crucial to consider, he said, whether there was any intention to disseminate *untruths*. The cause for non-facts appearing in dictionaries could be split most simply between those mistakes that occurred as a result of extra-lexical concerns and those that occurred through editorial misunderstandings. David was at pains to point out how other, rival dictionaries botched this: for example, early in the history of the *Oxford English Dictionary*, all of the drafted definitions that began with the letters *Pa* written up on slips, ready to be edited, were accidentally used for kindling. This error was blamed on an inattentive housemaid. Moreover, only after the first edition of the *OED* appeared in print was it discovered that a fugitive *bondmaid* (n.) entry had been completely left out from the proofs due to misfiling. This kind of unfortunate occurrence was not limited to dictionaries and encyclopaedias, of course. In an interview, the creator of the popular *London A–Z Street Atlas* described how she momentarily lost possession of 23,000 index cards out of a window thanks to a sudden gust of wind. Many of those hand-completed cards flew onto the top of a bus as it sped down Holborn High Street. This explains the absence of the entry for Trafalgar Square in the first edition. I had no idea whether this anecdote was true or not. I never checked, but David made a very compelling narrator for forgivable editors' oversights. He could write a dictionary of failures, I thought.

David continued: unfortunate coincidences and misjudgements of this kind could cause an *incomplete* dictionary but certainly not a deliberately incorrect one – there is no evidence of malicious intent in these instances that contributed to a wrong dictionary designed to mislead the user. Reader. Chance-upon-er. Plain errors of definition as well as mistakes could just sneak into a dictionary or encyclopaedia, and such blunders were contributing factors to the unwitting summoning of so-called *ghost words*. David spoke about *ghost words* for some time, grabbing a text from his shelves and quoting directly from it: 'Yes, *ghost words* – "words which have no real existence" *dum de dum, blah de blah* –' he thumbed through the paragraph – ' "being mere coinages due to the blunders of printers or scribes, or to the perfervid imaginations of ignorant or blundering editors." '

I had no idea what he was quoting.

Such fruits of 'perfervid imagination' were represented by the ghost word *dord* that 'famously' appeared in five consecutive editions of *Webster's New International Dictionary*. In 1931, *Webster's* chemistry editor submitted a slip that read 'D or d, cont./density', intending to indicate that the letter *D* in upper- or lower-case could stand as an abbreviation for the value of a density in scientific equations. Miscommunication between different editorial bodies within the publishing process meant that *Webster's* typesetters received the editor's slip and assumed that *Dord* was a headword, defined as 'density', rather than an illustration of upper- or lower-case – it was only when *dord*'s lack of etymology was noted in 1939 that the entry was questioned and eventually expunged.

Dense dense dense. God knows how many people must have used *dord* in that time. I know I used it at least four times every week, dorddawdledoodling my way through the day.

Many lexicographers and encyclopaedists drew upon their predecessors in a sleight of standing-on-the-shoulders-of-giants (unacknowledged or scandalised as those giants might be by the presumption), and we should count ourselves lucky that *dord* hadn't worked its way into *Swansby's* pages.

At this point in his lecture, David Swansby gave a nervous cough. He went on, avoiding my gaze.

Some dictionaries deliberately constructed and disseminated fictions in order to protect their contents, whereby the violating act of inserting a fictional entry enabled that entry to become an anti-violation device. Think of it this way, David said: if (if!) you were compiling a dictionary, it would be very easy to purloin another person's work and pass it off as your own since words are words are words, etc., etc. But if they made up a word and put it in their text and then saw that it had bobbed up in your pages, they'd know you copied their stuff.

Mountweazel: the noun that refers to these bogus entries cooked up and inserted into a dictionary or encyclopaedia as a means of protecting copyright. Misinformation, fake news – gotcha, pal.

This was a strategy also used by cartographers to safeguard their maps: just plop a non-existent 'Trap Street' in amongst the roads and byways in order to tell upon tracing replication in other publications whether other maps have copied yours.

I permitted Tits the cat to curl up in my lap as David went on. He explained that *mountweazels* were named after one of the most famous fictitious entries, printed amongst the pages of *The New Columbia Encyclopedia* (1975). Lillian Virginia Mount-weazel sits unobtrusively in the company of the composer *Mussorgsky* in the foothills of *Mount Olympus* and *Mount Rushmore*:

> *Mountweazel, Lillian Virginia*, 1942–1973, American photog-rapher, b. Bangs, Ohio. Turning from fountain design to photography in 1963, Mountweazel produced her cele-brated portraits of the South Sierra Miwok in 1964. She was awarded government grants to make a series of photo-essays of unusual subject matter, including New York City buses, the cemeteries of Paris and rural American mail-boxes. The last group was exhibited extensively abroad and published as *Flags Up!* (1972). Mountweazel died at 31 in an explosion while on assignment for *Combustibles* magazine.

I liked the sound of Lillian Virginia. It was a shame she didn't exist.

'So there are some of these fake words in *our* dictionary?' I said.

'In a manner of speaking,' David said.

'One?' I asked. 'One or two? What are they?'

'Herein lies the issue,' David said.

He handed a printout to me. Tits was excited to see movement across the desk and perked up beneath my hand. The piece of paper was slightly coffee-damp around the edges.

It was a scan of a *Swansby's* dictionary page. The scan was not a good one, with the spectre of David's fingertips visible at its sides. A single word and its definition were circled halfway down the column.

cassiculation (n.), sensation of walking into spider silk, diaphanous unseen webs, etc.

A good word, I thought. I can see the use for that.

I brought the page close to my face as if trying to sniff out the fraud. 'This is one of those fake words? These mountweazels?'

'I've cross-checked as many dictionaries as I can bear: it's not in *any* of them.' David indicated his bookshelves, then ran his hands through his hair in such a way that seemed to imply that he was used to pulling it out.

'I mean,' I said, turning the word over in my mouth, 'just one little word. *Cassiculation*. What's the harm in—'

'I went back to the archives,' David interrupted. He was not usually an interrupting man. He held up a faded index card on his desk. 'I went back to the original slip of paper that we had in storage. Each word has its own "slip" with its definition written on it. Have a look at it, here: no example usages given, there's no etymology – it's been written on the card in a completely non-standard way. God knows how it got through the editing process and was included, but this bloody word has been squirrelled away in the dictionary in every copy ever printed.'

'If it's one of these mountweazels,' I said, picking up the index card, 'and if I've followed you, surely there must be some record of it being inserted? Otherwise the trick doesn't work. It wouldn't work as a copyright trap. You need to know you've lain a trap to catch anyone out.'

David nodded. 'That's what I'm holding out for – that there's a list somewhere in storage that we can scoop up, then tick off and winnow out all of these fake words before I digitise it.'

'A *list*,' I said. 'So you think there might be more than one?'

David sank behind his desk. 'I'm afraid so.' He twirled his finger dejectedly. 'Turn the page. I made it my project at the beginning of the week to see whether another one surfaced – I opened the archives at random and found one after about three hours of checking for the same handwriting on the index card.'

I turned my A4 sheets. Another scan, another circled word and definition. It might have been my imagination, but the circle looked slightly more frantic.

asinidorose (n.), to emit the smell of a burning donkey

'Jeez,' I said. 'Whoever came up with that must have been – a little bit – a little bit out there.'

'I mean, it's completely embarrassing,' David said, gesticulating. 'Mountweazels are common enough, but each edition only requires *one* of the damn things. And an editor needs to *know* about them, otherwise it's just pointless. Pointless falsehoods! It's inexplicable why they would just be sprinkled in there.'

'Makes it look like the dictionary has a mind of its own,' I said.

'How embarrassing,' David said.

'You know what, I think this is fine.'

David looked up. '*Fine?*'

'Sure,' I said. 'This is great. Make it an *asset* of the digitalisation. Digitisation. Whichever.' I warmed to my theme, seeing an opportunity to be people-pleasing. 'Totally – hoick these up on the old socials, use them to shine a light on the –' I cast around for the right words – 'I don't know, the idiosyncrasies of dictionaries. Kick up a bit of a stink on *Countdown*'s Dictionary Corner or among the cryptic-crossword community – you can't *buy* that kind of USP. It's zany, it's out there, nice traction with new demographics.' I had warmed so thoroughly to his subject, object, verb, that it seemed to me quite the hot topic.

I had no idea what I was talking about, and this kind of language seemed to cause David physical pain. He visibly aged at the mention of *USP*. 'It makes the whole of *Swansby's* into a laughing stock, that's what it does,' he said. 'I'm not going to be the editor who not only sees the end of the line for the dictionary but also ensures it's remembered as some kind of barmy sideshow.'

Tits yawned and I rubbed his ear until the purrs began. I thought it might alleviate the mood.

'So what do you want us to do?' I said. It occurred to me that David might have called me in for actual bad news. 'Do you want the digitisation to stop?'

'No!' said David. 'God, no. No, that's not going to happen. But while I carry on digitising, updating, I *do* want all hands on deck going through the archives to rout out all of these index cards.'

Tits yawned again.

'By all hands on deck, you mean—'

'I've seen you reading the *Dictionary* at your desk,' said David. 'I've noticed the pages spread out in your office.'

A guilty pang that I had been caught in my slacking. 'Just out of curiosity,' I said. I felt myself redden. Boredom. The word was *boredom*. 'Just incidentally.'

'I want you to just – well!' David clapped his hands. 'Just keep reading, but cross-check the index cards from the arch-ive. Read the 1930 edition, the nine volumes, and the proofs. If there's anything there that seems amiss you – you just, well, you let me know?'

I stood up, holding the index card. Thoughts of spiderwebs and burning donkeys filled my head.

'Certainly,' David said, to nobody at all. He looked pleased, and somehow a lot lighter on his feet. It was as if passing on the confession had unburdened him. 'So, if you wouldn't mind. I've brought up most of the *A-word* boxes and put them down by the – ah – by the litter tray over there. I'll help you bring the others up to your desk. Not a moment to lose: how about it?'

H is for *humbug* (n.)

Winceworth's mind returned yet again to the previous night's party and the reason for his headache, his current life defined by the ringing of his head. To trace the history of this particular headache meant following Winceworth-of-yesterday as he made his way through an evening crowd, vying for space between the hats and shoulders and shawls of Long Acre. All this time the word *curriebuction* kept rising in his thoughts. He ate a chestnut loudly, as if to dislodge the word.

He had not wanted to be i) late, or ii) there at all because it would involve celebrating Frasham's birthday.

The last thing that man needed was more attention. Winceworth planned to visit for half an hour, make his excuses and leave sober and informed and thoughtful and better for the exercise. Maybe he would go home and read some poetry, or philosophy, or take up a study of art history. He had been curious to attend the meeting place of the 1,500 Mile Society, however. According to the invitation, one could only be a member once the requisite 1,500 miles had been travelled from London. Winceworth had never heard of such a club.

Once he had located the right building near Drury Lane and made enquiries of the stern-faced, bow-tied doorman as to the society's whereabouts, he was marshalled down a corridor and then to a brightly lit oak-panelled room. It was hot with chatter and jangling with the sound of bracelets against champagne flutes.

The room was large but Frasham was difficult to miss. Surrounded by his university friends and fellow Swansby's employees, he sat in one of the 1,500 Mile Society's leather armchairs in a fine grey suit and bright pink boutonnière, playing with a cigarette case. Frasham had completely lost the Spotted Dick, boiled-pork bulkiness that, at a younger age, must have been an advantage when barrelling across a rugger pitch or sitting on a first-former. Siberia obviously suited him – he seemed an irritatingly attractive mix of rugged well-put-togetherness, with a fine new red moustache and his black hair waxed close over his ears in thick liquorice loops.

Winceworth greeted Frasham with a handshake, forcing himself to seem jovial. The handshake was oily and over-long. Somehow it seemed Winceworth's fault for being so.

'Winceworth!'

'Frasham.'

'Winceworth! Thank you, thank you: twenty-seven years young!' the birthday host hooted, unprompted. They were still shaking hands. Winceworth stared at their wrists rising and falling. He congratulated Frasham on attaining membership to the society.

'Oh, *that.*' Frasham pumped their hands and drew their heads together. 'I *formed* the club on my return. Had a word with my uncle—' He opened a palm towards a man sitting by the window who had exactly the same air of charismatic gentility as his nephew. This depressed Winceworth, who had privately hoped that this demeanour might be pummelled out of Frasham by the progress of time.

Frasham continued, leaning in too close: 'My uncle and I managed to secure these rooms – not a bad set-up for a soiree, don't you think?'

Heaven knows the rooms' intended purpose before Frasham and his uncle appropriated them for this ridiculous society. There were phantom yellow nicotine stains on the ceiling that spoke of masculine company, with corresponding grubby haloes above the armchairs. There were cartouches and black bulb-buttock Hermes statuettes dotted about in alcoves. Frasham had presumably added some small props to convey the society's claims to the *outré*: Winceworth almost tripped over an elephant-foot umbrella stand on the way in. He was also fairly sure that Frasham must have family connections with Kew Gardens who were not above loaning out some specimens from their Palm House – scattered about the wide room were swathes of potted reeds and long grasses, so thick and lush they could conceal a panther.

From what Winceworth could remember from previous conversations, Frasham's uncle and the family money had something to do with rhubarb – rhubarb jam, preserves, conserves and marmalades shipped all over the world from a family estate. Winceworth never completely understood the difference between all of these things, but the emphasis was on cloying sweetness and teeth-on-edge, sour, tongue-curling congealments.

'So,' Winceworth said, smiling brightly, too brightly, consternation already broiling in his stomach. He worried that if he had to keep forcing this smile, the corners of his mouth would meet around the back of his head, and that then his head would detach and roll away. 'So!' he said again. 'You are not only a member and founding member, but also, in fact, the sole member of the 1,500 Mile Society?'

'One of two thus far, dear boy, one of two.' Frasham beckoned a waiter to his side and Winceworth was suddenly holding a warmish exclamation mark of champagne. 'When you manage to fling yourself further than Battersea you will be able to join us up there, what do you say?'

Winceworth followed Frasham's extended hand – the man seemed incapable of pointing with a finger directly, gesturing instead as if he was taking part in a louche, dandified version of a Renaissance court dance – and let his eyeline be trained towards a wooden plate on the wall. It looked like a School House Prize commendation board.

In gold lettering, there was Frasham's name (*Cantab*) above that of Ronald Glossop.

Glossop was at that moment stationed by the door and making sure everyone signed their name in a guest book as they entered. Winceworth must have walked right past him without noticing, and certainly without being asked. As he watched, Glossop passed his lime-green handkerchief across his face and caught Winceworth's eye. He raised his glass, Winceworth sipped his champagne, Frasham quaffed. A clock struck somewhere.

A band was playing in a corner of the room, punctuating the air with occasional blarts of oboe. Winceworth considered making some uninformed compliment on Frasham's choice of music, but even as he opened his mouth, Frasham was buttonholed by another guest and steered away. Thankful for the lull, Winceworth relaxed into his usual social routine – counting paces as if he was in a cell.

He completed an uninterrupted lap of the room before switching tactics. He decided to spell out certain invisible words against the room's carpet. By making his way across the two parallel sides of the room and then cutting across the centre, he executed an *H*. He then endeavoured to complete an *E*, then traced two *L*s across the room before concluding with another lap: a final *O*. As well as taking up time, this had the added benefit of allowing his face to tighten with genuine preoccupation. By spelling out letters on the carpet like this, Winceworth found he could successfully evade conversation without seeming rude – by looking genially but intently in the direction he had set his abecedarian course, nobody thought to approach and engage him in discussion. This became a slightly more awkward affair once the serving staff recognised his isolation from the herd and Winceworth became aware of them tailing his progress. To credit the 1,500 Mile Society waiting staff, they were wonderfully attentive – after two further glasses of champagne, Winceworth tried to dissuade the waiter's advance by requesting the most outlandish drinks that he could imagine. He hoped the task would prove a long-winded one and that he would be left in peace, but almost immediately he was presented with an elderflower spirit and something that apparently was derived from rhubarb honey served in a glass urn. Thwarted. It tasted of soap used by a despot with a secret. He changed tack, and decided to be frank with the waiter. He asked for whisky. It was all going on Frasham's bill, ran Winceworth's logic, so who was he to argue with such generosity? He also ordered drinks for the musicians in the corner – they bobbed their instruments in thanks.

Across the room one could tell that Frasham had said something witty because a fairy ring of sycophantic university friends burst into applause. Then from a side door a cake was produced, so massive and heavy it required pallbearers. The cake was mocked up to look like a book, covered in blue royal icing with the host's name picked out in white fondant letters in the place of a title. The band struck up the first notes of 'For He's a Jolly Good Fellow', Frasham cut into his cake with a huge knife and the 1,500 Mile Society rang to the clank of ice against glass, cufflinks against glass and canes upon the carpet. Glossop bent over the guest book, smiling.

Slices of cake were handed around by waiters and Winceworth, successfully spelling out the whole alphabet twice across the floor and now feeling quite drunk, decided that he would attempt one further circuit of the room before he left. He convinced himself that pacing rather than conversation brought out the best in him, reasoning that it was a product not of nervousness so much as flâneurie. He helped himself to cake from a tray and had a flash of inspiration – he could pace out an alphabetic diagram of London's streets beyond this room. Holding on to the wall, he began to devise specific routes through the city that would trace graphical Roman letters. Walking and alphabets could be, he decided, a marvellous distracting therapy. To pace the letter *A* he could begin at Cambridge Circus, trot up Earlham Street, turn at Seven Dials and follow St Martin's Lane (with Tower Street forming the letter's central spoke). Some letters were clear in his mind – *D* would be the perimeter of Billingsgate Fish Market, for example, and St James's Square could form the *O*. If he ran its perimeter five thousand times, he thought, he too could enter the 1,500 Mile Society. A general snooze of *S*s and *Z*s existed between the newly pulled-down church on Finsbury Circus and the lunatic asylum at Hoxton House – he added all these to his expanding index.

Winceworth was dimly aware of passing Glossop. The man was licking his thumb and turning the guest book's pages.

Winceworth often had cause to remember a textbook from his schooldays filled with grammar exercises and tables. One page required students to rank the following verbs according to their pace: *jaunt, stride, amble, lumber, strut, patrol, plod, prance, run, saunter, shamble, stroll* and *traipse*. Winceworth swept by the band once more. He jaunted *marcia moderato*. He strode *allegro*, he ambled *adagietto*. He caught the eye of the waiter and signalled for another whisky. Everyone was laughing and toasting, blurs of sleeves revealing bands of naked skin and teeth bared. He lumbered *larghissimo*, he strutted *ad andantino*, he patrolled *moderato*. There must have been two hundred people in the room by now and they all seemed to be having quite a time of it. He plodded *grave*, he pranced *vivacissimo*.

Perhaps the hope that he might trickle out through the door once a necessary hour of social grace had been observed remained a possibility. He decided to stand behind one particularly lush potted plant in order to evade the further attentions of the serving staff and Frasham. Here count down the minutes in the relative safety of the potted plant's leaves. It was a huge plant, as tall as a lexicographer and with large flat drooping leaves. He did not want it to appear as if he was *sidling*. He had spent the day in the office defining this verb, and was keenly aware that to *sidle* can convey a certain sinister intent if one happens to be observed. It pleased him that *sidle* (v.) could slide into *slide* (v.) – the surreptitious becoming the graceful. It was just a question of bearing, and perhaps the same reason that Frasham seemed more charismatic than he. Winceworth thought a good trick to counter any accusations of *sidling* might involve bouncing slightly at the knees and keeping elbows close to the body. So it was that Winceworth, now obsessed with the fact he was one of humanity's natural sidlers, slid bouncingly into what he might at his most thesaurusial choose to call the potted plant's *arboreal verdancy* without disturbing a single leaf.

He sidled straight into a young woman already hiding there.

The woman was crouching slightly and caught in the act of eating a slice of birthday cake. They stared at one another – both of their eyebrows went up at the same time and tilted into identical angles of surprise. Their expressions changed simultaneously: their eyebrows were at once a grave accent, then acute, then circumflex ò ó ô signifying *shock* then *furtiveness* and then an attempt at nonchalance. She deposited her cake into a beaded purse without breaking eye contact and then set her shoulders and Winceworth, drunk enough to interpret this as an invitation to dictate proceedings, cleared his throat.

'—' he said. He considered and then continued, whispering, 'I beg your pardon. I had not realised this plant was taken.'

She was dressed in dove-grey stuff with pearls as big as eyes or frogspawn, no, something nicer, it doesn't always have to be approximate, they were large pearls around her neck. Her neck was very white. Why was he staring at her neck? He had forgotten to lisp. Winceworth's head snapped back to the crowd visible through the potted plant, but not before he noticed the three leaves bending against her hair as she stepped back a pace under the plant's shadow. He shook his head to force concentration.

'Don't worry about that,' the young woman was saying. 'This plant has the distinct benefit of coming fully recommended.' She held her hand towards Winceworth. 'Dr Livingstone, I presume?' Their expressions changed from distrust to shared, good-humoured conspiracy: ō ŏ. Winceworth, quietly and implausibly and in a frankly impractical way, suspected he had fallen in love.

'I'm not sure the good doctor was invited.' He drew closer into the plant and brought his heels together.

'In which case,' she said, 'one might say some people have all the luck.'

'You do not want to be here either?' He wondered whether he was standing upright properly and tried to rearrange his spine.

'I could not possibly comment.' She adjusted her gaze so that it mirrored his own, directed back out into the room. 'I suppose you're staging an escape too?'

The plant's trunk had a label nailed into it bearing the name of its species. The label was slightly askew and he realigned it with a thumbnail. The room seemed to be chanting *rhubarb, rhubarb, rhubarb.*

'Hardly that,' he said. 'I'm a desk man.' He trialled another glance at her face and found it puzzled. 'Rather than a man of the field, that is,' he clarified, poorly. 'Unlike Terence. Mr Frasham, I mean. I am sorry, have we met?'

Leaves rattled around them. The label on the plant read Do Not Touch.

'I do not believe so,' said the woman. 'Have you travelled fifteen hundred miles?'

'Not this evening.' Two men walked past their plant discussing politics, loud enough for Winceworth to gather they were using parliamentary terms incorrectly. From this angle, Winceworth could see that one of the band's musicians had concealed a hipflask in his viola case. 'I wonder,' he said, 'have you dropped anything?' Her eyes were brown and one of them had a curious green notch in it. Why was he looking in her eyes? At her eyes. He felt that if he did not look at her he could not be blamed for whatever rubbish he was saying.

'I only asked in case you were in *here* —' and he gestured at the leaves surrounding them — 'for any specific reason. If you had dropped something, for example, I might assist you in retrieving it.'

'I am not at my best during busy social occasions,' the woman said, or words to that effect, bluntly but gently. 'But I do know a good vantage point when I see it. I am enjoying watching people from here,' she said. She lowered her voice still further. 'Manet's scene through a Rousseau jungle. And for the most part it allows me to avoid small talk.'

'You must continue to do so,' Winceworth said. He withdrew and raised a glass between them, promising himself to look up any draft *Manet* and *Rousseau* biographical entries in *Swansby's* at the first opportunity. 'Hiding behind plants is the closest I get to intrepid, but I can do so quietly.'

'Let us intrepede together, then.'

He considered *intrepede*. This was the longest sustained conversation he had kept for months. He considered starting every day by drinking whisky or whiskey and maybe everything would always seem this cogent and easy. 'What have you observed so far?'

'A great many things.' The young woman appeared to have perked up and nodded towards the scene before them. 'The migratory patterns being made, the watering holes being chosen, the different calls used within different groups. I had, in fact, been watching you until quite recently.'

'Nothing untoward, I hope.' He felt his cheeks.

'You will forgive me —' she said (*perhaps she is drunk too*) — 'I

concluded half an hour ago that you are a very good negotiator of meaningless paths.'

Winceworth detected a slight accent on the way she pronounced the letter *t* in *negotiator*. He tried to place it.

He said, attempting charm, 'I suppose we all are, in our
own small way.' He pressed the whisky glass again to his lips –
somehow, he missed his mouth but his wrist kept going,
propelling the glass all the way up to his eye. For a second,
glimpsed through the angled glass, her dress appeared as if
stained yellow. He kept the glass there for long enough for the
Glenlivet fumes to make his eyes burn.

She did not take her eyes from the room. 'That man over
there has been doing the same perambulations as you for the
past hour but in the opposite direction – you went clockwise,
while he is quite widdershins.'

Widdershins immediately became Winceworth's favourite
word in the whole world.

'And *that* woman—' the young lady pointed, and Winceworth followed her finger – 'no, not her, that one, with the
prominent bump on the back of her head, like her pons is trying to escape out of her skull—'

'*Pons?*'

'Wearing the curry-coloured hat. She has been pivoting on
alternate feet every seven minutes. And Glossop –' she indicated the man by the door – 'why, he has not moved at all.'

'You know Glossop?' Winceworth asked. 'Well. Well!
Glossop is famed for his –' Winceworth took another gulp of
whisky and considered his phrasing – 'his stolid permanence.'

'I should be making a spotters' guide. Where would you rather be right now? I wonder?'

The question threw Winceworth off balance and he blurted the truth before he understood where it came from: 'Sennen Cove.'

Her face registered a crease of confusion. 'I'm not sure I know—'

'It's in Cornwall. Near Land's End – never been, myself, but I once saw a picture of it in a newspaper clipping. It had the caption,' and Winceworth affected a slightly different voice for quotation, rolling his eyes back involuntarily with the small effort of memory, '"Sennen Cove boasts one of the loveliest stretches of sand in the country". Lots of tales of mermaids and smugglers. I could have a little whitewashed cottage.'

'You could,' the woman said.

'Shipwrecks too, of course – a place filled with ghosts. Sorry, am I wittering? I'm wittering. Thank you for asking. I've looked it up since, Sennen: I confess, now I think on it, I became quite fixated for some while on a fantasy of upping sticks and living there.'

Winceworth had never disclosed these dreams or thoughts to anyone before, but he realised the words and truth of this daydream, this desire, were always on the cusp of being said. He had not known how close to the surface of every waking thought this daydream lurked, ready to spring out.

He went on: 'There's a rock formation nearby called "Dr Syntax" and another called "Dr Johnson's Head" on account of its peculiar silhouette – isn't that marvellous? Or tedious.'

'Marvellous,' the woman emphasised. She repeated it in case Winceworth could not hear her over the band. 'What a pleasure to learn these things.'

Usually, Winceworth would be sure he was being mocked by such a sentence, but tonight he believed that perhaps all these thoughts were worth the sharing. '*Marvellous.* I hope I am not boring you, I'm so sorry. Since reading about the place I haven't been able to get the idea of escaping all this—' Winceworth took in the whole room, the whole capital, his whole life in a sweep of his arm, 'and making my way there.'

The woman beamed at him. 'You should do it,' she said. 'Escape.'

Winceworth let his shoulder sag. 'Thank you. That would be—' He sighed. 'I could keep bees.'

'You could learn chess,' she offered.

'Keep bees, learn chess. Peacefulness on my own little underlooked stretch of the world.'

'But wouldn't you miss all your lexicographicking? I assume you are here with the rest of the Swansby lot?'

The woman laughed at the expression he made. The sound thrilled him, and he found himself screwing his face even tighter for the sake of her delight. 'I think I'd rather disappear entirely and stop pretending I know what's best for language.'

'I like your candour, sir.'

Winceworth blushed, coughed, but words were tumbling out faster than the rhythm of normal speech, almost a splutter, the uncorrected proofs of sentences. He was acutely aware that his words might be coming out as a mess. He saw it all, how easily it could go: his vowels tangling in the air and sibilants snagging on his lips, garbles treacling in the corners of his mouth.

The woman locked eyes with him and Winceworth trailed off: the unformed words got caught in her eyelashes or in the shadowed notches on the edge of her iris. He opened his mouth to attempt a regroup, or an apology, or anything resembling another sentence to reel out into the space between them, ready to apologise for over-speaking or speaking out of turn.

'So what is it that stops you?' she asked, cutting through his unravelling thoughts. 'What keeps you from the shipwrecks and the bees?'

'No funds for it.' He did not say it wistfully, because already the daydream was dissipating, and the sense that he had prattled became more important than the thoughts themselves. 'It is no matter. Just something nice to dwell upon.'

'How much would you need?' the woman asked. 'How many countless riches to have the life you want?'

Winceworth played along, and made a show of calculating on his fingers. 'For a small cottage, a beehive and a chessboard? Throw in some new clothes perhaps, and maybe a bottle of whatever best champagne is doing the rounds—'

'It wouldn't do to die of thirst even though you are so close to the most lovely of beaches.'

'Call it six hundred and ninety-nine pounds exactly,' Winceworth said, and he twirled his hand, 'with maybe a shilling or two spare for the train.'

'A bargain,' she said, and they touched their glasses. They shared the smile of strangers who felt no longer strange. They looked out once more at the figures at the party.

'You are not going to ask where my dreams would take me?' she asked after a while, and Winceworth almost yelped his apology.

'What where and how would you—?'

But before he could get his mouth around his question, Frasham and his bully's bloodhound-nose for awkward situations chose that moment to notice the top of Winceworth's head peeping from the leaves of the shared potted plant. Winceworth raised his glass to his face again, but it was too late – Frasham was striding towards them.

'Winceworth!' he cried, 'Stop scaring the cobwebs and speak to me properly.'

Neither Winceworth nor his companion moved.

'Discovered, alas,' she murmured.

'I could always just ignore him,' he replied, not entirely joking and not entirely undesperately.

'Winceworth, old man!'

It was not worth reminding Frasham that greetings had already passed between them and Winceworth admitted defeat.

'Frasham.' Winceworth emerged. 'A joy.' He was enfolded into the host's broad chest. A shirt button bruised his eyelid.

'Taking in the local flora and fauna, I see,' Frasham said. He seemed as if he too had been enjoying the waiters' attentions. Frasham motioned to the young lady emerging on Winceworth's arm from the plant. 'Sophia, has he bored you so much you're trying to blend in with the props?'

Sophia! Winceworth's new favourite name.

Her gloved hand tightened on Winceworth's sleeve in what he decided was a show of camaraderie. 'We have travelled,' she said, 'from the very depths of the wildest woods together. We are now closer than siblings.' Winceworth swallowed and tried to focus.

'The old dog.' Frasham eyed Winceworth appreciatively. 'And has Peter explained how we know each other, I wonder?'

'He has not yet had the opportunity.'

'Winceworth's the one I was telling you about,' Frasham said, and his voice raised somewhat. 'The man with the lisp working on the letter *S!*'

Winceworth wondered whether his blush would scorch through the fabric of his shirt.

'How precious,' squealed one of the party attendants eavesdropping nearby. Winceworth recognised him vaguely from the desks at Swansby's, a scholar of oral linguistics. Winceworth couldn't for the life of him remember the man's name. For some reason this man was wearing a fez and turning glassy eyes from Winceworth to Frasham with sloppy bonhomie. 'But,' continued the man, 'Terence, you simply must tell us all more about your Siberian adventure.'

Frasham grinned. Winceworth wondered how difficult it might be to club someone over the head with a 400-pound potted plant. 'It was quite extraordinary,' he heard Frasham say. 'And, at the same time, often completely preposterous. I mean! Watching some Cossack in a suit fracturing his tear ducts pronouncing *czar tsar* or *sdzar* in any fourteen hundred different ways, and poor Glossop scribbling it all down.'

Winceworth helped himself to another drink from a tray swung by his elbow. He smiled but his mouth felt stiff, snappable. He believed that he could hear every tiny movement of bone in his jaw in syrupy clacking sounds. There was small gratification that his shrub-mate looked absolutely bored by this turn in the conversation.

Someone across the room produced a balalaika, an instrument that Frasham had apparently mastered on his travels, and this gave him cause to peel away from their little circle and resume a position on the club-room's sofa. He played a version of 'The Boy I Love is Up in the Gallery' without looking at the instrument's strings, fluttering his eyelashes at Glossop. The old rogue. Good old Terence.

Winceworth nosed his whisky.

He considered leading Sophia back to their plant and explaining – how might one set down the phonetics of a hiccup? – that this lisp nonsense was far behind him. It became, befuddledly, crucial that Sophia not only be made to understand that he *wanted* to apologise, but that he was a Good Sort. He could not play the balalaika but he had other talents. He could spin the etymology of the word *hello* from its earliest roots.

Frasham was by now miming to a delighted crowd the way in which he had wrestled the walrus in the famous photograph received by the office. Lamplight caught his hair, clinking off his teeth and making gold chevrons in the fabric of his suit. He was singing again.

'A dreadful, handsome show-off, is he not?' murmured Sophia. They watched Frasham turn his head upward and serenade the ceiling, his throat was exposed. Winceworth could not help but think that Dr Rochfort-Smith, connoisseur of mouths and mouthparts, would probably call Frasham's throat a perfect specimen.

Þrotobolla is the Old English word for a man's Adam's apple, Winceworth wanted to say. It means *throat-ball* – no poetry there, just etymological pragmatism. The jutting shape of the letter Þ enacting the jutting swell of the gullet. He blinked at Sophia in front of him and she momentarily doubled in his vision.

What was I saying? Winceworth thought. Ignore what Terence said about my lisp, Sophia. Do not think about my tongue as a buzzing, fat proboscis like that of a fly. Do not think of my tongue at all. I am more than that.

A fresh whisky was held out to Winceworth. The hand offering it had extremely freckled fingers and bloodless nails. The knuckles formed a row of white *M*s spelling out a mumble along the cusp of the fist. Let me tell you about the etymology of the word *hello*, Winceworth thought, taking the drink. I cannot sing and I cannot be handsome, but I can perhaps charm you with a fascination with the particulars rather than the general, that's my talent. This tendency to drift off and delight with small details, the transformative power of proper attention paid to small things.

He really was quite quite drunk.

'Are you feeling quite all right?' Sophia asked.

Helloa, pronounced like *cocoa*, from an emphatic imperative of *halôn*, *holôn*, to fetch, used especially in hailing a ferryman, a distant or occupied person, or said with surprise at an unexpected meeting, such as within the shadow of an expensive potted palm. *Hallow*, as in the ground, cf. demonstratively splendid. To shout 'halloo' at dogs in order to urge them on. *Lo! Hullabaloo*, from *bas, là le loup!* (down there, the wolf!), hallelujah! Ah, etymologies, the speculative pedigree of a word. *What do you think of me as a lexicographer, Sophia?* Winceworth wondered as she doubled once in his vision. What would that knowledge prompt you to ask? What is my favourite word? Or, more particular still, my favourite letter? Allow these private fictions to a boring lexicographer. Ask me something, Sophia, Winceworth thought.

Terence Clovis Frasham was again by their side. 'Of course,' he was saying, pulling his arm about Sophia's shoulders, 'there was one particularly fine acquisition I made on my travels.'

Winceworth noticed the two small details of Sophia and Frasham's matching rings and something tightened just beneath his Adam's apple.

Winceworth made his apologies and stumbled down the stairs out of the society.

In a phrase of which Dr Rochfort-Smith would no doubt be proud, January sun had long since sought solace, silently, amongst some small scudding cirrus clouds. Winceworth ran – *prestissimo*; he shambled – *lento*; he trudged – *andante moderato*.

With some birthday cake shoved deep into his pocket, Peter Winceworth wove his way across the road and began his journey home.

I is for *inventiveness* (adj.)

'And *that's* the moment when you should have quit,' Pip said emphatically down the phone. 'Threat of hellfire is one thing, but an actual threat? Are you kidding me?'

I thumbed through the index cards in front of me. 'Leaving David in the lurch doesn't feel quite right,' I said. 'Do you know, I've found another one already? Listen to this, I came across it almost by accident: "*agrupt* (n. and adj.), irritation caused by having a dénouement ruined."'

After a pause, 'Sounds like a real word,' Pip said.

'That's what I thought, but I looked up *agrupt* on my phone to see whether it existed. The results took no time at all. That's not true: 694 results appeared in 0.41 seconds. And it said, "Did you mean: *abrupt, agrupate, agrup, agrupe*?"'

'Phoney as a three-dollar bill,' said Pip.

'Right?'

'Nice catch. How did no one see any of these?'

'Overlooked, I suppose. They are just nestled in random places.' Down the phone there was the hiss of foamed milk and a close-distant clink of teacups from Pip's café. 'Everything OK at work?' I asked.

'Who the hell cares. What word are you up to?'

'I'm starting from the top,' I said.

'*Aardvark* strikes again?' Pip said.

'Currently up to –' I glanced down – 'apparently *abbozzo* (n.)'

'Definitely fake,' Pip said. 'Or a kind of pasta. A head monk, but also a bozo. A funny way of pronunciating the first three letters of the alphabet.'

'Pretty sure *pronunciating* is not a word.'

'Touché. Touchy.'

I adjusted my mobile against my ear. 'According to this,' I said, 'it means "an outline or draft of a speech or piece of writing. Obsolete. Rare".'

'No shit,' said Pip. 'And you're checking each one individually? Every word?'

' 'Fraid so.'

'Have you eaten your lunch?'

'Yes.'

'Cupboard egg?'

' 'Fraid so,' I said again.

'I *admonish*, verb,' Pip said. 'I abdicate all responsibility.'

We had met three years ago in the coffee shop: her working behind the counter and me a customer having just started at Swansby House. At that time I was still dazed by the city and tired from drafting CVs for any job I could get, imagining my internship there would not last out the year. *How long could digitising a dictionary possibly take?* Sweet innocence.

I remember the day we first spoke. I was desperate for caffeine after a morning staring at my terrible computer hourglass. I was first in line. However, a man behind me in the queue chipped ahead of me before I had delivered my order. 'Three cappuccino – sorry, *cappuccini*,' he said. He made a fingersnapping motion. He was a busy man, clearly. The busiest.

'Coming up. Any food?' asked the girl behind the counter. I remember looking at her thinking, This is someone who knows how to keep her cool. Here is someone who is unflappable.

'Yeah,' said my queue-jumper. 'Three croissants.'

'Three *crrrrrroisseaux* on their way. *Crayz-onts*. Three *quwah-surnte*,' she said. She caught my eye. 'And that was one coffee for you. We only have takeaway cups today, is that OK?' and she asked this charitably as if the customer could ever do anything about this. The napkins by the sugar sachets and milk jug had *Geography is a Flavour* printed across them and a drawing of some coffee beans.

'That's amazing,' I said. Why? *Shut up, shut up.*

'And what's your name?' she continued. She tapped a pen to a Styrofoam cup in her hand and I lost four years off my life.

'Adam,' said the queue-jumper.

'And yet not always the first dude, dude,' Pip said, quick as you like, and it didn't really work as a joke but the thinking was there, and I was watching her forearms in a way I didn't understand. It didn't feel right. It felt too right. I read the homily on the napkins again.

'And you?' she said to me, Sharpie poised. 'I need it for the cup.'

'Mallory,' I said. She nodded, yawned and covered her mouth. She had knuckle tattoos. Did she? It looked like they spelt TUFF TEAK, but her hands were upside down and I couldn't crane my neck in time to read them properly, and she had turned away and started roughing up the coffee machine before I could work it quite out.

It couldn't be TUFF TEAK, I thought. Unless that's some hot carpentry slang that I'm not queer enough to understand. Probably that. Stop staring. I tried to break down the scene into words that could be carried around on one's hands.

TRIC / KY!!
CAFÉ / GIRL
MANY / TIPS
POLY / DACTYL

'And I was literally *dying*,' said Adam into his wireless headpiece.

'I just drew them on this morning.'

The girl had come around the bar area to give me my drinks. She presented her knuckles to me.

'Ah,' I said. The girl in the café stretched out her hands and placed them in mine, turning them to show me. Which was preposterous, but she did. They weren't tattoos at all, not even letters: just meaningless scribbles in pen, the same pen that had been used to write my name on the Styrofoam cups.

'You were staring hard enough to rub the ink off,' she said.

And it was *not* a good line but it was meant to be an almost-good line, which in a way is kinder. She turned away to pass me the coffee.

'Thank you,' I said.

'And what time do you clock off?' the girl behind the café counter asked me. And 'the girl behind the café counter' became, more usefully, the pronoun *you* in the same way that many small details are not necessary but can become everything.

'And are you going to be bringing the index cards back home?' Pip asked down the phone. 'Am I going to have to shore up our bookshelves and just accept that you won't be able to raise your head from the pages for the next fifteen years or so?'

'Thems the breaks,' I said.

Aberglaube (n.), *aberr* (v.), *aberuncate* (v.)

'And you're OK?' Pip asked. 'For real, though. Really.'

'A little over my head,' I said, 'Maybe. Long day to go.'

'I just like the idea of some guy in a . . . I don't know, what do Victorians have?' Pip said, and I imagined her throwing her hands in the air. 'Top hats and deerstalkers and cholera. Hansom cab chases. Steam trains and telegrams. And then him sitting down and having the brass gall to make your life a misery by fabricating words for a dictionary.'

I said, 'That's very helpful, thank you.'

'Here's a spoiler: the *zebra* (n.) did it.'

'Neat,' I said. 'Nice.'

'See you later,' Pip said.

'Yes.'

'And you're OK?' she said again. 'After the morning?'

'Hmm,' I said, not listening.

'I love you,' Pip said, and I ended the call and picked up the index card in front of me.

J is for *jerque* (v.)

After some hours at his desk and beneath his headache, Winceworth slipped away from Swansby House to get some air. He took his satchel filled with made-up sketches for unusual words slung across his shoulder. He did not wander far and soon settled on a bench in St James's Park, his shirt still slightly damp thanks to the cat and its eruptions. He stared at his knees. He stared at his hands. In his rush to reach Dr Rochfort-Smith's appointment he had forgotten his gloves and his fingers chapped slightly in the cold.

Winceworth drew some remnants of birthday cake from his trouser pocket and turned it over. The slice was flatter and more compressed than any baker would appreciate, and sheened over with a kind of post-party next-day sweat. With a pang of fellow feeling, he inspected the slice of cake, cupping stray crumbs and brushing them from his knees. The first letter of Frasham's name was iced onto the surface of the fondant. Keeping his eyes trained on the fricative, Winceworth brought the slice up to his face and bit down hard. At the pressure, an almost imperceptible spiderweb-fracture made a mosaic of the icing.

St James's Park was the closest green space to Swansby House, and idling members of the staff often spent time there, depending on the season, gazing into flowerbeds or feeding the ducks. The correct placement of St James's Park's apostrophe on the boards and fences was a bane or boon to the members of Swansby's editorial team. In Winceworth's first year at Swansby House there had been a war of attrition between some younger members of staff and the park-keepers concerning this apostrophe. During this time apparently many of the park's signs dotted around the lawns and grounds were defaced (and consequently re-faced) in line with whether one or many St James's ownerships were being asserted.

Never a dull moment.

Winceworth's chosen bench sat tucked in a bend of a path with no good view of the lake nor any interesting sweeps and vistas. He would not be disturbed by colleagues and it was less likely to be on the route of winter-hardy courting couples or wandering tourists. The time of year also meant many of the planted beds were unremarkable, russeted-over and presenting a manicured kind of dreary. In fact the only flowers he could see near him were some early puff-faced dandelions at the feet of his bench. They had survived the rain and the cold – he would have to ask someone at Swansby House whose studies covered botany to know whether these were freaks of the season or to be expected. A freakish weed is just a flower that has not asked permission. Winceworth kicked one of the dandelions appreciatively with his heel and its head exploded.

Away from the Scrivenery, Winceworth felt the muscles in his shoulders loosen and he able to take deeper breaths. The air of the park helped clear his head and of course with this came a certain new confidence and *l'esprit de l'escalier*. He imagined potential, missed ripostes: Look here, Appleton, you ridiculous bore, Coleridge probably died before Frasham's father was even born. Bielefeld, you daft-necked carafe of a man, don't peacock about *romanticise* (v.) to impress Miss Cottingham; Coleridge also came up with *bisexual, bathetic, intensify* and *fister* if you thought you had an interesting weekend.

The birthday cake made his back teeth sing with sweetness and he closed his eyes against the pain. His day had already taken its toll on him. *Pons pons pons.* Toothache would have to wait its turn.

Somewhere across the way an unseen bird was trilling. Weak sun fooled something light across his face, and he felt a yawn slip electric beneath his tongue – he shook his head, dog-like, to summon alertness, but then drew out his watch for nap calculations. Waning nausea and exhaustion had caught up with him. All he wanted right now was to sleep, to curl up like the cat in corners of the Scrivenery without a care for anything.

But falling asleep now would muddy the rest of the day and spoil any chance of rest this evening. Finish the cake, he told himself, take one more turn about the park to get the blood going and face the day renewed. He dug his glasses into the bridge of his nose and winched his face to the sky, willing himself into wakefulness. Two birds veered overhead, chatting and braiding the air. It might have been his imagination, but a dandelion seed seemed to drift through his line of sight and join them. He wondered whether anyone would miss him if he just stayed put amongst the weeds, kicking the clocks of dandelions until facelessness and spending the afternoon not amongst paper and letters and words but instead here, head to and in and of the clouds counting birds until the numbers ran out. There were funny, oily little wild birds in the park, some of which he recognised. Surely too early for starlings. Starlings with feathers star-spangled and glittersome. One brave bird hopped about his feet for cake crumbs while still more were flitting above his head with the dandelion seeds, blown wishes finding a smeuse in the air. The best benchside exoticisms January could offer were all on show – the starling, the dandelion, the blown seeds and the birds skeining against the grey clouds, hazing it and mazing it, a featherlight kaleidoscope noon-damp and knowing the sky was never truly grey, just filled with a thousand years of birds' paths, and wishful seeds, a bird-seed sky as something meddled and ripe and wish-hot, the breeze bird-breath soft like a – what – heart stopped in a lobby above one's lungs as well it might, as might it will – seeds take a shape too soft to be called a burr, like falling asleep on a bench with the sun on your face, seeds in a shape too soft to be called a globe, too breakable to be a constellation, too tough to not be worth wishing upon, the crowd of birds, an unheard *murmuration* (pl. n.) not led by one bird but a cloud-folly of seeds, blasted by one of countless breaths escaping from blasted wished-upon clock as a breath, providing a clockwork with no regard to time nor hands, flocking with no purpose other than the clotting and thrilling and thrumming, a flock as gathered ellipses rather than lines of wing and bone and beak, falling asleep grey-headed rather than young and dazzling – more puff than flower – collecting the ellipses of empty speech bubbles, the words never said or sayable, former pauses in speech as busy as leaderless birds, twisting, blown apart softly, to warm and colour even the widest of skies.

Winceworth awoke with his head slumped to one side, rumpled and oblique on the park bench. A boy was standing in front of him, holding a toy boat and staring. Presumably the boy had been staring for quite a while, for as Winceworth shivered himself more upright and an involuntary *harrumph* left his body, the little spectator started. The wooden boat fell from his arms onto the path and its mast snapped the moment it hit the gravel. Winceworth's apology knotted in the air with the boy's yelp of surprise.

Dropping the boat and howling, however, did not break the child's staring. His eyes were wide, mouth slack and he looked as if he had seen a ghost – the wail carried an edge to it, a cry not borne of anger nor shock at the self-scuttling of his boat, but a shriek of real horror.

Winceworth shook the sleepiness from his head and stared back. The child was looking *through* Winceworth. He had finally become invisible. His colleagues might overlook him or hardly ever notice that he was there, but since leaving Swansby House something had obviously changed in him, had gone further or had clarified – Winceworth had finally, somehow, been tempered into nothingness, thin air with no more traction than a breath. The child's mother drew up beside her staring charge, and as she came level with Winceworth her face too registered the same look of shock. He must just be a suit and clump of birthday cake suspended in the air on a bench in the park.

Winceworth trialled a gentle, spectral wave.

Both faces' expressions changed to one of distracted displeasure. It then occurred to Winceworth that perhaps he was not the object of the boy and mother's attention, and he pivoted in his seat to follow their eyeline.

Some feet beyond his bench, one of the Royal Park's huge white pelicans was rearing up and silently hissing. Not only that – it appeared to be covered in blood, and a woman was strangling it.

The pelican was huffing, straining, its absurd head bent upwards and pale eyes rolling back and forth. Both bird and attacker were making grim little growls and burbles with effort as they circled across the lawn. The woman's hat had been knocked off and sat trampled between them.

The woman had her hands about the bird's neck and her fingers were tucked under its wagging pink dewlap pouch – she had to keep rocking on her feet and ducking to avoid the panicked beating of bloody wings hitting her face.

Winceworth heard the mother say behind him, 'They can break a man's arm!'

'You are thinking of swans,' corrected her staring son in a high voice.

Both woman and bird were strangely matched in appearance and there was something ridiculously ballroom about their skirmish – the bird's plumage was stained red, its bill a hot yellow, while the woman's skirt was made of some candy-stripe coloured stuff and she carried a yellow umbrella wedged beneath her arm. They waltzed, irregularly, tugging and gasping, moving closer towards Winceworth and his companions.

The pelican made an obscene, wheezing call.

'Ought we to call—' said the mother, pulling closer to Winceworth's bench.

He fiddled with his glasses, still groggy from his nap. 'I really have no idea who—'

'She must be mad!' interrupted the mother and pulled her son closer to her side. The boy struggled and in turning his head, caught sight of his broken boat on the path. He let out a screech and Winceworth found he was all at once caught between two quiet, ludicrous brawls. His mind turned to how best to slip away.

'Do something!' The mother clearly had decided that Winceworth was the one who should take charge of the situation. She looked at him with stern expectation as her scarlet child jigged up and down.

Winceworth stepped forward. There was no etiquette for this. He tried a small, 'I say—' but the pelican-woman was too engrossed in combat to notice. Half-heartedly Winceworth hefted the small remaining nugget of birthday cake at the fighting pair. The piece bounced off the woman's elbow and had no effect whatsoever. Mother and child gave him a long look. The pelican's pupil – round, human-like and panic-widened – fixed upon Winceworth for a split second at his voice, and its body appeared to stiffen. Taking full advantage of this momentary pause, the woman attacking it either had a change of strategy or a sudden surge of courage – she lifted the pelican bodily off its feet and seized it in a kind of chokehold. The faint sunlight behind them made the bird's pouch glow a soft rose, branched veins swelling dark and angry within the membrane.

The boy, the mother and Winceworth goggled.

This tableau lasted for less than a second and the pelican's neck suddenly flexed and darted like a serpent – it struck upwards, catching the woman across the chin with its beak. She shrank back but kept her hold about the pelican's throat.

'Let it be, can't you?' cried the mother. 'Don't look, Gerald. She means to kill it!'

At this, the woman turned her head to look at them. There was a small cut above her eye and some of her hair had come loose and was sticking weirdly to her forehead, and—

Sophia from the party?

Winceworth didn't know how he vaulted over the bench so quickly nor how he covered so much ground in apparently one step but all at once he was face to face with the pelican on the ground and hitting it and hitting it and hitting it, pinning it between his knees and landing punches against its large white body. It was scrambling beneath his weight while behind him the mother and the child were screaming but all he could think of was the small cut above Sophia's eye, bleeding; a thin line of blood ran down the side of her face so that its symmetry was thrown completely off, and the bird had not been bleeding at all as he had thought but was in fact covered in *her* blood, and he hit it in the chest over and over and over—

K is for *kelemenopy* (n.)

When a cartoon character is represented swearing or cursing, there is a word for the series of hashtags and exclamation marks and toxicity symbols in their speech bubbles: *grawlix*. @#$%&! It is a growling grunting irk of a work of a word. That's what my brain felt like on days like this one, with tasks like reading through index cards. Asterisks lodged in my thoughts, upside-down question marks *grapplehooking* and *winching* the sides of my brain. My head as grawlax, grawlixed. Plural *grawlixes* or *grawlix* or nitpicked obscene *grawlices*.

I could feel myself growing bored. I doodled a small drawing of me screaming on top of one of the index cards. We all have that at our fingertips, don't we: an image or design to which we unconsciously return and use to fill stray bits of paper. I used to draw thousands of boxes and little cartoon cats over my university notes. I wondered whether they ever doodled, the errant lexicographer or lexicographers who had gone so off-piste in the index cards of Swansby House. There might have been a better way to assuage their boredom, rather than making up fake words for me to hunt down.

There is a kind of snow blindness that descends during repetitive tasks. Pip described it happening at her work too – coffee orders no longer make any damn sense and you have to trust muscle memory to get the task done.

I started picking index cards at random from the pile. I checked the definition and if I didn't recognise the word I cross-checked it on my phone.

I held one up to my window and read the beautiful looped handwriting.

> *crinkling* (n.), a small precocious apple. *Notes*: Compare
> with other *crinkles*. Compare also *crumpling* in widespread
> English regional use. Compare also with *craunchling* in
> the same sense

I double-checked this word, sure that it must be an error and I had found another false word but damn damn *damn* it did bear some scrutiny.

I was tired, and the page on my phone listed in my vision. I had enjoyed-endured interesting, transformative and very boring discussions since sixth form about the instability of language but this task felt different – looking at the columns of online and pretty much infinite definitions, I was no longer sure which words were real nor why anyone had ever bothered trying to contain them. This was a failure of the imagination on my part. This was giving up. But surely compiling a dictionary or an encyclopaedia, even one as ramshackle as *Swansby's*, was like conceiving of a sieve for stars. I was daydreaming about audiobooks for dictionaries. I was daydreaming about literally browsing and pulling my lips over the words and routling or rootling or etymolojostling and chewing the cud of these index cards littered across my desk just to see what stuck in my teeth and could be removed. *Cud* and other ruminations.

I held up the index card. *Crinkling*, I read, a type of small apple. A precocious apple. What did that mean? What the hell. I associated *crinkling* as a verb or adjective with the corners of eyes, or Mr Blobby, or the unseen recesses of a wastepaper basket. How dare *crinkling* apples have unseen roots. This meant that someone once held a fruit in their hands and rather than say *whatchamacallit* or *thingy* or, indeed, 'small apple' to describe it, they had announced *crinkling*. And someone else had written that down. Adam and Eve naming the beasts of the field and the birds of the sky and the tricky precocious crinklings.

Not for the first time at that desk, I looked up 'Symptoms of adult ADHD' on my phone and flicked through the first few results. I then tried searching 'What is an adult?' The first link on the search page showed up purple, so clearly I had looked that up before.

I glanced at the cards strewn across my desk. Oh, my God, shut up, you are too interesting and too much, I wanted to tell them. That's what people say to belittle women in workplaces, isn't it? Or women in general. I wanted to say it to the materials of a dictionary. It was because I was intimidated and I hated it.

Oh, my God! shut up! you are too! interesting! and! too!

much! was precisely how I fell for Pip because I was intimidated and I loved her.

Where did that thought come from?

I held up two of the index cards. I squinted.

All of the cards that contained *made-up* words were written
in a quite different type of fountain pen. All the rest were in
different handwriting, sure: the work of hundreds of hands
filling in thousands of index cards. But they all had the same
uniform scratchiness, the same kind of line and flourish. On
these false entries, however, it was as if the person writing
them had used a completely different type of nib.

There was a knock on the office wall.

Like like the sun or like a shock or the least agrupt thing in
the world, Pip's head craned around the door.

L is for *legerdemain* (n. and adj.)

Sophia's umbrella smacked Winceworth across an ear. He rolled to the side, released the pelican and lay on his back, panting slightly.

'It's choking on something,' Sophia said. She was panting too and kneeling beside him in the grass, eyes fixed on the bird lying prone to his left. All three were winded like wrestlers, Sophia moving one hand against the bird's cheek and another feeling along its neck.

Winceworth scrambled to sit up on his haunches.

'Look—' Sophia said. Winceworth watched something beneath the skin of the pelican's throat buck unmistakably out of time with its pulse. This close to the bird, he could see its eyes were also starting from their sockets.

'I was trying to open—' Sophia panted, 'open the beak – put my arm down and dislodge—'

The pelican lurched forward suddenly and its foot-long bill swung across like a jib. Winceworth and Sophia only just leapt out of its path in time.

The spectating mother and child were nowhere to be seen.

'It looked as though you were trying to throttle it,' Winceworth said. 'I thought it was attacking you.'

'Trained in *bartitsu*,' Sophia said, as if that explained anything. She pushed her hair from her eyes with her wrist. Either she had not realised or did not care that she was bleeding. 'Are you strong enough to hold it down?'

'Of course,' Winceworth said, lying.

'I still think,' she said, gnawing her lip and calculating, 'I could prise whatever it is blocking the passage – if only it wouldn't move about like this—'

'Of course,' Winceworth repeated, with even less certainty. The waist-high bulk of the pelican baulked and lowered its head, weaving from side to side. Winceworth removed his jacket and approached with the inner fabric facing him, stretched tight.

'Like a – like a matador—' he said for no good reason whatsoever.

'"The light-limb'd Matadore,"' quoted Sophia, apparently for her own amusement. She was smiling, madly, and Winceworth's heart became a nonsense.

The pelican grasped this opportunity and gave a rollicking, panicked feint and ran past him, gaining speed as if in order to make an attempt at flight. Winceworth leapt just at the moment that the bird leapt – on instinct, he clamped the fabric of his jacket about its shoulders and together they rolled headlong along the grass.

'I have it!' he shouted.

He hoicked the sleeves of his jacket in tight as the pelican gamely batted and jabbed at him. The pouch under its beak was soft and warm against his hands. Winceworth sat up, tussled more firmly with the bird until it was jammed beneath his knees and swaddled in his jacket, neck extended like a hobbyhorse. It seemed a lot quieter, weaker. Quelled, it met his eye again, and he looked away.

Coughing to mask his hard breathing as Sophia came closer, 'It's still too – I wouldn't go near its beak,' he warned. 'It's a – nervy, I think – bit of a brute and I'm not sure it won't have your eye out.'

By now a number of geese had appeared from another part of the park and were honking and hissing their own disapproval at the uproar. One of the geese came close enough to punch Winceworth on the arm with its head and, more by accident than design, he raised his elbow and slapped this goose full across the face with the pelican's beak. The goose retreated, wailing and showing its tongue.

'Where is everyone? This park is usually a damn thoroughfare—'

Sophia approached with her yellow umbrella extended. 'I daresay that if you are able to keep the bird just there—'

The pelican gave a muffled irregular gagging sound. It swung back and its beak gaped open. Its pouch folded back and, head lolling, it sagged inside out against the bird's spine at an obtuse angle. It looked impossible, imploded. A bloody tuft of feathers pushed against Winceworth's neck. There was something tender to this brief touch. He felt dreadful.

Sophia took the pelican's beak in her hands and, finding no resistance, pushed the two mandibles apart. She stared down the bird's throat.

'I can't – I can't see anything,' she said. 'But it is hard – to tell—'

The pelican was inert but still breathing, shallow and rumbling next to Winceworth's chest.

'Did you see it swallow anything?' he asked. The pelican's thick feet gave the smallest of kicks.

'It was walking strangely,' Sophia said and turned the pelican's head from side to side in her hands and squinting. 'It's clearly not – look, it's clearly not getting enough air.' She added, 'I'm not sure you hitting it will have helped—'

Braver members of the geese contingent made another honking incursion and she shooed them away with her umbrella.

'I don't imagine so.' Winceworth hoisted the pelican up against his chest and slightly to the side, as if a bagpipe. 'Perhaps – maybe it would be best—' Fleetingly he imagined taking the bird's head under his arm and twisting it, the pelican growing limp and the whole business being over. The pelican's eye met his own one more time. A translucent purple eyelid sluiced sideways across its vision.

'I have it,' said Sophia, face shining. 'Do you have a ribbon? Or – may I remove a shoelace?' She was not interested in an answer and began plucking at his Oxfords. The geese and the ducks laughed at Winceworth. He pulled the pelican tighter against him. Sophia *tsked* and tutted. Adrenaline made her fingers awkward. Winceworth felt his shoe loosen and Sophia was there binding the pelican's beak together with the lace in quick, tight loops. Her face was close to his, just the pelican and the new smell of pelican between them.

'I can use this?' Sophia said.

She had reached for the exposed lining of his jacket that was banded across the pelican's swaddled belly. She plucked at something there – the stem of his hollow metal Swansby House pen that he kept in the pocket there. She slid the pen free and flexed it in her hand. No, she was not flexing it, she was bending it. It snapped with a dull *crack*.

Sophia grabbed the pelican's beak and felt down its throat with her hand. She found its collarbone. Pelicans almost certainly do not have collarbones. Sophia pushed the broken pen into the pelican's throat.

There was a loud hiss of expelled air – the pelican swelled under Winceworth's grasp and a second later they both heard it take a huge gulping heave of a breath.

The geese cackled and hooted.

The bird, the man and the woman panted.

'Do you come here often?' Winceworth asked.

M is for *mendaciloquence* (n.)

'I'm here to help,' Pip said, simply.

She drew a tray of index cards towards her from the pile on my desk.

Clarity is her talent and part of the reason I ever fell for her. Pip was often a person of actions. Action is often better than words. I was a person of anxieties rather than anything. 'How did you get in here?'

'The door was open, and let me tell you when I see that boss of yours I'm going to give him an earful about security. Aren't you meant to be under siege or something? Expecting a tankful of homophobes through the door at any moment?'

'But the café—'

'Everyone will have to deal with a sign that says C L O S E D on the door,' Pip said. She looked around my office, eyes searching for the office phone.

'Is that the one they call you on?'

'Don't worry about that,' I said. 'You're really staying?'

'Try and stop me,' she said. She hugged me. It meant more than words can say.

'You should leave.' I said it with authority, drawing myself up to my full height mid-hug.

★

We got into a system at my desk, Pip perched up on the window-sill and me on my chair, both looking for the handwriting and distinctive penmanship that crossed the *i*s and dotted the *t*s on the definition index cards. Pip had brought me lunch from her café, and for a while we passed the time in busy, bored silence.

An hour later, Pip was flipping through a volume of *Swansby's* in *tsk*ing fury.

'I've just spent about five minutes staring at the word *pat* without taking anything in.'

I knew exactly what she meant. My eyes and my brain had severed any meaningful connection and it was tricky to concentrate enough to recognise even the most regular of words. The array of handwriting on the index cards appeared to pulse if I maintained eye contact for too long.

'I think we can safely discount *pat*,' I said.

'*Pat*, begone.' She flicked the index card across my desk to join a growing pile. We had decided to put the 'found' fictitious words in an envelope.

'Words: What Are They Like?'

'Thanks for helping,' I said. 'I have no idea how David expects me to know I've found every false word that could possibly have snuck in. But two heads better than one.'

'Are you kidding? My pleasure,' she said.

'Sure.'

'Can't have you doing all this spelling-bee research on your own: what if we ever play Scrabble and you've got all this advantage?'

She did not need to say it, and I recognised the deflection. Since I had told her about the threatening phone calls coming in at work, she had told me how worried she was, how helpless she felt. At the time I laughed it off and said it was nothing, but knowing she was nearby somehow made the sight of the office phone immediately less terrifying.

'I don't think we've ever played Scrabble,' I said. A vision of a future Pip – same unpiplike figure bent only a little with age, a tartan blanket over her knees and sitting across from me, squinting at boardgame tiles. The same smile and the same haircut, a little greyer. What words might we have for each other then, with all the possibilities of where that *then* and *that* might be?

'A girl can *dream*, can't she,' Pip said. She picked up another sheaf of index notes and a groan escaped her lips. 'Dear God in heaven, I've found a whole flock of *pelicans*. No language needs so many different meanings for the word *pelican*. Listen to this—' Pip read from the cards, slapping them down on the desk as she went through them. 'We've got *pelican* (n.) as you'd expect – although this is a bloody detailed entry about them, not sure we need to know they have human-like pupils. And which is *not* great editing by the way: I assume they mean human-*eye*-like.'

'Swansby's isn't famous for being the best at that type of thing,' I reminded her.

'Fine, right, but anyway, then, then!, we have *pelican* as a verb too, to be *like* a pelican.' Pip pelicanned to underline her point. 'And I'll accept that, I suppose I kind of see the need, but, BAM, we've got *pelican* (n.), second meaning, "an alembic with curved tubes on opposing sides of the vessel, used in distillation."'

She glared at me. 'It's not my fault!' I said.

'What the hell is an *alembic* is for starters? I guess a beaker?' She groaned again, more intensely than before. 'Is that a *pun.* Don't answer that – *and!* once you've processed *that,* woah *pelican* as a third noun: "a pronged instrument used for extracting teeth."'

'The English language's rich tapestry,' I said. 'You'd hope that the context would help you work out which one you needed at any given time.'

'Surely one of those is *made-up,*' she protested.

I waggled my phone at her apologetically. 'I've cross-checked while you've been talking,' I said, 'and they look legit.' I showed her images of historical prongs and flasks.

Pip leaned over and faux-angrily gave me a high-five. It was the most *alived* (adj.) thing that had ever sounded in this office in my whole three-year internship. 'So that's at least one down, the rest of language to go.'

Pip pelicanned again, gulping down words and annoyance. 'Nothing like knowledge to make you feel thick. Up next: *pelike.*'

'*Pelike* checks out.'

'Once you start knowing there are *made-up* things in here,' Pip said, launching the index card across the room, 'this whole dictionary is just a – I don't know what to call it.'

'I know,' I said.

'*An index of paranoia.*'

I had texted Pip about the concept of mountweazels after my meeting with David. More to complain than anything else. She had compared it to customers who came into the coffee shop and asked for some outrageously confident mangling of coffee terms and expected to be taken seriously. A grandêe wet latte-frap all-foam half-soy with soft-hedge, to leave, please. Pip added that the word for the cardboard sleeves that go around the takeaway coffee cups is *zarf*. I sent her a shocked emoji.

I brought this up now we were together in person. 'There's a word I would have been *sure* didn't exist.'

'That's their *official* name,' Pip said.

'It doesn't feel official if no one knows it.'

'Well, you know it and you'll never forget it. Like my *official* name is Philippa.' She made a face.

'A wonderful name.'

'It means *lover of horses*. Can you imagine.'

'I refuse to. And Pip suits you better,' I said. She leant over the desk and kissed me on the cheek with a small tough squeak.

Another half-hour of flipping through the index cards, and she sat back. 'I've looked up all the swear words I can think of and I've learned loads about things beginning with *J*.'

I rubbed my eyes. 'There might be a way of being a bit more systematic.'

'What words would you put in?' Pip asked. I'm not sure she was listening. I'm not sure that I blamed her. 'Are there things you've always wished there might be a word for? Put better grammar into that sentence,' she added. 'My head's fried.'

'I was happy when *precariat* gained some traction,' I said. 'That filled a niche.'

'Tell me about it,' Pip said, 'But combining words feels like cheating. Portmanteauing. *Port-man-toe*. God, there should be a word for when words make no sense.'

'Nonsense,' I said.

Pip aimed an index card at my head.

'Is a picture of the guy emerging?' Pip asked. 'I mean, from the kind of stuff he's been inserting: do you get a sense he had any special interests? I just read a really long entry all about chess and I suspect whoever wrote it took that hobby very seriously.'

'Learn anything new?' I said absently. I held two index cards up to the window, staring at the handwriting in hope of a clue.

Pip rolled her shoulders as she read aloud. '"In the four-teenth century, a variation of the game was developed, characterised by the fact each pawn was delegated a particular purpose."'

'Sounds lovely,' I said, tapping away at my phone.

'It goes on. If I am reading the handwriting correctly "Ivan the Terrible died while playing chess, as depicted in a painting by Konstantin Makovsky." Why on earth would anyone think that was relevant detail to put in an article about chess?'

'The internet seems to think that's entirely true.'

Pip drummed her hands. 'Whoever wrote this must have

been *bored*. I bet there are words all about elaborate boredom in there that he's cooked-up just to pass the time.' I waved at the *Swansby* volumes in front of me as if to indicate that she should be my guest. 'What about – what were the ones that David found? One about walking through cobwebs, and something about a donkey burning?'

'The *smell* of a donkey burning,' I corrected.

'Got to be into something, I suppose.'

Somewhere above us came a distinct scuttling in the ceiling. A piece of plaster floated down and landed square in the coffee Pip had brought me. It was a flake the shape of Hy-Brasil.

'This place is falling apart,' Pip said. 'Is that rats above us?'

'I can't imagine David will do anything about it if it is. I don't think he really manages to cope with how much it must cost just to keep the place running as it stands: I doubt he's going to spring for speculative mousetraps.'

'Maybe it's ghosts,' Pip said cheerfully.

'They can pay rent like the rest of us.'

Pip returned to the desk. '*Chess, chess-apple, chess-board, chessdom, chessel* – I resent alphabetical order,' she said.

'Welcome to my world. What's a chessel?'

'It says here that it's a vat of cheese.'

'Nice.'

'Dictionaries should arrange everything by nouns, then verbs, then moods, then – geographically. I don't know. Shut up.'

'I didn't—'

'I was talking to the ratghost.' We were possibly being driven word-mad by this point in proceedings.

'I had a professor,' I said, massaging my temples, 'who once told me that rats were the first archivists – ripping strips of paper from early books and manuscripts and taking them away to their nests.'

'Do rats live in nests? Dreys?'

'That's squirrels,' I said, uncertainly.

'*Squirrel* a better verb than *rat*,' said Pip. 'It's a shame that cat with the awful name can't do anything about whatever it is up there. Everyone slacking at their jobs!'

Some more moments of reading.

'You once told me that the office cat is descended from a load of office cats,' Pip said.

'That's what I've been led to believe.' I was becoming a little annoyed by her interruptions: it was difficult to concentrate with someone unused to the need for brain-crimping silence when intensively word-sieving. 'Masses of them. Chowders.'

'You mean clowders.'

'It doesn't *matter*.'

'If there were so many cats about, I wonder whether *that* might have inspired him,' Pip said. '*Say what you see* and all that. Define what you know.'

I gave her a thumbs-up, unconvinced, and returned to my pile of index cards.

N is for *nab* (v.)

Immediately post-pelican, and leaving the scene in the capable hands of a park-keeper, Sophia took Winceworth's arm and sallied forth beyond the park's gates. 'I demand, in the words of Hippocrates, to be fed eclairs and served hot tea before the day proves all too much.'

Winceworth at once forgot any local knowledge and his brain pitched with dither. Sophia did not seem to notice – as he stuttered and glared at their surroundings and every point on the compass, she took the time to fuss over the blood on her sleeves. She picked up her stride and before Winceworth knew what was happening they were browsing nearby streets and market stalls for shawls. He was unused to shopping quite so casually, and hung back as she made easy conversation with the retailer, touching textures of fabrics with her fingertips and nodding with interest as they extolled different cloths' virtues and characteristics. A new shawl duly acquired, Sophia promptly announced that she would now like to visit a stationer's. Her arm looped through his, and before long Winceworth was walking just off Pall Mall with a bottle of Pelikan-brand India ink and a new silver fountain pen in his pocket just above his heart.

'You mustn't feel so uncomfortable accepting gifts!' Sophia

said, laughing at his twisting and squirming shoulders. 'Especially since you sacrificed your Swansby pen for such a noble cause. It is only right that I replace it.'

He suggested that he really should be returning to work. In doing so he suffered a small coughing fit as if his body rebelled against his getting any words out at all. Sophia pulled her new shawl more snugly about her to obscure the more obvious daubings of pelican-blood. 'The dictionary can spare you just one more hour. Besides,' and she quickened her pace. 'After a shock it is often good for the constitution for one to sit somewhere quiet.'

Winceworth thought of his desk in the Scrivenery, flanked by Appleton and Bielefeld.

'To drink something hot and to eat something sweet,' Sophia said.

The image of the paperwork strewn across on his desk. 'I wouldn't dare oppose your medical advice, given the previous patient, no. Not without some kind of suit of armour.' He mimed the gait of a spar-chested pelican with the martyred dignity of a waddling St Sebastian.

'I have simply no idea what you might mean,' Sophia said. 'And, do you know, I think you should probably explain it to me, at length, somewhere warm?'

He felt the arm tense gently beneath his.

The *Café l'Amphigouri* was Sophia's selection, picked at whim down a side street some way towards Whitehall. Despite its proximity to Swansby House, Winceworth was unfamiliar with the place or must have overlooked it whenever he passed it on his walks through town, discounting it as a destination not meant for him. The tablecloths were as thick as royal icing and the bowl of sugar came with a pair of ornate silver tongs. The café's owner applied some baking powder to the cut above Sophia's eyebrow as they were seated. They were placed by the window and soon a spread of tiny cakes, buns and dessert forks was laid before them.

'Back home,' Sophia said, turning a plate to examine a delicate layered confection, 'we would call this a Napoleon cake.'

'Looks nothing like the man,' Winceworth said, playing with an eclair on his plate with his fork.

'Very good,' Sophia said, and he beamed. She tapped the side of the cake with her fork, counting the strata of cream and thin sheets of pastry. She removed a wisp of icing sugar from the corner of her mouth with a fingertip. Winceworth leaned forward in his chair in order that he might have the best chance of catching her words, but whatever thought she might have been framing seemed to leave her within the same instant. She raised her teacup to her lips instead, leaving Winceworth confronted with a face eclipsed by floral china. The base of her teacup bore the manufacturer's hand-painted name: *HAVI-LAND & Co., Limoges*.

He wanted to commit the whole scene to memory as accurately as possible. Every detail of the tearoom was laden with significance now that Sophia was a part of it. From the angle of shadows amongst the curtains to the number of faceted cubes within the sugar bowl. The arrangement of the chairs and the postures of the other diners suddenly seemed of critical importance. The exact pitch of the bell as they passed through the door was a crucial fact to be treasured and privately indexed away.

Perhaps all encyclopaedic lexicographers experience love like this, Winceworth thought – as a completist might, a hoarder of incidence-as-fact. It was not that he even particularly liked the details: he wanted to dash the teacup to the ground for coming between them – *damn you, blasted furnaces of Limoges!* – but he wished he could identify the blue, twist-leafed flower that patterned its porcelain. If he knew the flower's name he would run to the nearest florist and fill his lodgings with armfuls of the stuff, plug his rooms to the rafters with posies, bouquets and tussie-mussies of it. He wanted to glut on every detail, block out any not-tearoom scented light that dared to come anywhere near him ever again.

Sophia was still concentrating on the cake.

'All these layers, you see, meant to symbolise the Grande Armée. And this —' she raked the cake's surface and crumbs kicked back against her fork – '*this* represents the Russian snow that stalled the French advance, helping to defeat the little Corsican's troops before reaching Moscow.'

'Pelican surgery, military history expressed through cakes – you are quite the dissector.'

'What would *you* call it?' Sophia asked. 'This type of cake?'

Winceworth tried to usher some poetry. He failed. 'A variant on the custard slice.'

Sophia nodded, sympathetically, and cut herself a portion.

Winceworth felt so unused to this gentleness, this back and forth. It all felt a complete nonsense. He would not have been surprised if a Mad Hatter joined them from another table or if a Carollian dormouse appeared over the lip of the sugar bowl and started talking about mousetraps, memory and muchness. That, or the other diners had hidden their haloes and stowed their angelic harps. He was worried he might forget how to use cutlery correctly.

'A certain pragmatism to *custard slice*,' Sophia said. 'Is that the term for it? When a word just sits there, entirely fitting but somehow flat?' She glanced out of the window at the passing Whitehall traffic. Winceworth recognised the way she flicked her eyes from passer-by to passer-by at random. He did that too when he was trying to find the right word for something, to coax the word forward from a forgotten part of his mind. When she spoke again she did so slowly, carefully. 'When a word has *pragmatism* mixed with *stolidity* mixed with *bathos* mixed with *clunk*: what is that called?'

Me, Winceworth felt moved to say. He felt drunk. Was *she* drunk? This was awful. This was lovely. What was she talking about, and had he started this? Was this what conversation should be, or could have been, all along? Conversation as meaningless and wonderful, and terrible.

'So, tell me all about your work,' Sophia said. 'Have you always loved language?'

'Do you mind if I do not?' Winceworth said. 'You will excuse me: I am not good at talking about myself.'

Sophia raised her eyebrows. 'I appreciate that in a person.'

'I'd much rather talk about you,' he said.

'Nothing I can tell you,' came the reply, which made no sense at all but Winceworth concentrated very hard on his cake and tried to look pleased with this answer. She looked pleased to have given it. Winceworth hoped he hadn't somehow allowed an impasse.

'And secretly, between you and me, I am glad to not have to hear much more about Swansby's. Do you know how many names I had to memorise for the party last night? I ended up having arranged them in my head alphabetically: *A* is for anxious Appleton, *B* for bloviating Bielefeld, *C* is for the curious Cottingham twins.' Sophia counted down on her fingers. 'I believe I have a space left for *E*, but then there's Frasham of course, followed everywhere by that strange little gurgle of a man Glossop—'

'This is quite scandalous,' Winceworth said, enthralled.

'I should not defame the good dictionary. All power to its eventual publication. Do you play chess?' Sophia asked, helping herself to a canelé.

'No, but I would like to try.' Conversation as meaningful and entirely wonderful precisely because it *means* nothing except to the two people involved. Terrible because of the pressure to fill the silence with a special type of nothing-ing – a kind of everything-nothing – and make it seem artless all the while?

Sophia smiled at him. 'I would like to teach you! Do you know, I had a dream about you in your little longed-for

Cornish cottage.' Winceworth's fork twanged weirdly off his plate. 'I was visting you and we were playing chess.'

'That sounds – that would be—' he began, but she cut across him.

'You would love the vocabulary of chess too, I think,' she said. 'Have you heard of *zugzwang*?'

'*Zugzwang*,' Winceworth repeated, unlispingly. If she liked it, it would be his new favourite word.

'Wonderful, isn't it? It is the situation where a player is obliged to make a move to one's own disadvantage. Great word, horrible feeling, like being caught in a lie.'

> *love* (v.), to fill a void with icing sugar and healing weeds,
>   or with glib little shared lies

'I profess to know little of chess,' he said.

'There are many excellent phrases to be had there.'

'Much more than *check* or *stalemate* and I would be out of my depth.'

'I have much to teach you,' she said. 'It all changes with the fashions, of course. For a time, did you know players would announce *gardez* when the queen was under attack? Or *en prise*. But the warning is no longer customary. That's chivalry for you.'

Winceworth wanted to tell Sophia that the fear of seeming like an idiot had cured his headache. He just wanted to say that in this moment he aspired to be a fearful idiot for the rest of his life, and that he wished his life to be such meaningless moments, over and over, for ever.

The window next to them was hit with an awful bang. Winceworth, his fight- and flight- and freeze- responses engaged all at once, gripped the table and all the silverware clattered.

Terence Clovis Frasham waved from the street outside, his cane raised as he rapped on the windowpane once more. He was smiling with all of his teeth.

Sophia gave a start and then a smile settled across her face.

'What an extraordinary coincidence,' she said.

Frasham entered the café with great strides all abluster, making the tiny bell spring on its gantry above the door. He waved the owner away and placed his hat on their table, barely missing Winceworth's plate.

'Sophia!' He dipped his face to kiss the air above her ear. Winceworth looked away. Frasham was too big for the tea-room, too well-formed. Pulling a chair from another table, the other lexicographer sat down with his legs apart. He pressed the fingers of one hand in and across his fine red moustache as if framing a yawn or loosening his face. This was a mannerism Winceworth had forgotten. He found it indefinably repulsive. 'And Winceworth too! Why, man, you should be at work! Tea, cake, a man's wife-to-be – you devil!'

Sophia and Frasham and Winceworth laughed at such an idea. *Aha aha.*

'In fact,' Frasham said, clapping a hand to Winceworth's shoulder, 'I say, old man: don't you have a train to catch?'

'I beg your pardon?'

'Not that I want to break up your little tête-à-tête, of course, but,' and Frasham's face changed as he looked at his fiancée at close quarters. 'Good God, what's all this dust on your face?' He touched the silt of baking powder above Sophia's eye. 'You look ridiculous. Winceworth, why didn't you tell her?'

'There was a cut—'

'A cut!' Frasham took Sophia's chin in his hands and studied her. He seemed concerned, then amused. 'What do you get up to? Quite the buffet you've taken. Eating cakes when you know we are going for dinner this evening, and – what? – getting into fights? And leading young bucks like Winceworth astray all at the same time?'

'Did you say – what *train*—?' Winceworth tried. Perhaps he had misunderstood. He also realised that at the sight of Frasham, his lisp had automatically returned. He wondered whether Sophia detected the change. He wondered whether he could choose his words carefully enough that no s-words would be necessary in Frasham's earshot.

'And what is this shawl all about?' Frasham continued, regarding her at arm's length in mock horror. 'Darling, it is quite, quite awful! I have become engaged to a ruffian.'

'Mr Winceworth and I have been saving the wildfowl of London,' she said.

'I'm sure, I'm sure,' Frasham said. He dropped his hand, and Sophia's chin lifted slightly. Winceworth pretended to busy himself with a napkin, but he imagined Frasham's fingers resting gently on Sophia's knee.

'I ought to be leaving,' Winceworth said again, slightly more loudly.

'Yes,' said Frasham. 'Yes, old Gerolf has been looking for you back at the Scrivenery.'

'For *me*?' No one ever looked for Winceworth. There must be some error.

'You must stay, you must!' Sophia protested. 'I need someone to explain and corroborate the day's events.'

Winceworth began yammering. 'I was just – quite a coincidence, I ran into Miss – Miss—' He ignored the fact that the lisp caused Sophia to look at him at a new angle. 'I'm – I'm so sorry,' he said. 'Forgive me, only now do I realise that I do not know your—'

'Slivkovna,' said Frasham.

'Just so,' said Sophia.

'Soon to be Frasham,' said Frasham.

'Slivkovna,' Sophia said again. She laid a hand on Winceworth's sleeve.

'Sophia is teasing you, I'm afraid,' said her fiancée. 'What a word for a lisper to deal with!' Winceworth imagined grinding an eclair prow-first into Frasham's ear. 'Mind as fast as anything. I've promised her a visit to the British Museum this afternoon, and dinner near my club after theatre just to tire her out: too much energy by half.'

'And your first name, Mr Winceworth?' Sophia Slivkovna asked. 'I remember a *P* . . .'

She does not even know your name. To name a thing is to know a thing.

'*Wince* as in *flinch*,' laughed Frasham. He dug Sophia's fork into some of Winceworth's cake.

'I prefer *wince* as in *startle*,' Winceworth said.

'And *worth* as in "worse for wear",' Frasham lisped. He tugged at his moustache again, upward with his whole palm so that his smile seemed to slide onto his face beneath his hand, a conjuring trick. He brought the same hand down companionably on Winceworth's arm. Frasham became a conduit between the fabric of Winceworth's elbow and the fabric of Sophia's skirt.

'Your fiancé can see I am not, perhaps, running at full steam,' Winceworth said.

'*Startle dignity*,' Sophia quoted, quietly, looking out of the window again.

Frasham kept his hand on Winceworth's shoulder. 'And what was it – sorry, I interrupted – tell me, what was it that you two were doing today? Earlier? Away from the Scrivenery?'

'Is that what you call it?' Sophia turned to Frasham. 'The place where you all trap poets' words like spiders underneath a glass? *Scrivenery*.'

Conversation was about parrying now and concerned with feints. *Love* (n.), in the sport of tennis, the name given when any player has a score of no games or points. Etymology disputed, with submitted but speculative derivations including a French expression *l'œuf*, with an egg resembling the number zero on a scoring board.

Winceworth tried to catch Sophia's eye.

Winceworth failed to catch Sophia's eye.

'Where *is* your umbrella?' Frasham asked. 'That funny yellow thing.'

'I must have — I must have left it in the park. It's such a story — there was a bird, and I hit your friend here, and then we—' Frasham interrupted her with a large guffaw, making his laughter the main event of their conversation. He suited laughing, it made him seem younger. He had the relaxed posture of someone who laughed, youngly, often.

Winceworth asked Sophia, 'Does it hurt awfully? Your eye?'

She felt the side of her head. 'Not even a little. I had quite forgotten it.'

'Miss Slivkovna is made of sterner stuff than I,' Winceworth said, and he knew that it was a line Frasham would deliver with the dashing candour of a proffered cigarette, while in Winceworth's mouth it sounded like a criticism or as if he was appraising livestock. He reddened again to the roots of his hair. The ceiling of *Café l'Amphigouri* seemed a foot closer to his scalp and the walls were bending in. He concentrated on the metal scrollwork on his teaspoon.

'I was just thinking,' Frasham said to him, 'that you are remarkably alert, considering.'

'Terence—' Sophia said.

'The party yesterday,' Frasham continued, folding his hands in his lap and leaning back. He explored Winceworth's face and spoke as if this was a good shared joke but his eyes were hard. 'You really were in quite the state, weren't you? *Slurp, quaff, guzzle* — it appears I had forgotten quite how much a day of looking up words in one book and writing them down in another can create such a thirst amongst my colleagues.'

And Winceworth was back in the club room at the party, back in amongst the potted ferns and braying colleagues, speaking far too close to Sophia's face. What had he said? His hands and noticed they had balled up, without him meaning them to at all.

'Perhaps now would be a good time to apologise for my behaviour,' Winceworth said to the teaspoon. His reflection peered across the table at him, upside-down and swollen. Pelican-necked. He flipped the spoon over but the reflection on its reverse was one grown large, chinful and bug-eyed, even more ghastly. Sophia and Frasham regarded him. A lifetime of no one looking, and now this. He pushed the spoon away – it hit his cup at a strange slant and made what was left of his tea slop across the tablecloth. Winceworth scraped his chair back, and the stark ringing of china and metal made other unangelic diners stop and look round at the noise.

'No need, no need to apologise,' Sophia said. 'It was a pleasure to see so many of Terence's friends enjoying his birthday.' As she laid her napkin over the spreading dash of tea, her engagement ring gave Winceworth a pointed glint. 'If anything, I really think Terence should be apologising to you. I thought this at the party and now is as good a time as ever for me to say it: I think it was entirely wrong of you to make fun of Winceworth's lisp in the way that you did.' Sophia turned to Winceworth: 'In fact, I really have not noticed you speaking with one at all this whole time.'

Frasham put his head to one side.

'Is Mr Winceworth joining us tomorrow, Terence?' Sophia asked.

'Tomorrow?'

Frasham yawned. 'Oh, that. Perhaps you've heard that we are having another little soirée to raise money for the Swansby House coffers tomorrow evening. A more – ah! – a more intimate affair, shall we say.'

Sophia leaned forward. 'Terence has used his influence to get us a private party in the Secretum! Can you imagine: the most licentious place in the whole of London! Europe!'

Frasham smiled, so it seemed to Winceworth, directly at him. 'You do not know my dear Sophia's interest in the more esoteric side of art. She's quite the collector.'

'You are mocking me,' Winceworth said.

'I would not dare! No, poor unshockable Winceworth, do you know she has a chess set that was once owned by Catherine the Great? She hopes to exhibit it at the Secretum – it's absolutely repellent and quite wonderful.'

'Have you heard of the Pushkin Palace?' Sophia said. She genteelly tooled her dessert with the side of her fork. 'Golden doorknob shaped like a phallus, tablelegs positively burgeoning—'

'How very impractical,' Winceworth said.

'But we are making him uncomfortable,' Frasham said delightedly. 'Best not describe what the bishop, rook and knight in the chess set resemble!'

'A single pawn from the collection would sell for seven hundred pounds,' Sophia said.

'That would free you from the confines of the desk, eh, old thing,' Frasham said.

'I do wish you – I wish you wouldn't call me that.'

'Old thing old thing old thing,' said Frasham. 'What better soubriquet when we talk of solid-gold antiques. Honestly, Winceworth, you philistine!'

'Seven hundred pounds is not to be sniffed at,' Sophia said, watching Winceworth's expression. He felt like there was no air in the room, and all the lights were too bright.

'I – I really must be taking my leave,' Winceworth said, 'and I hope that you enjoy the rest of your stay in London.'

Frasham stood too and his arm was again on Winceworth's shoulder. 'Yes! I keep letting it slide – you've just reminded me! I stepped into the office on my way here, and old Swansby was there pacing and squawking and looking for you. You're supposed to be somewhere on dictionary business right now, old man! Something about a train?'

Sophia also rose from her seat.

Winceworth stared into Frasham's face. He knew the man was lying, but was trying to work out what the game might be.

'They just *know* Winceworth is usually a good bet when it comes to having nothing better to do,' Frasham continued. 'I'm joking, old man. But seriously, I can't believe I forgot! Can't believe *you* forgot, Peter, more's the point – lucky I caught you here, all told: you'd better hightail it back on the double!'

'What – what train?'

'To Barking.' Frasham did not waver.

'Barking,' Winceworth repeated.

'Barking?' Sophia asked, looking between the two of them.

'Yes, yes, Barking. Tell you what – I'll save you the trouble of going back to the Scrivenery for the tickets—' Frasham suddenly had some coins and was folding Winceworth's hands around them, pushing him slightly as he did so towards the door of the café. Winceworth's diet today had consisted exclusively of cake and he was beginning to feel the effects both on his pulse and vision. He vibrated gently, unsure if it was the sugar or the offence that Frasham thought he could be ushered away with such obvious a lie.

'Barking?' Winceworth asked again, staring at the money.

'Barking!' Frasham's tone was one of enthusiasm and mild jealousy, as if he couldn't quite believe Winceworth's luck. 'Gerolf wants you to clear up a little confusion about the place name. Or the, what, the adjective. You know: *with all that jabbering, Winceworth must be absolutely barking.* Gerolf seems to think it's worth you popping along and investigating any connections between the place and the word, however spurious.'

'However spurious,' Winceworth repeated. With his lisp, the word furred over like rotting fruit.

Frasham kept nodding. 'A meeting has been set up for you, apparently, with – oh, what was his name? Some local historian. Folklorist. Something along those lines.' Winceworth stared at him, clearly becoming florid in the act of improvising. '*That* should be enough to get you your ticket: Fenchurch

Street train should take you straight there.' He grinned again. 'Best not be late! Sounds like a marvellous research trip.'

Winceworth had never undertaken a trip for Swansby House before, let alone been sent on such a last-minute and vague expedition. That was the role of field lexicographers and linguists like Frasham and Glossop, not the desk-botherers of the Scrivenery. It was utterly absurd.

'I am working on the Ss,' Winceworth said, weakly, and Frasham spread his hands and shrugged.

'It was specified that it should be *you* that goes. You have clearly made an impression.'

'Barking.' Winceworth wanted to seize Frasham by the collar, *garbgrab* and scream at him. 'This is a fiction!' he wanted to shout. A fool's errand, a wild goosechase!

Frasham smiled. 'No need to thank me. But, time might be of the essence?'

And Winceworth was backing out of the door and into the street, apologising and nodding and holding his new bottle of ink. For just a moment he turned to look back through the café window – the pair had turned to their own private conversation and were taking their seats. Frasham moved into his vacated chair and was laughing at something Sophia had said. They looked happy, they looked as though they matched.

Winceworth kept watching as the third, unnecessary chair at their table was moved away by a waiter.

O is for *ostensible* (adj.)

Perhaps a sense of narrative is one of the first things to degrade when you spend a long time looking though dictionary entries. Certainly ('certainly'!) chronology no longer matters as much as it used to, and links between pages seem either entirely contrived or simply impossible. Patterns emerge but they are often not to be trusted.

For this reason and although they are tasked with bringing about order and a degree of regimentation, I can't help but think many lexicographers must go through something of a breakdown from time to time. As I flicked through the blue index cards, I wondered if my nineteenth-century mountwea-zelling interlocutor knew the word *breakdown* (n.). I wish I could have extended my hand through time and offered it to him. He might have found it useful.

Surprising everybody, Pip's policy of looking for any word remotely related to cats paid some dividends. She busied herself making a small stack of the cards we could identify as mountweazels by the door frame and into an envelope.

'You little prat,' she hissed. 'Listen to this, Mallory: "*peltee* (n.), a hairball, or matter disjected from the mouths of sleaking beasts (SEE ALSO: *cat*)." Honestly, he's trying a bit too hard there, I think.'

'Honestly.'

'Honestly. Ah, but here's a nice one: "*widge-wodge* (v.). Informal – the alternating kneading of a cat's paws upon wool, blankets, laps &c." A sappy so-and-so, then.'

I did not like thinking of our obscure mountweazeler in that way. I preferred him as bent on chaos, disruption, as some-body thrilled and motivated by sneaking around and having the last laugh. If I let a more tender portrait of him emerge, I ran the risk of liking him. Him, her, it. Him. Let's say *him*. Odds are.

I did not want to feel protective of him. I didn't want to invest in that fact that many of the words showed small sweet observations, inconsequentialisms. As I flipped over the index cards I found myself hoping that nothing ever entirely terrible or perilous was being termed. I didn't want that to be his remit, the world he was casting to define. It was fine if that meant his world was small. He didn't have to make grand claims. I'm much more comfortable with people who just about manage the bare minimum.

We continued to pore and paw and pour over the index cards, seeking out the distinctive pen nib and any other clue. We swapped between who got to sit on the chair and who bal-anced on the window-ledge every half-hour and compared how many mountweasels we each could find. I had slightly more than Pip because I was faster at spotting the distinctive penmanship, but she was quicker at checking online to see whether the words appeared anywhere else documented in the English language. Pip gnawed her lip as she read. Her dentist had told her that she ground her teeth as she slept – *bruxism*, she had repeated to me through gritted jaws that same evening with a flourish of distasteful new vocabulary. The dentist told her that if she kept grinding her teeth they would be eroded down to half their size. This had shocked an unconscious self-preservation response in her body: ever since then, she made sure to tuck her lips between her teeth and grind them together instead. Mouth as mangle and buffer.

'Do you think David will be pleased with our haul?' she asked.

'Pleased he can winnow them out, sure.' I arranged the most recently uncovered fictitious entries together, taking them out of alphabetical sequence.

skipsty (v.), the act of taking steps two at a time
prognostisumption (n.), belief, as made by glimpsing aspects
   of something from at a distance
pretermissial (adj.), the quality of being unbearable, particularly as pertains to silences
slivkovnion (n.), a daydream, briefly

'Whoever jotted these down clearly had his mind in the *S*s and the *P*s,' Pip said.

We went on sifting.

'Quite an odd man, that boss of yours,' Pip said after a while. 'Don't you think?'

I shushed her. 'He's just down the hall.'

'It was interesting to put a face to a name this morning. I gave him a good once-over while he was eating his ice cream and waiting for the police to give the all-clear.'

'What did you make of him?'

She shrugged. 'I mean, I understand this is his passion. Life work. But trying to digitise all this – it's not like *Swansby's* is ever going to really replace the *OED* or the *Britannica*, is it? I mean, *Swansby's* is only known for not being finished. Having mistakes and being a bit eccentric.'

I agreed, but felt I owed the place some benefit of the doubt. 'David has a line he likes to trot out about mistakes. Tell you what: I wrote it in my phone so I could quote it back at him if I made an error when helping him with the digitisation.' I scrolled to find it. 'Right. From Sohnson. That's a typo. Here we go. Johnson: "Every other author may aspire to praise; the lexicographer can only hope to escape reproach, and even this negative recompense has been yet granted to very few."'

'Snappy,' Pip said, barely listening. 'But that doesn't excuse him putting you in the line of fire with those phone calls.'

'There will always be someone looking to ruin everything,' I said.

'Not good enough,' she countered. And I believed her I believed her I believed her.

I found another false definition about idling, dreaming:

alnascharaze (v.), to force oneself to fantasise

and then another, a touch more cynical:

Mammonsomniate (v.), to dream that money might make anything possible

Small little extracts revealed a state or state of mind. Briefer
than an anecdote, more overworked than a passing thought.

'What do you think about when you think about a dictionary?' I had asked Pip on our first proper date. It was a clunky
sentence. It was an evening of shynesses and clunky hopeful
approaches.

I remember that she had rubbed her ear and I thought it
was kind she took time to answer such a dumb question. It's
not like I had a good answer for it either. And she cleared her
throat, raised a fist in mock mic-stance and in her terrible
singing voice warbled an impression of Sinatra's hit 'Too Mar-
velous for Words' and I remember she winked and twelve
glaciers' worth of tension melted beneath my throat and
some new desire beneath that developed its own Brinell
scale over the pub garden table, and yes, every flower in the
Red Lion's hanging baskets might as well have swapped
their stigmas for bugles and their petals for clappers in that
moment, and it was fine, it was fine, to be here with her,
thinking about the difference between 'being out' and 'going
out' and she was still singing in that moment and my mind
was getting ahead of itself and I remember that I knew I
should be concentrating, should stop staring at her mouth

for anything other than listening very precisely or definitely, and then a wink could have been a mistake or a tic, and I smiled as she sang off-key.

I probably said, 'That's nice.'

'You use that word too much,' Pip said. And she ground her teeth a little, *very very*.

Five years later, helping me sort through index cards for God-knows-what because that is what love sometimes had to be, 'There's no noun *pornography* in here,' Pip said abruptly, fanning a spread of blue definitions across the desk. 'Do you think that's significant?'

'Why on earth are you looking that word up?'

'No reason,' she said.

'I'm sorry you're bored,' I said, tetchily. 'This is what my job is. Boring.'

'I'm having a whale of a time,' Pip declared. She pelicanned. 'A *prodigious* time.'

'I'm pretty sure that's not what prodigious—'

'It can't be that they didn't *have* pornography,' Pip mused on, regardless. 'Perhaps they just didn't have the word for it.'

'Or they did and *Swansby's* just didn't include it.'

'Jesus Christ, never mind that: did you know *pip* refers to various respiratory diseases of birds—'

I had looked up *pip* (n.) and (v.) very early in what once might have been called our courtship. Our stepping-out or not-out out-going outings. 'Various respiratory diseases of birds, esp. poultry, when accompanied by a horny patch on the tip of the tongue.' I decided to keep this definition out of the three years' worth of Valentine's cards.

I preferred *pip* (v. transitive) of a chick: to crack (most likely the shell of the egg) when hatching.

It felt good to watch Pip discover this pipfact for herself, pip me to the post before I could tell her.

Love is often using words like *maybe* or *most likely* to soften a blow, or using words like *like* when really you mean *indefinitely* and using the word *definitely* to imply anything can ever be anything other than a suggestion or an impression.

I often had cause to remember this line while working in *Swansby's*: 'Too precise a meaning erases the mystery of your literature.' I think I first came across it in one of my pointless essays for a pointless degree for a pointless internship at an end-of-the-line encyclopaedic dictionary. I had underlined the – what, *axiom*? *motto*? – on my essay notes.

'What would be in your personal dictionary?' Pip asked me from her position by my office window. It was January so the light had vanished from my window, and we were working as long a day in Swansby House as I could ever remember.

I stretched my arms and pinched the bridge of my nose. 'I don't know if there's anything new to say.'

'That's the ambition of the woman I love,' Pip said, and came around the back of my chair to wrap an arm gently about my shoulders.

What things in the world do I want to define for other people that might otherwise be overlooked? Coming up with words is a particular kind of weird creative peristalsis: memory is involved, and self-awareness and absorption. The image is of someone tapping your brain as one might tap a trunk for syrup.

'I've no idea,' I said.

I thought: a word for how I always mistype *warm* as *walm*. Silly things. A word for knowing when the pasta is perfectly cooked just by looking at it. Crucial-silly things. A word for when you're head-over-heels in love with someone and you're both just burbling nonsense at each other, forgivably. A word for mispronouncing words that you had only ever seen written down. A word for your favourite songs that can never be overlistened to. A word for the great kindness of people who, unseen, take care to release insects that are trapped in rooms. A word for being surprised by an aspect of your physicality. A word for the way that sometimes thoughts can sit unpenetrable but snug like an avocado stone in your brain. A word for the strange particular bluish sheen of skin rolled between the fingers.

'What about a word for not being out?' Pip said.

We never fight, not really. Not about the expected stuff: not about ambitions, not about our future, not about exes. *Ex* is included as verb in *Swansby's* – it is defined as 'to obliterate character by typing *x* over it; to cross out in this way' – and as a noun: a mark made in lieu (of a signature). Often witnessed.

In three years the closest we come to a row really came down to one of us wanting the other to take definitive action.

'Where did that come from?' I said.

'Forget it,' she said.

'I'm out enough,' I said.

'Are you?' Pip asked. *This face is left intentionally blank*, her tone seemed to say to me.

I get on-the-tip-of-my-tonguish when it comes to being out. For a start, the tenses go all wrong and my thoughts all come disjointed and panicked, disarrayed like an upturned box of index cards. I've been gay since I can care to remember but haven't been able to tell other people. I say it's because I haven't got around to it, and maybe one day this will be true. I hadn't told my parents even though I don't think they would mind. They would *care*, I think, but I don't know if they'd mind. Compared with so many places in the world etc. etc. it is a good time to be out. I know that. It's nice out. That's what I know to be true and yet *and yet*.

Pip has been out her whole life and can't understand why I would be uneasy or unable to. My brain loops round and through and in and in and in on itself if I try to put it into words. It's not interesting. It *is* interesting. It shouldn't define me. It definitely should. I wish I had an easy way to remember how to spell *mnemonic*. I wish I could remember how to use 'surely' and 'definitely' when it came to finding words for myself.

'Just tell me what's wrong,' Pip would ask at home. 'I'm here, I'm listening.'

You're unbelievable, a voice in my head whispers.

I can never quite get the thoughts and words in order. 'Maybe I'm not ready yet' feels like cowardice, or strangely prissy, I am a special rare bud or fruit.

The word *closet* is flimsier than *cupboard* or *wardrobe*, right? No one would miss a closet and its unstable walls. No one cares about a closet. I hate that it matters. I hate that I matter, sometimes. I haven't got the right words for me.

Swansby's defines *closet*, amongst many things, in terms of a 'closet of ease (n.), a toilet, a privy' and a 'closet of the heart (n.), the pericardium, which encloses the heart; a chamber within the heart, the left atrium or ventricle. Obsolete.'

'It's not lying to not be out,' I said, slowly.

'I never called you a liar,' Pip said.

'I don't know why you're crying,' I said.

'No,' she said. She wiped the corner of her eye with her sleeve, not-angry but not-not-angry, and then she squared her shoulders. 'The sooner we can get this done, you know, the sooner you can leave this job. I don't feel comfortable with you working somewhere where you're being threatened.'

'Is this about the phone calls? I've told you, it's just some idiot.'

She stared at me. '*Just* is doing a lot of work there. Look, forget I ever said anything.'

'I don't want to fight,' I said.

Pip hugged me again. I wished there was a word for

marshalling a loved one to safety. I wish that I could be the one to coin it.

'I'm sorry.' She perched again on the window-frame and patted my seat. 'I'm tired, I love you, and I'm feeling on edge. Come on: we can do another hour or so. Let's find what else is up the garden path.'

P is for *phantom* (n. and adj. and v.)

On the train to Barking, if he concentrated, Winceworth believed that he could almost hear the genteel roll of the dessert trolley and the squeak of waiters' feet in the rock and rumble of the carriage. He used to only ever daydream about the picture of the cottage in Cornwall. The salt on the breeze in his hair, the soft hum of bees. It seems that this dream had been ousted and replaced.

Perhaps he should think of it as a badge of honour that Frasham felt compelled to send him on such an obviously made-up errand. It was absurd, of course – *imagine anyone being jealous of me*. But there was some comfort that Frasham had noticed Sophia's interest in him, or friendship, or tenderness. It clearly was significant enough to cause him to intervene.

Barking. Honestly.

He tried his more familiar daydreams and to think about a whitewashed cottage with a bare table, a window overlooking a bright, clear stretch of sand. He had mentioned the Sennen Cove fantasy to Sophia in a moment of madness. It was a silly thing, a flippant cipher for the idea of being left alone and clearheaded. He would be at no one's beck and call with no responsibility other than for himself. It felt an unambitious fantasy but an honest one. What would he do with all the money in the world? His immediate thought: disappear. The train shifted a little, and with it his mind changed tack. Would anyone miss him? A scruffy lexicographer, who left no real mark on the world? He reeled back to the idea of a cottage, and the sound of bees in a garden.

As he daydreamed, or tried to force himself to daydream, Winceworth leaned his head against his seat and watched a moth make its way up and down the window of the swaying carriage. He had read somewhere when researching for a Swansby article that some species of moth had no mouthparts. *Mothparts.* At the time of reading he had been overcome with sadness at this fact. A case of too much information not always being a good thing. He never realised that he needed to believe a moth could shout in rage, for example, or find comfort in eating its favourite moth-snacks or even have a chance to yawn. Winceworth yawned now and regarded his mouthless companion with sympathy.

A thought intruded: Frasham leaning in and his red moustache close to Sophia's neck.

Of course, when *Frasham* left the office it was with full fanfare and pomp, and he got to gallivant around Siberia as language's knight errant, its swain and suitor with his damned hollow Swansby House regulation pen and headed notepaper. While I am sent thirteen miles to Barking, Winceworth thought, with my regulation pen irregularly lodged in a pelican's throat. Winceworth's gifted, new silver pen would have to do. The stationer had filled its cartridge in the shop. He used it now to doodle on the cover of the attaché case – *barkBarkBARK K* – and as he ran the pen across his lap and the train gave little skips, his writing jumped with jolts and shimmies on the page.

Winceworth returned to the moth at the train window and brushed absently at some pelican blood on his shirt. He wondered whether the moth had ever been beyond the confines of this train. Like the mice and rats he sometimes spotted on the underground sections of the Metropolitan Railway, perhaps this moth was born here and would die here, had no moth-memories of tree-bark or woollen jumpers or moonlight to fall back on. Winceworth imagined a moth-eaten volume of *Swansby's New Encyclopaedic Dictionary.*

Every time that the moth reached the wooden lip at the top of the window frame where escape was possible and the world appeared in a brighter strip, it missed its opportunity and slowly head-butted its way back down the windowpane. Up and then down, up and then down, taking in the view as the train cut a journey through London. Tattered clouds, black brick and gutters. Winceworth thought of all the moths that he had trapped beneath tumblers and deposited outside over the years. The moth reached the top of the window and again turned on its heels and began its descent. Winceworth slid an eye to the passenger sitting opposite him – a mixed metaphor of an older man, tamarin-moustache jutting a few good white inches beyond his cheeks with liver spots like giraffe skin and the surface of Jupiter on his hands. The man was watching the moth too, apparently unperturbed.

Winceworth got to his feet, unsteady with the pitch and

roll of the carriage, and opened the window by pulling on the leather strap.

'Come on, old thing.' He tried chivvying the moth out with his document folder. The moth refused to take this advantage. Up and then down, up and then down again as cold air snapped around Winceworth's ears.

'Close that, won't you?' said the other passenger and Winceworth acquiesced at once.

Winceworth's later recollection of this train journey would be hazy. The train ran through East Ham with its glue factories and sad-faced, easily led horses. The marine paint factories disgorged columns of steam and a smell that you first sensed in your stomach before any flavour hit your nose. The moth made its way up and down, up and down the window. He knew that bombilating was the verb for bees – what of moths? His human carriagemate leaned forward and produced a newspaper. The page facing Winceworth featured an advertisement in bold italics: *Don't Mutilate Your Papers with Pins or Fasteners, but Use the Gem Paper Clip.* A nap curdled in Winceworth's mind and did its thing to senses of time, place and space. January beyond his window had made the sky above the city paperclip-coloured. The moth continued to rumble up and down the window, up and down.

Later, Winceworth would not be able to recall the scene very clearly.

The train carriage bucked and swayed a little and Winceworth would recall that he had been quite cold and his crumpled jacket was thin. He would remember closing his eyes, and that briefly there was nothing but the swaying of the train, the smell of the leather seats, previous travellers' cigarettes and the paint factories outside. The moth's coat at the window was attracting dust and cobwebs, growing infinitesimally heavier, up and down, up and down. The train worked out its shunting *solfeggio* as it coursed along, the telegraph posts and buildings flicked past the window and caused weak afternoon sun to the-opposite-of-flash through Winceworth's eyelids. The undersides of his eyelids shifted from a deadened ruddy colour to bursts of red light as each post passed by. There was a false sense of depth to the shapes that he began to see forming there and he experienced an instant, pleasantly terrifying giddiness. The silver of his new pen flashed in the sun. He added *Barking* as a title to the notepad page, and he underlined the word twice, with a flourish.

The moth humming its way up the windowpane – that detail he would remember. He would remember coming out of his nap just as the tamarin-faced, Jupiter-giraffe-skin man opposite made a noise, rolled up his newspaper, and smacked it against the glass, against the moth, and at that very moment that the world went

whumppp

A number of Winceworth's colleagues cut out and kept some of the headlines from the following day's papers: TERRIBLE EXPLOSION, MANY KILLED AND INJURED – GREAT DESTRUCTION OF PROPERTY. Later articles listed the injuries and the damage: 'parts of the body were found 60 yards distant', 'the dome of the boiler is lying in an adjoining field'. The lexicographers who kept these papers would stress that they collected the snippets not out of some new-found desire to chase souvenirs of awful events, but to help account for Winceworth's movements and assist in putting the narrative together. He had no memory of alighting from the train, nor of how he might have made it to the site of the explosion. Bielefeld found one photograph in the press that featured a figure that if you squinted might well have been Winceworth at the scene of the disaster. At least, the man in the photograph had glasses and was pictured carrying a slim paper folder. There was certainly a corresponding stain over his chest where, say, a new and unopened bottle of Pelikan ink had smashed in a breast pocket of his jacket. Everybody else in the photograph looked either infinitely more capable than this figure, or was lying under a sheet on a stretcher.

Winceworth could only remember a batch of moments out of sequence. He could remember every detail of a moth at a window, but not how he got down from the train to the site of the explosion. From the snapshots he *could* remember, he might construe that the afternoon was spent with his sleeves rolled up in dust and masonry and wood and steam, being shouted at by a fireman. He remembered kneeling in order to throw up, and finding a man's face next to his. He had been holding a man's jaw in his hand. The man was trapped under some sort of girder or column or beam: it was a very straight line made of very black metal that was too hot to touch. The man's jaw was not where it should have been on his face. The angles were all wrong and at odds with conventional perspective. Winceworth might remember that he had got a small stone in his shoe and that somehow dust had got behind his back teeth. He remembered thinking that the firemen's brass all looked remarkably clean amongst so much soot. Everyone except for the firemen had been entirely silent. He would not remember seeing the fire engine.

He remembered the dampness of ink against his chest, that there was broken glass in his hair and that, at the time of the explosion, the colour that he had seen through the zoetropic train carriage window was one he simply could not name.

The facts are these: in the hour after the blast, Winceworth came-to in the middle of a line of firemen and bystanders, coughing with smoke and rheumy eyes. He was on his feet and did not think he had fainted but he had no idea where he was or how he had got there. That was how shock was supposed to work, wasn't it? In his hand was a pail of water. He looked behind him and saw frightened, drawn or soot-blackened faces. He was so close to the centre of the blast that Winceworth could feel the warmth of fire beat against his cheek. He helped pass buckets of water into the heart of the heat. Above them, as it coiled away into the dusky pink-sliced sky, the smoke was a purple tinged with the red of the flames.

Winceworth's knees were unsteady and for some reason, even as he watched the bucket of water leave his hands and pass on down the line, he had no sensation in his fingers. All of a sudden he was watching a reflection of his face distend and warp in some kind of gold flux in front of him. He accepted that the world had entirely changed and that natural processes and dimensions no longer applied. He concentrated and shook his head as if dislodging something. His reflection in the fireman's helmet shook back at him. He looked dismayed. The fireman was leaning down and shouting something at him, pointing, but Winceworth did not understand the words.

'He says we should leave,' another voice then said, calmly, in his ear. It was the man with the impressive moustachios with whom he had shared a train carriage – he too must have climbed down to the site of the newly ruined factory to help. He was also caked in debris and ash. All of the people around him were panting and one was being silently, violently sick by a sweetshop's storefront.

Winceworth let himself be led away by the group. He murmured agreements to their *No more we can do*s and *Gave it our best shot*s. He allowed his face and hands to be towelled clean by a bystander. Despite this kindness, more dust fell. He felt the grit in his face stiffen as he grimaced. The world came to him muted and muffled – he hoped this was due to dust plugging his ears, or else his hearing must have suffered in the blast.

Fragments of masonry lined the streets: spars and splinters of wood. The group he joined milled for a while, communicating by nodding and catching each other's eyes. They walked aimlessly down side streets with no destination in mind other than trying to be *away*, at times doubling back on themselves. Some seemed to join the party, others to leave it, until eventually they stopped outside a public house where people were taking an early supper. Patrons put down their papers and their pies as the group entered, all grey-faced and caked in cinders and soot. The landlord either must have known what happened or recognised a look in their eyes, for immediately Winceworth had a drink in his hand and found himself pushed into a wing-backed chair by the fire.

Distantly, the sound of a fire engine: whistles and hooves.

A dimpled glass mug was lowered in front of him.

'Sharpener – get the blood going,' said the landlord, and Winceworth drank it all in one pull.

'Where are you meant to be, lad?' the landlord asked.

Winceworth did not have a good answer. He felt for his new pen in his loose jacket pocket and saw that its nib was, miraculously, unbroken.

'Volume *S*. Back in Westminster,' Winceworth said. He patted his pockets for his train ticket. 'Sorry, I don't know what's come over me. I'll walk.'

'To Westminster?' said the man. He looked at the sky through the window, which was turning apricot and black. 'Don't be daft, you'll keel over by the time you reach Plaistow.'

'I don't know where that is.'

The man gave him a long look. 'I say, you really don't look well at all.'

And Winceworth, whose veins were full of a nervous fire and who was tired of not finishing his sentences, tired of not being heard or having a chance to speak, wanted to seize the man by the ears and hiss that all he had managed to eat today was cake and that he was impossibly, nonsensibly, intractably, irreducibly, awfully in love for no good purpose and the woman that he loved-with-no-good-reason was, for no good reason, probably right now at this very minute being led around an obscene, beautiful statue by a man with a bright red moustache and perfect posture who had all the time in the world, time Winceworth would never have, with that laugh of his and that laugh of hers, and yet here *Winceworth* was with his hands shaking, on a road, *barking* or something ludicrous like that on account of a dictionary where nobody knew he existed and that he loathed because to bottle up language, to package language – he! Who was he to love her and to make passels of words! – to attempt to confine language is impossible and a fantasy and loathsome, it *was* like trapping butterflies under glass, she was right – and yet yet yet yet yet yet even in loathing it the dictionary had trained him so well; it had trained him so well he was halfway even then itching to reach for his notes, his little Swansby's headed notepaper, so that he could ask a landlord about his use of *sharpener* just then, and make sure he took good, neat dictation down for the specific six-by-four index card on which the word would be housed, and *in* it would slot, *in* would go an example of an incidental, but somehow meaningful aside ready to be consulted when the *Sh*-words of *Swansby's New Encyclopaedic Dictionary* were compiled. Congratulations, it's a verb! they would say. How did everybody manage with this responsibility and complete lack of agency? Was it that no one saw, or nobody cared? Every word investigated, every fact taken into account. Everything anyone said mattered, and the matter at hand was not why they said it, or where they learned it, or the specific pull of their tongue against the palate of their mouth as they said it that is individual only to them – did you know that the palatal rugae pattern on the roof of a mouth is distinct to each and every individual, like a fingerprint, and every word one says has been loosed and polished and buffered and bruised by it in a unique way? Would the dictionary know he'd associate *sharpener* for ever more with the taste of ash? With wanting to cry? With men with white moustaches and dead moths in a terrible window onto the world?

Winceworth didn't say any of that. He cleared his throat. 'I am fine, thank you.'

'I'll tell you what,' said the landlord. 'My good deed for the day: I'll call you a cab back to – what did you call it?'

'Swansby House.' Winceworth did not know how the man could possibly seem so together. He reached into his pocket absently, but the man waved him back down.

'No, don't mention it – it's the least I can do.'

'What's your name?' asked Winceworth. And the man told him.

'Thank you,' said Winceworth simply. An idea had suddenly formed in his mind. 'And – one last thing – did you see the colour?'

'The colour?' the man asked, picking a sliver of wood from

Winceworth's sleeve and crumbling it absently between his fingers. 'Colour of what?'

'Of the explosion – did you see it from here, through the window?' Winceworth sat up. His head felt suddenly clearer. 'What colour would you call it, the explosion? What exact colour?'

Q is for *queer* (n. and adj. and v.)

We found some more fictitious words. They seemed to be getting more and more obscure but maybe that's because my tolerance for them was becoming weaker.

Here was one about the 'guilt of having a false speech impediment'. Here was another noun specific to 'the dream of retiring and keeping bees'. More usefully, perhaps, Pip was very pleased to find a noun for 'the hardened callous on your middle finger caused by years of ill-use': she liked the ambiguity of it, even though I guessed this was a desk-bound lexicographer just complaining about his lot.

Pip left her index cards for half an hour to find some coffee. On her return, she came back panting slightly and holding something in her hands. It was rectangular and framed, and as she swung it in through the office door she peeped over the top of it.

'I found it in one of the storage cupboards downstairs,' she said. 'Tucked behind a yoga ball and some old posters.'

The light through office's windows fell at a slant across the picture's glass and the reflected glare made it difficult to quite work out what it was that I was being shown. Its frame was old and the photograph inside was at an angle on its mountings as if the sun had taken a swing at it on Pip's behalf.

'A yoga ball?' I repeated.

'It was purple. I know, who knew David Swansby had it in him. But never mind that, look at this – a proper line-up for you,' Pip said. 'A real rogues' gallery.' She brought the photograph closer to me and crouched slightly behind it. 'Take a look! *The Usual Suspects 1899*: *This Time It's "Personnel"*.'

I rolled closer. 'You think he's in there somewhere?'

'*"Personnel"*,' Pip said again. She lowered the picture and looked at me expectantly.

'That's really good,' I said.

'I thought so. Go on then – get a load of these potential culprits, detective ma'am.'

A caption was printed under the picture on a ribbon of yellow paper: *Swansby's New Encyclopaedic Dictionary Staff, S–Z – 1899.*

The photograph featured three rows of crossed arms and unrelaxed faces. Two figures at the bottom were lying propped on their elbows in a stiff attempt at a sprawl. It's an unlikely posture that's usually relegated to commemorative photos of sports teams or lion-slumped big-game hunters, one that only ever really suits drunk Romans handling grapes in frescos or walruses sunning themselves on ice floes and tundras. The men's suits, ties and taper-straight moustaches all implied that striking such choreographed floppage came rather less than entirely naturally.

Presumably for the photograph's benefit, a number of posh-looking carpets or rugs had been dragged out onto the floor as a stage for the ensemble and they lay there overlapping and runkled on the ground just above the caption. I was actively suspending the moment of looking at the staff members' faces, taking in every detail of a carpet instead, its tassels and bunched-up wrinkles. I wondered where these carpets had come from, whether they were the photographer's own and, more particularly, where they had got to by now, or which storage cupboard was affording some moths the best meal of their soft-bodied lives. Nowadays, the Scrivenery was all about scratchy purple, nylon-pile, tiled modern flooring: thick enough to trip over but thin enough to allow an office chair to wheel over with a few extra leg pumps. Too thin to absorb coffee-stains particularly well, as I knew to my cost. These carpet tiles ran at waist height along the walls throughout the building, too. I imagine that the same carpet lines flimsy cubicle partitions in offices across the capital. I imagine people across the city pinning family photos into the pile of these fake walls, to help keep their work space a weird approximation of home.

'Are you holding your breath?' Pip asked from behind the photograph. 'I can tell from here.'

'No,' I said. I exhaled.

Every person captured in the photograph was looking in a slightly different direction and nobody seemed to know or have been told what to do with their hands. Some had gone for a just-bagged-a-brace-of-pheasant dip at the hip but, for the most part, all the members of the Swansby staff had arms pressed firmly across their chests, not wanting to give the photographer anything of themselves. They also all looked quite daunted as if ill at ease with being outdoors, or as if they could sense Pip's hands, giant and white at the untattooed knuckle around their frame.

The only two women in the photograph stood together in the middle, fussy collars and satellite-dish hats; one had black hair and the other entirely white. The photograph itself was that mottled kind of sepia that is not quite grey and not quite brown, ash and moth-coloured. It is a colour that leads you to believe that if you were ever moved to lick the photograph it would taste of toffee and bourbon and bookshop dust.

The beaming man on the far left-hand side of the picture sported a huge beard: the focus in the picture was sharp, so much so that even the crinkles around the man's eyes and the links of his pocket chain were distinguishable, but for whatever reason his marvellous beard sat beneath the glass as heavy and matt as a gravestone appended to his chin. I recognised the first Prof. Swansby from the portrait in the lobby downstairs. I could almost see something of *Swansby's* current editor David in this man's posture or in his wide eyes. The beard was quite a distraction. Also, the current editor was about three feet taller; clearly some non-Swansby, more dominant genes had blossomed along the line.

Spurred on by the familiarity of Prof. Swansby's face, I found myself trying to recognise the features of people that I knew replicated beneath the glass, and to think of period actors who best resembled them and could step into their roles.

One of the figures in the photograph had his whole face

blurred there was just a feathered smudge of paleness. His head must have snapped up as the camera's shutters did their work. Or maybe a fault when it had been developed, a thumb slipping and dredging ink in the darkroom's developing tray? No, there was still a trace of face there within the distortion, the shape of a head that had turned too soon. This figure was looking up and across, staring somewhere above the camera and off to the left as if in horror at something hitched in the clouds.

'It must have been taken in the courtyard outside,' Pip said, lowering the frame. 'If you imagine it without the bins and the air vents.'

She was right. The ivy lacquering the wall behind the figures still clung to Swansby House. I could crane my neck at my desk and looked down at that courtyard, the ivy leaves glossy and bouncing behind them in a light spritz of rain. Those leaves were often the only reason that I could tell one season from the other from my desk, whether they were rustling with raindrops or winter moths or nesting finches. I peered again at the photograph: the ivy was thinner there with fewer branches splayed across the brickwork.

Pip handed the photograph to me. 'But it's good, right? What do you think, do you have a good eye for cheating bastards?'

I rolled my chair back over to my cubicle and to the window. I spun on my chair midway: you have to take your perks when you can get them. I overbalanced slightly by the potted plant.

I extended my arm and tried to best match my view of the yard with the orientation of the photograph. If the alignment was correct, the blurry-faced man must have been looking directly up at my window just as the picture was taken. `

As Pip continued looking for fake words, I propped the photograph in the centre of my desk, where usually an employee might have a photograph of their partner.

R is for *rum* (adj.)

Winceworth waved goodbye to the landlord and the cab pulled away from the Barking kerb. He had shaken off most of the dirt from his clothes. He looked down: ink, crumbs, muck, cat-sick, blood. It was an archive of a day that seemed to be from a different life. For years he had kept his head down, worked with words silently and cleanly. As the cab hurtled through unfamiliar streets he felt a strange new energy lodge and jangle in his lungs and heart. It was a reckless energy, manic, tightening and reverberative, rebarbative, *verve surge urge*, one that felt not so much like something renewed as deranged.

The cab dropped Winceworth by the gates of Swansby House just as Westminster chimed seven o'clock. He muttered thanks to the driver and ducked beneath the steaming horses' noses. He hauled up to Swansby House and wrenched the gates open. The clunk and rattle of his arrival caused a panicked of Titivilli cats in the halls. At this late hour, it was unlikely that many lexicographers were still at work: the building was the cats' empire.

Gripping his satchel in his hands, Winceworth took to the stairs and into the Scrivenery hall. *Pons pons pons.* It was eerily quiet and his footsteps rang with odd shadows of noise and unexpected echoes. When the place was not teeming with people keeping their noses to their respective lexicographical grindstones, it was not so much that the place just felt empty – the air was oddly pressurised, the Scrivenery's shelves and bookcases impossibly high, filled with an impossible number of books filled with an impossible weight of words. As Winceworth rounded the corner, he spotted one of his colleagues still working, hovering by his desk. Bielefeld looked up from his papers, visibly paled – 'Dear God, man! What happened?' – and scrambled over tables and around chairs to reach Winceworth's side. He took a firm grip of Winceworth's elbow and steered him through the rows of desks. Bielefeld wanted to position him under one of the lamps fitted between the desks so that he might bear closer inspection.

Winceworth adjusted his jacket as Bielefeld plucked at him. Some cats came and sniffed at his feet. He wondered if they could detect pelican on him under the grime and smoke. 'Do I look entirely awful?' he said. 'People were crossing to the other side of the street.'

'An absolute state. What on earth have you been up to?' Before Winceworth had a chance to reply, Bielefeld continued, 'You're lucky to catch me – I'm only here so much later because I've been chasing a reference to *scurryvaig* and not making one bit of headway.'

'Yes?' said Winceworth. Despite the Barking landlord's brandy, his throat still felt coated with dirt and ash.

'Pesky thing to hunt down. Noun. Seems to be in a translation of the *Æneid*, and I'm assuming it has something to do with *scallywag* – say, I don't suppose,' and here Bielefeld coughed lightly and looked up at the rumpled Winceworth through his lashes, 'I don't suppose you have any ideas about it? For *scurryvaig*, I mean – with an *i* after the—'

'None whatsoever.'

'Only ask because I've got a backlog on *swingeouris*, and *swanis* too and it looks like I will have a rather rum couple of weeks ahead of me.' Bielefeld caught Winceworth's eye. 'But, I say, what on earth *has* happened to you? You look like you've been settling punches with a volcano. And is that ink down your shirt?' He flapped at Winceworth's chest. It puffed back a reply with brick dust. 'Should I – should I get you to a doctor or somesuch?'

'I'm fine,' Winceworth said. 'There was an accident – it doesn't matter, I don't think. I just left some work that needs finishing up here and then I will be right off to bed.'

Bielefeld regarded him. 'You have bags under your eyes that I could carry pens in. You'll look dreadful for the staff photograph tomorrow.'

'Oh, dear *God*.'

'But are you quite certain you should be here? I would stay with you but—' Bielefeld pointed over at his desk, all its papers neatened up for departure and his Swansby attaché case waiting. He attempted an apologetic smile. 'Was all set to go, you know. And I've bought tickets for the ballet.'

Winceworth flicked dust from an ear. 'I'm only here because I've been absent most of the afternoon. Tying up some loose threads.' He smiled ghastily. Bielefeld did not seem to notice.

'Frasham mentioned that he ran into you dining on tea and

cakes,' Bielefeld said, and he angled his face towards Winceworth to see if an account would be forthcoming. Winceworth kept his eyes fixed. He wondered whether Bielefeld could smell the Barking reviving alcohol on him. 'And his fiancée!' cried Bielefeld, and he laughed and clapped a friendly hand again to Winceworth's shoulder. 'Well,' Bielefeld continued, going over to his desk and picking up his things, 'if you're sure. Just as long as you're not – I mean to say, you look like you've been hit by an omnibus. Always *scribble, scribble, scribble! Eh, Mr Gibbon* and all that. Make sure that you do not overdo it.'

'I shall endeavour to not do so.' Winceworth watched Bielefeld slowly take his leave. He stopped to pet one of the Swansby cats on the way out and humming some bars of Tchaikovsky. The cat avoided his hand. Winceworth wondered what anecdote Bielefeld might be composing for his colleagues about the whole matter.

Winceworth was left alone in the echoing hall of the Scrivenery.

He moved to his own desk, and out of habit he reached for his pen in its usual place in his jacket. He drew out the new fountain pen Sophia had bought for him.

He spun the pen across his fingers. Two sleepy Swansby kittens were draped over the neighbouring bureau and both moved their heads slowly in synchrony, watching the pen twirl back and forth through his hand. He waved it around for their benefit until they appeared to lose interest. Tiredness yawped and tangled across his vision as he reached into his case and placed his idly doodled, fictitious entries on the desk.

His little diversions, sketched-out underminings and skits. He rubbed his eyes and saw again the strange, blasting, indefinable colour snarl around the edges of his vision.

A daydream, tinged by anger, became a surreptitious hope. His imagination stumbled and flew a little as he looked around at the pigeonholes filled with entries ready to be filed. The pen felt a devious weight in his hand. He flicked through his notes for dawdle-scrawled false definitions. His handwriting there looked so much more relaxed than when pressed into official duty. He looked again from these secret, silly words to the Swansby House pigeonholes. There was grit in the thumb-nails and traces of blood. The thought became clear and clean: it would take just some small strokes of pen to transfer these doodled drafts onto the official blue index cards and he could pepper the dictionary with false entries. Thousands of them – cuckoos-in-the-nest, changeling words, easily overlooked mistakes. He could define parts of the world that only he could see or for which he felt responsible. He could be in control of a whole universe of new meanings, private triumphs and soaring new truths all hidden in the printed pages whenever the dictionary was finished and (absurd notion!) *others* might find his words in print. He would never be known as a poet or a statesman, never be known as anything really – but if Prof. Gerolf Swansby's vision for *Swansby's New Encyclopaedic Dictionary* was achieved, Winceworth imagined his personal words and thoughts on every bookshelf up and down the country.

One of the Tit cats approached his desk. He couldn't be

sure if it was the same one that had soiled his shirt earlier in the day. He pulled his elbow around his work automatically, protecting it from even the cat's prying eyes.

He would be consulted. His words might be someone's first words, or last words. And if he was clever about it, there'd be no way to trace it back to him. Some value in his anonymity, at last: even if some poor clerk or printer's devil was tasked with winnowing out these entries, Winceworth would be long gone. He thought about this figure discovering his private words and definitions in – what, he hazarded – five years? Ten years? A hundred? Would they resent him, or cheer him on?

Winceworth tapped his pen from Sophia against the glass of his inkwell.

winceworthliness (n.), the value of idle pursuit
unbedoggerel (v.), to elucidate from nonsense, to free from
    darkness or obscurity

Winceworth slipped the blue index cards into the existing, completed deck on his desk. His mouth was dry. A private rebellion, a lie without a victim – what claims for truth did anyone really have, anyway? What right to define a world? Some trace of his thoughts surviving him was not so bad a thing. He would live for ever.

Where did that thought come from?

His face bowed in the glassy reflection of his unnecessary inkwell once more. It was puffy with sleeplessness.

He thought of Sophia and the words he would never say to

her. He thought of Frasham, and words he had for the feeling of these thoughts. He thought about the indescribable colour of the explosion and how he had felt it in his bones.

Winceworth reached for the silver pen once more.

The words spooled out of him. Etymologies suggested themselves in constellations of thought and conjecture.

abantina (n.), fickleness
paracmasticon (n.), one who seeks out truth through guile in
    a time of crisis

These felt like spellwords: Latinate, finickity and florid. There was a coltish joy to not feeling limited to using the letter S, which for so long had been the start of everything for him at this Swansby desk. He remembered his past couple of days: the shames of them, the leadenness of boredoms and required etiquettes, the spritz of energy and shocks. He felt them form as puns or logical morphing of semantic units. He felt that impulse fall away. He felt the new words bloom, sag, scratch.

agrupt (adj.), irritation caused by having a dénouement ruined
zchumpen (adj.), the gait of a moth

Winceworth imagined once more the person who might discover his false entries, his surreptitious fictions. Perhaps readers would no longer need dictionaries or any reference books in the future: print and writing might be impossible in the future's steam and smog, spoken language inaudible over the sound of engines. Maybe in the future people would communicate through touch and smell and taste alone. Maybe there would be dictionaries for that. All this learning of vocabulary for a world he would never see and sensations he would never know, Winceworth thought, patting the index cards on his desk so their edges aligned.

He veered from imagining the mischief he would cause with this non-thing, this practical joke, this overlookable nonsensing, to accepting that his hoax entries were the one act that he would ever be (not) known for and his only chance of leaving a trace on the world. He regretted he could not share a wink or something more permanent with the person who might find them.

He turned back to his work and added a final full stop to the entry he had been writing. He let the ink dry. It flashed a lively blue sheen for a moment in the light, and then the words set into the fibres of the card. The ink bled only a little; if one raised the index card to one's eye, it was possible to see the microscopic wisps and flicks seep out from the intended lines and curves out into the paper's grain.

New words came to him easier than breath. He had only to set them neatly down in the official way and then jimmy them into the appropriate pigeonhole in the hall. It was that simple.

★

Winceworth closed his eyes. The colour of the explosion blazed behind his eyelids and, just for a moment, he was gasping, an instant fizz of sweat across his back. The colour pinch-stung his vision in a bolt exactly as it had through the train window earlier that afternoon. And it was not a memory of the colour's intensity nor its sudden blast across his vision that had him passing his hand across his face and loosening his tie: it was the colour itself that terrified him. It flared with all the oranges of Dr Rochfort-Smith's rooms and all the mottled yellows of the Swansby cats' coats; it had the January greens of St James's Park somehow within it too, the blush of a pelican's blooded feathers, the blue of Café l'Amphigouri's twist-leafed Limoges china. It was a colour that made no sense. It sneered like red, milk-mild and lemon-brash and tart and tangy on the eye, singing with white-hot curves and slick, abrasive purple licks.

There was a scraping sound, distant but also somehow close, followed by a self-censoring hushed curse. Winceworth started – he must have fallen asleep at his desk. He glanced at the Scrivenery's clock and clutched his attaché case to his chest in one movement, expecting that its chime had woken him and that at any moment his colleagues would come filing through the door for their morning work. It was still evening.

He realised the sound that had made him stir was some kind of rhythmic thumping coming from the floor below.

'Hello?' he called into the silence of the Scrivenery.

The thumping ceased. And then, softly, there was a laugh

from the corner. There were stairs there that led down into the cellar. The sound was floating up the lift shaft.

Winceworth looked at the thick stacks of blue index cards. There were hundreds, thousands there – each identical when shuffled together, his words amongst all words.

That is that, he thought. *That that is, is. That that is not, is not. Is that it? It is.*

There was another laugh and Winceworth felt no triumph whatsoever. He staggered to his feet and made his way towards the noise.

S is for *sham* (n. and adj.)

'There's something pressed on this one,' Pip said, and she tilted a card in her hand towards the light. I wheeled my chair closer to get a better look. This action was not quite as fluid as I would have liked: the threshold was just across a small stretch of carpet but it still took about six heel-punts to get there.

'It's probably just dust,' I said.

'*Victorian* dust.'

'Probably Tits's fur,' I said.

We had been looking for words for hours, were questioning the authenticity of every single entry. Once-familiar and expected words became uncanny and absurd, impossibly new-fangled: *quack* and *quad* and *quiddity* all looked stupid. Why would a monarch be called a *queen*, a word so squeaky and keening? It was as exotic and unlikely to see *quick* as *Quetzalcoatl*.

'I think it's a dandelion seed,' Pip continued, holding a remnant of something between her fingers and futzing with it. She blew.

In our second year of dating and once we had moved in together, Pip bought a book called *The Language of Flowers* (1857). Arranged alphabetically and with whimsical illustrations, it outlined the 'meaning' of certain blooms, *floriography* (n.), and what might be intended by their inclusion in a bouquet. Some I remember: an azalea means 'temperance', white clover means 'think of me'. Less sweet, but memorably, cardamime means 'paternal error' and Fuller's teasel means 'misanthropy'. We laughed about these last two and then spent quite a lot of money at our next anniversary ordering armfuls of cardamime and Fuller's teasel as a private awful joke. They did not arrange well together and the teasel pricked our thumbs.

The first two in the book's list were the flowers called 'abecedary' (meaning 'volubility') and 'abatina' ('fickleness'). I've never found a florist or nursery that stocks them or admits to knowing what they might look like.

Pip let the old maybe–dandelion maybe–nothing remnant fall from her hand to the floor and returned to her index cards.

'I see *queer* gets a look-in,' she said after a while.

'That's one of the first words I looked up when I got the job.'

'That's the gay agenda for you. Find your people,' Pip said. Then, 'Oh!'

'What?' I tensed, pen poised and ready.

'Did you know *queest* is a word for wood pigeon?'

Another entry from *The Language of Flowers*: cedar leaves meant 'strength'.

At home, we considered where to put this book on our shelves. We told each other that one day we would get around to arranging the shelf alphabetically or by spine height or colour but somehow we never did. It ended up next to a Greek cookery book and a translation of *Lesbian Peoples: Material for a Dictionary* (1979) by Monique Wittig and Sande Zeig. Pip found this book in a flea market or a thrift store or a jumble sale. She had riffled or rifled through it, laughed like a drain or a spout or a gargoyle and right there and then began texting me morsels from its pages. I had to hide my phone from David whenever he popped his head around the door in case he thought I was slacking off at my desk.

I had heard of Wittig during my degree. Zeig was Wittig's partner and formerly – and, I hope, both throughout and latterly – her martial arts instructor. The book is a playful, speculative, excoriative almanac for a fabled island populated by lesbians. It's a send-up, silly and amazing all at once, a manifesto and a flipglib thumb to the nose. Deep in its pages, the book features the neologism *cyprine*. What does it mean? A translator of the book rather tentatively explained the word as 'the juice'. In the French, *cyprine* is defined as 'le liquide sécrété à l'entrée du vagin de la femme lorsqu'elle est en état d'excitation sexuelle'.

Pip sent a photo of this page from the flea market stall. She included a ;£ in the text. She meant to type ;) but I think her thumb must have slipped.

It felt nice to suddenly have a word for *that*. Reading Pip's text, it struck me that all the words I had that approximated *cyprine* were either associated more with men or with stuff coming out of my nose.

Cyprine in the dictionary of Wittig and Zeig was intended to have linguistic connotations with the island of Cyprus, Aphrodite's home. It's a spry and glistening kind of word.

At the time, I texted Pip back: *It's a spry and glistening kind of word.*

Pip replied: *And you know the gays love an island – cf. Lesbos, cruising, etc.*

Are you flirting with me? I had texted.

Are you out at work yet? Pip replied. I had put my phone in my desk drawer and returned to whatever intern task of the day was required.

Wittig and Zeig's book was brimming. That's part of what I loved about Pip. We could talk about brims between ourselves, Brims and misunderstandings and their different pressures.

I had looked up *cyprine* in the Swansby dictionary out of sheer curiosity. It was an idle thought, an idling thought. A scurrilous voyeur kind of thought but also without much hope. I did find it there, but only because the word also describes a variety of a mineral first discovered adjacent to lavas on Mount Vesuvius. Boom clouds and bodies transfixed: yes, that Vesuvius. I will never guess the correct plural of *lava* right first time. It does not come easily. What does? *Sensu stricto*, the breeze might call through the curtains, so I'll follow its scent and read, yes, multiple laval shifts surge hot and impossible like hands reaching out from rock.

Swansby's New Encyclopaedic Dictionary states the mineral *cyprine* is also known as *idocrase*. I *do* craze sometimes, I thought, when the fan was merely stirring the air into something silicate and nacreous, stars or suns peacock-bright outside. '*Idocrase* occurs as crystals in skarn deposits.' *Skarn* referred to chemical alteration of a rock via hydrothermal means. The notion here was of hot fluids that had been subjected to contact metamorphism. Hot stuff, and changing out of hardnesses and feet-on-the-groundnesses. I read that cyprine's crystals could be cut as gemstones. 'Cut your teeth on this' always sounded to me like the most violent-hot turn of phrase.

How many serious books and websites did I consult before I went to serious bed with a serious woman? There were diagrams in those books as there might be for DIY furniture construction or jewellery repair. All the books were bought and not from the library. This syllabus was undertaken and taken under with an earnest and terrified sense of revision. I certainly did not have the word *cyprine* to hand. There's a pun here but I'm not sure I can make it indelicate-delicate. Pursuit of a word's meaning or a meaning's word making me sound a little unhinged.

I read there was a mollusc called the Icelandic cyprine (*Arctica islandica*), also known as an ocean quahog. *Quahog*. A bubble of a word, snug and ugly and great. *Quahog* is a word for saying underwater or with a mouthful. Some words are made for speculative onomatopoeia. Have I ever spelled *onomatopoeia* correctly on first time of typing? Have I fuck. *Onomatoepia* is onomatopoeia for mashing your hands unthinkingly but hopefully onto a keyboard.

Swansby's New Encyclopaedic Dictionary claims that the Icelandic cyprine is a species of edible clam, which in terms of Wittig's *cyprine* word was an excellent suggestion: you can right or wrong the punchlines as you like. I migrated to Wikipedia and found that an individual specimen of Icelandic cyprine was recorded as living for 507 years, which made it 'the longest-lived non-colonial metazoan whose age was accurately known'. Cyprine and accuracy, mud in your eye: 507 years ago Thomas Wolsey drew up plans for an invasion of France. The article about ancient edible clams specified that 'it is unknown how long [the specimen] could have lived had it not been collected alive by an expedition in 2006'. I imagined a dredging naval vessel, its bad radio full of that year's worst hits as they dug up the noble, ancient clam: Fergie's 'London Bridge', JT's 'Sexy-Back', P!nk's 'U + Ur Hand'. You should not rake for these things, I thought at the time. I then thought: this job is killing my attention span.

I wondered how you date an edible clam, and other sentences.

There are certain words that have such a pleasing consistency, texture, taste, colour, odour, network, milieu, stance, poise, arch, crane, comfort, peak, trough; limpid, tepid, torpid, torqued, liquid, lacquered, honeyed, latched, thatched, throstle-sungèd, spangled words. The normal pH of these words is between 3.8 and 4.5, so there is some bite to them.

I supposed there was a man with the surname 'Skene'. I supposed there was a man called 'Bartholin'. Glands and ducts named after them, in the same way men name mountains and creatures after themselves. I hoped these men were kind.

I preferred *secrete* as a hiding verb rather than anything concerned with outwardliness. *It is secreted about my person.*

Have you ever heard the word *Spinnbarkeit*? I hadn't. Why didn't we all have these words at the tips of our fingers? Who had been stockpiling them?

'They have an entry for *queer bird*,' said Pip, looking up from her dictionary page. 'But, ah, "Obsolete". Poor word's extinct.'

Obsolescence itself was just another beautiful word for a nothinging. Secrete it about your person and pearlgrit your teeth with a new vocabulary.

My office phone rang and I jumped on instinct – Pip did not have the same Pavlovian response to this sound. The peal ricocheted off the surfaces in the office.

'Don't—' I said, but it was pointless. Pip was already there, hand on the receiver and lifting it to her face.

'Hello,' she said and with a brightness that was purely for my benefit. There was only a slight hesitation when she improvised what she *should* be saying. 'Mallory's office phone?'

I watched her expression change. She did not want me to see her concern so she angled her body away from mine as though a glancing blow had turned her shoulder.

I wanted to ask if it was the hoaxer. I wanted to tell her to put down the phone and felt a rush of defensiveness. He was *my* problem, not hers. He was *my* threat, my reason for waking up with my heart in my mouth and horror pinching my throat.

She was meant to be doodling on her hands or singing in a pub garden or holding me: his cartoon voice and his malice shouldn't touch her. His words should stop an inch from her ears and wilt in the air.

I realised that I had no words for what I'd do to protect her.

T is for *treachery* (n.)

Winceworth descended to the basement of the Scrivenery in a creaking, cage-like lift. He had only glimpsed down to the cellar once before – as far as he knew it was an untouched, unbothered part of the building, sequestered and sectioned away until the first edition of the dictionary was ready to print. It was full of damp and shadows, the scuttle of strange unseen unnameables alongside the ready-for-use printing presses. He struck a match as he descended and in the flash of light saw the pristine presses sitting waiting in the dark. He could not have told you what the parts of machinery were called nor their intended function – they looked hulking and sleek in the dark and somehow open-jawed. They made the air stink like metal: a foretaste of the steam and inksweat of printing to come whenever *Swansby's New Encyclopaedic Dictionary* was ready to roll out volume by volume, word by word.

Something skipped over his foot and Winceworth shrank back in the lift. What was the point in all these cats if a burlesque of mice was able to hotch beneath the floorboards? What he thought he had heard from the Scrivenery hall was no pest, however, or a mere clank of pipes expanding or floorboards flexing. He stepped forward into the gloom and struck another match as another *mnmun*muffled laugh crept from behind one of the nearest printing presses. He rounded the corner and looked down. The woman scrabbled to cover herself as he lowered the match to her level, and she rolled away and bobbed behind a pile of boxes in the shadows. As she did so, she gave another titter.

Frasham had no such scruples. He was dressed in only his shirtsleeves and socks, everything unbuttoned and encyclopaedic. Winceworth swept his match in an arc and saw his colleague reclining odalisque on the ground, propped up on one elbow and using his jacket as a blanket.

Frasham extended his arms: 'The whispering lisper!' He seemed unruffled and either genuinely delighted to have been caught or delighted by his companion's embarrassment. 'My good man, descend and join the party!'

There had always been rumours about Frasham and his friends carrying on in this way. *Carrying on in this way* – Winceworth's mind became prissy and frilled with euphemism. He heard plenty of gossipy mutterings about Frasham's dalliances, with talk of lewd boasts and comments and tally charts. Winceworth picked up on this chatter because people talked over his head in the Scrivenery and it was impossible not to rake through the ashtrays and berms of conversations. He had always assumed that these tales of trysts and encounters were just swagger and braggadocio, or, if indeed real, they occured in grotty hotels or alleyways in Whitechapel. But *of course* that was not Frasham's style – *of course* he would use the Scrivenery as his own bordello once everybody else had gone home. It rankled that even the private and unexpected, scurrilous luxury of after-hours Swansby House had been taken away from him the very evening that he made use of it. Terence Clovis Frasham had been there the whole time beneath the floorboards, snuffling and rutting and doing what he did best with not a care in the world.

Winceworth turned to leave. As the match guttered he noticed again the woman who had shrank back to the side of the room. She was not cowering from Frasham, necessarily, but from discovery. Winceworth recognised her salt-white hair as the match burned out.

'I trust you are well, Miss Cottingham,' he said. She tutted and drew some piece of clothing under her chin.

'Now really,' Frasham said, smiling through his moustache in such a way that his teeth caught the light, 'you'll embarrass her. A drink?'

There was a *tfft* of flame and Frasham lit a lamp by his side. It revealed a table with an open bottle on it and two glasses. The clothing on the floor tripped Winceworth slightly as he came forward. *Pons pons pons.* His head was splitting.

'You are all right, Miss Cottingham?'

'Perfectly well,' came the reply, snapped and guarded. Frasham laughed.

'I would say *please, sit down* but perhaps your company would not be entirely appreciated. Another time, perhaps.'

'Until tomorrow, Frasham.' Winceworth made for the stairs.

'I'll never get tired of how you say my name, dear Winceworth. *Fraffth'm.* You make me sound positively effervescent.'

Winceworth heard a dutiful snicker from Miss Cottingham. 'Leave him alone,' she chided, but went on laughing.

Frasham went on: 'You look completely ludicrous: like you'd been in the wars with a hedge.' Winceworth moved again to leave but Frasham called after him. 'Completely battered – a rum job, old man, rum job. And to think it was because of my little prank you were anywhere near Barking. You'll forgive me, won't you?' Winceworth didn't say anything. Frasham did not seem to notice. 'Especially since your battle of wits with the bird earlier. And I must say, I'm surprised to find you still in the building: why is that, do you think, darling?' He directed this to Miss Cottingham. 'Working over-hours? Got your own little projects to attend to?' and Frasham raised an arm and indicated the underground room that he occupied, his little kingdom.

'I bid you both a good night,' Winceworth said.

'I'd be pleased if you didn't mention to anyone your bumping into us,' Frasham said. The tone was gentle, with no sense of pleading or shame in it, but had an extra edge.

'I am sure you would be.' Frasham regarded him. Then, smoothing down his shirt so that it just grazed past his knees, he approached Winceworth. Winceworth took a step back, closer to the lift, but untrousered Frasham pulled his arm and brought them together into a loose embrace as if they were the oldest friends. His breath was sweet and clear.

'I've been meaning to say—'

'You do not need to make jokes about my lisp.'

'You misunderstand!' Frasham recoiled, hurt, then closed

back in. 'My uncle has a friend who has a friend,' he said, his moustache close to Winceworth's ear, 'who knows a man about a dog who knows a man who works in the British Museum. He has keys. Keys to rooms you wouldn't imagine.'

'I'll take your word for it,' Winceworth said.

Frasham gave a conspiratorial, boyish wiggle of his shoulders. He had never spoken one-on-one to his lowly desk-man counterpart at such length before, and Winceworth felt adrift in the dynamics of power at play. He felt all vulnerability, vulning.

'You must have heard of it,' Frasham continued. At school we used to talk about nothing else. Stuff straight from Burton's translations, Pisanus Fraxi and all that – sculptures and everything.' Across the room, the Condiment pulled a chemise across her shoulders and fidgeted with hair pins. Frasham seemed to have completely forgotten about her and their discovery. 'All sorts in there that the public is not allowed to see.' Frasham studied Winceworth's face. 'Well! My uncle and I have been pulling some connections and tomorrow night we have a private viewing! To properly celebrate my being back in the Great Wen!' He laughed, open-mouthed. 'What do you make of *that*?'

'Sounds quite the evening.'

For his contribution, Winceworth earned another laugh. All Frasham seemed to do was laugh. 'Elizabeth will be there,' Frasham said, nodding at Miss Cottingham. She kept Winceworth at a firm distance, jaw set and tight.

'And Sophia?' Winceworth asked.

Frasham smirked. 'Well, now, certain subjects and activities are not perhaps best suited for one such as she. These evenings can get rather raucous.'

'As if that would keep her away,' Miss Cottingham snorted. 'Isn't she selling some of her collection? Brought all the way from the wild and savage Steppes?'

'But!' said Frasham, rolling back on his heels, 'I see I have been remiss!' He brought his face so close that Winceworth could have kissed him, their legs planted one against the other. Frasham smelt lightly drunk, his chest slick and cooling. Winceworth felt grimier than he ever had before. 'But you simply *must* be part of our merrie bande, I think. Shake something loose, my good man – you always look so uptight. It was good to see you with a drink inside you at the 1,500 Mile Society – what do you say? Do you fancy it? Find something there for you? My uncle can lay on quite a festival when he puts his mind to it.'

Of course, Frasham was not a week back in London before he was organising orgies in a museum. Of course, he would be standing there half-naked, caught with his trousers not only down but way across the room, yet still have the upper hand!

The colour of the explosion scorched the backs of Winceworth's eyes.

It would be good for his career to accept this ridiculous invitation. The thought disgusted him, but it was invariably true. If he could be in Frasham's inner, trusted circle, who knows what new futures his life could hold: what escapes, what wished-for possibilities?

'That's kind of you,' he said.

'Then that's settled! Come by the museum after midnight – we'll show you how a relaxing evening progresses.'

Miss Cottingham laughed again, and Frasham held Winceworth's gaze for many seconds more than was at all necessary. The lamp sputtered once more and made the shadows waver across the scene – Swansby House's desk-man and the field-man, one covered in dried blood and soot and the other hot with lust for life, momentarily arm in arm in their Westminster basement.

U is for *unimpeachable* (adj.)

'Mallory's not here right now.' Pip's tone sounded bright and businesslike on the phone. I strained to hear the robo-voice of the hoax caller, its rasp and tininess and tinniness. I tried to sidle closer but she moved the phone cord over her shoulder and swivelled away from me on her chair, out of reach.

'Who am I?' Pip echoed. I made *cut-it-out* gestures near my carotid artery but she dismissived them with a wave. She was grinding her teeth and I wondered if the caller could hear it down the phone.

Another flake of plaster fell from the ceiling. I watched the blister of it settle its pace in the air and land on my shoulder.

'No, yes, I've heard all about you,' Pip said. 'And do you know what – sticks and stones, mate. You're worried that a dictionary is going to change the definition of a word? You know that we laugh about you, right? Your little squeaky vowels and your threats. You know Mallory goes home and thinks about you every day? And, I'm not a violent person, but I ask her what is wrong and when she tells me, I imagine you sat in your little house and I imagine feeding your hair into a lawnmower. You know what other words have changed over time? Wash your mouth out. What else has changed? Words like *girl*. *Sanguine*. *Spinster*. No, don't ask me how or why, I have no interest whatsoever: frankly I've not the slightest interest. Mallory explained it once over a delicious dinner and I was concentrating on not tripping over my own tongue – look it up yourself if you're so invested. You clearly have the time. Who else do you ring up and bully? Weather forecasters? Tide-tablers? Whoever tables the tide. I bet you resent that we're not still speaking Latin. No, actually, I bet you resent Latin's influence on the language and wish we could just be speaking in good old whatever came before. Anglo-Saxon. Jute. I've no idea, please don't try and correct me on this, I haven't the foggiest. You're just a gross little troll who likes freaking people out, like something from the Grimm brothers. They wrote a dictionary too, didn't they, Mallory? Did you tell me that once?'

'I—'

'*So you listen here,*' Pip said to the caller, and she stabbed the air in front of her with a finger. Colour flushed beneath her collar and across her neck. 'You silly little man. No, don't apologise to me. I didn't call sick off work to have you, what, *snivelling* on speed-dial. I'm not sure what your deal is – homophobia? Fear of change, or language, or gays, or both, or is it you feel like you're left out or behind and there might not be a place and time for you in a book that no one reads, that you can't abide – got me using words like *abide* – the smallest thing that makes no bit of difference to you? I learned a new word for wood pigeon today – *that's so much more important than you.* You know who you're speaking to? This may as well be the dictionary, right. You want to tell me that there's a bomb in the building because you don't want a word's meaning to change and get with the times? Well, I'm the dictionary today and I am telling you in the strongest possible terms to get bent.'

She slammed the receiver back down into its cradle.

'He hung up ages ago, didn't he,' I said.

'The second he realised that it wasn't you on the phone,' Pip said.

I came around and hugged her, burying my face in that yard of closeness between the top of her head and her shoulder. 'Into a *lawnmower*—?'

'Felt good to say,' Pip said. She hugged me back. 'Oh!' she said into my hairline, 'I think I found another one.' She pointed at a place in the index cards, finger grazing the paper.

The phone began to ring again.

There was a noise above us, a creak or stamp or thuddery. We stared at the ceiling tile above us.

paracmasticon (adj.), one who seeks out truth through guile in a time of crisis

'I'll take a look,' Pip said. 'Don't pick up that phone, OK?'

'OK,' I said.

And Pip swing-swang-swung from the room. The phone kept on insisting. I waited until I could hear her feet on the stairs and then picked up the receiver.

'I'm a man of my word,' the digitised voice said. The voice disguiser meant that I could not tell whether the tone or pitch of it had heightened. It might have been my imagination, but the words seemed to be tumbling out more quickly. 'I hope you enjoy yourself.'

'Enjoy?' I asked.

'*Enjoy*,' the voice echoed.

'Enjoy,' I repeated.

'Hello?' said the person down the phone line. Then, 'Oh – hold on a second—' and then there was that obscure sound of a phone being dropped from a small height and a sad, robotic, flatted autotune string of *shit-shit-shit*.

There was a corresponding thump from above. Then there came the shriek of a fire alarm, blaring at such a volume you could feel it in your blood.

V is for *vilify* (v. transitive)

As the cab pulled up outside his lodgings, an exhausted Winceworth tipped the driver far too much because the idea of weighing out or counting coins suddenly seemed an impossibly intellectual and physical undertaking. He race-dragged up the stairs to his front door, fell inside and slammed the door behind him with as much energy as he could muster.

Before undressing for bed Winceworth threw his Swansby House attaché case across his bedroom. He withered onto his bed so that his shoes came away from his feet. The very essence of him became simple and synonymous with *drooping, flagging* – he sagged on the counterpane and as his clothes slid to the floor puffs of masonry and grit leapt into the air. Between the birthday-cake-icing-sugared pockets of the morning, the cat vomit, tiny pieces of dandelion clock, the pelican blood mixed with ink and Barking's brick dust, his clothes were ruined with documentation of the day. He compared his own pale forgettable body, already goosepimpling in the cold of his bedroom, with Frasham's easy half-nakedness in the dark beneath the Scrivenery. He dwelled on this for some moments – too many moments – before pulling his bedsheet over his face. Bedsheets, he thought, negate the need for time. He burrowed deeper and he tried some of the breathing exercises Dr Rochfort-Smith recommended to him. He exhaled and inhaled, inspired and aspired according to his pulse and within seconds he fell asleep in his socks. There should be a word for how horrible this will make him feel upon waking.

On waking, Winceworth forgot every aspect of his dreams but for the record they all featured a mad kind of aviary and a desperate urgent need to escape – tiny orange birds in cages and pelicans on stilts, the air around his dreamhead filled with nonsense songs and the clattering of wings. It was the first night for years where he did not dream about a dictionary. His immediate thought was of Prof. Gerolf. He pictured the professor turning over the day's filed powder-blue index cards, and thought of each of his false words lying there in amongst the real entries, each one nodded at, appreciated as if valid and sound, and then filed away in the hush of the professor's study above the Scrivenery at the top of Swansby House.

Winceworth did not know whether he had expected to feel *relief* or *guilt* or *anticipation* upon waking – one of these emotions, at least, and possibly a combination of all three. Should it feel like he had pulled a prank? Should it feel like revenge? Devilment? Instead, all Winceworth felt was a new kind of numbness. The world had not changed and dawn was living up to most accepted definitions. He gave himself a moment longer beneath the covers before rising. Lying hidden, there, his eyelashes brushed the underside of a blanket. He concentrated on that small inconsequential pressure. He tried again to access how he felt. He was less exhausted, but it was not a kind of restfulness. He did not feel anything like at peace.

He fetched his book of matches from his jacket on the floor and attended to the lamp and enjoyed the rasp of the match strike and the sudden heat. A daydream came briefly and unbidden, of the Scrivenery on fire. He imagined flames passing from desk to desk. He imagined the stink of ink peeling across pages as a fire made its way up the folders and pigeon-holes, crawling brightly across to create a fretted, heavy ceiling. Winceworth moved away from his grate and there was no tune in his head nor any stray word ricocheting in his mind as he set about the practicalities of a working day. Ties still needed to be straightened and bluing chins still required fresh shaving.

He remembered it was the day of the Swansby House staff photograph. His grey face loomed in the mirror above the washstand, and he saw for the first time that the wire bridge of his spectacles had collected silt from yesterday's explosion: a tiny stripe of warpaint across his nose. There was a corresponding mark stamped against his pillow. He rubbed the stain, absently, then sluiced his face and underarms with water. Every action felt deliberate and slow as he worked the small nub of pink soap between his hands until it was thick and fat-bubbled. He rubbed away, closing his eyes against the shock of water, until the world smelled of suds and fresh skin. He shaved and, as was his habit, he nicked his jaw. Always in the same place. *Not concentrating*, he chided himself. *Prone to error.*

It had rained in the night and the window had a slight frost on the outside and inside of the pane. He felt the chill of it in his hair and against his face.

The morning at Swansby House was spent in the usual way with all the clerks and lexicographers quietly chasing their various entries and wrangling definitions. Bielefeld went on humming under his breath and Appleton kept up his campaign of sniffing while Winceworth picked over the bones of s-words and kept his head low at his desk. Some members of Swansby House's staff had heard about the events at Barking and visited his desk to express sympathy, curiosity or intrigue. He was not a good raconteur and these conversations were brief. He told everyone who disturbed his work that, honestly, he could remember very little of what had taken place out in Barking. They expressed surprise, regret and boredom and then moved on and let him be. Winceworth shot occasional looks at Frasham and the white-haired Miss Cottingham whenever he spotted them across the hall or their work took them anywhere near his desk. When the boy with the post-barrow, came to take the index cards from his desk, Winceworth did not show a flicker of emotion.

Prof. Gerolf emerged from his study at exactly one o'clock and addressed them from the gallery above the Scrivenery hall. He stood directly above the clock, beard cascading over the balcony as he announced in a headmasterly tone that the photographer was ready in the courtyard. *No need for the gentlemen to wear hats*, he declared, *let the brains cool off*. The Cottingham sisters exchanged glances and kept their headgear secured in their white and black hair. *Pons pons pons.* There followed a stutter of chairs scraping back across the floorboards and the dull tinkle of many inkpot lids being replaced: everyone began shooting their cuffs and smoothing their hair and emptied the Scrivenery in an orderly fashion, column by column.

In an effort to keep warm, the Swansby staff jogged up and down on their toes in the courtyard. Winceworth noticed that Appleton had bought a new watch chain for the occasion and Bielefeld had shined his shoes and parted his hair in a different way. Everybody was absorbed in neatening their moustaches and putting their shoulders back, standing slimmer and taller than they ever did in the Scrivenery. The lexicographers' shoulders were used to stooping over desks. They arranged into height order and positioned themselves in front of the camera against the Swansby House wall. Winceworth noticed that despite Gerolf's instructions, Frasham kept creeping into the centre of the photograph with the assurance of one compelled to do so by some ineluctable force – Frasham's expression did not waver and he did not say a word but his colleagues parted to let him through. Less seamless a negotiation of elbows belonged to Glossop beetling in Frasham's wake so that they might stand together.

'Excuse me!' The photographer was having none of it. 'Little man! Yes, you, green handkerchief! Back to the front, if you please!'

The photographer had a stentorious, magisterial tone

Glossop could not help but obey. Winceworth was jealous that one could possess such a voice. The photographer busied himself behind the camera with fabric and tripods. He looked at the amassed lexicographers with clear disdain. Martinet-lunged and growing red in the face, he explained that he had come from another appointment earlier that day with a particularly boisterous football team from Kennington and he was *simply not in the mood* for any *blithering* or *messing about*. All the Swansby staff looked at their feet and tugged at their collars.

Prof. Swansby, a sensitive man, tried to clear the air by enquiring about the names for the different parts and processes required by the camera ('Potassium chlorate, my goodness!'). This had a conciliatory effect and the tension between photographer and subjects lifted. The Swansby staff shuffled and the photographer lowered his head beneath his dark cloth. Behind the camera tripod, he was transformed into a new, slouch-shouldered creature, a glassy Cyclops with a concertina snout.

'When you're quite ready . . .'

Winceworth's neck stiffened and his mouth ran dry. He never coped particularly well when attention was trained upon him and this was almost as bad as his appointments with Dr Rochfort-Smith. He allowed his gaze to shift slightly towards Frasham. He saw the sharp clean lines of Frasham's suit, the brightness of his shirt collar, his tennis player's shoulders and imagined his face carrying a winning, winning, winning smile.

'Watch the birdie!' the photographer said. The flash powder

flared hot and bright off the brick wall of the courtyard, a brief, indescribable, terrible and familiar colour.

There was a movement from above them – tiny, inconsequential, but enough to catch Winceworth's attention. A rustling in the ivy, perhaps, or someone opening a window? Winceworth looked up at the Swansby House windows. He blinked.

Clear and white against the dark beyond, Sophia Slivkovna's face was framed in the window, staring down at the group. She looked calm, regal, as relaxed as an audience member glancing down from their box at the opera.

It was not fancy on his part: even at this distance, Winceworth could tell she was looking directly at him, her finger to her lips.

W is for *wile* (n.)

The fire alarm was so loud it made my teeth hurt – the kind of sound that makes every neuron sit up and beg, and forces shock to fizz along your gums.

'Pip?'

I dropped the telephone receiver, grabbed the fake-words envelope and sprang for the office door. I made it into the hallway before the surface of my eye began to itch. Out in the passage my vision became milky as if the walls and balustrades and skirting boards were in a state of flux, unsteady in my eyeline. I tried to focus and a familiar shape dashed past my ankles. Tits the cat, faster than I had ever seen, striped down the stairs and out of sight.

Smoke was filling the hall.

My heart dopplered. There was a muffled clatter from above as if something falling to the floor, and then the sound of wood or metal or stone lurching. I covered the ground in record speed up to the stairs, their banisters smoothed by the wear of century's past lexicographers' hands, and ran up to the forbidden upper storeys. A door was open some way down the corridor and I charged towards it. When I think back about this moment, there was the smell of something chemical burning in the air – but that might just be the mind playing tricks. I raced to the door, saw smoke pluming in creamy hurtles around its frame, and I lurched inside.

The smoke was thick in the room and the struggling figures I found there appeared as if through fog: I was able to first make out the darkened angles of their elbows and their knees. Both figures were coughing. I could recognise Pip's cough from over 1,000 metres – another way perhaps of defining love – and I made my way towards it, repeating her name. It sounded like bleating. The proportions of the contents of this room were unclear and impossible, transformed into bitter clouds and shadows, its details all completely lost. I knocked into a desk or a table or a ghost with my hip as I stumbled forward, calling Pip's name.

'Here!' Pip said. 'I've got him!'

And I was by her side and coughing in time with her, pushing my hands out in front of me and scrabbling at her shoulder, at some unknown fabric, at another's shoulder within it, within the smoke. All was greys and heats and angles, at our feet a shattered spray of glass. I rubbed my eyes again, focused on the floor and saw the remnants of a small flaming parcel of wiring. It stank and popped and gushed more smoke, and a man – *David*, I recognised his height and his movements now at such close quarters – stamped and stamped and tried to shake Pip from his elbow while bringing his foot down upon the package.

He was saying, hissing, desperate, '*Shit-shit-shit*—'

That voice without the robo-disguiser: I'd be able to pick it out of a million.

There was a roaring, zipping sound above our heads and we all twisted to stare through the fog above us. The smoke was thickest there and running up the corner of the room and to the ceiling tiles, we saw a terrible line of flame. Yellow and red and amber, apricot, auburn, aurelian, brass, cantaloupe, carrot, cinnabar, citric, coccinate, copper, coral, embered, flammid, fulvous, gilt, ginger, hennaed, hessonite, honeyed, laharacish, marigold, marmaladled, mimolette, ochraceous, orang-utan, paprikash, pumpkin, rubedinous, ruddy, rufulous, russet, rusty, saffron, sandy, sanguine, spessartite, tangerine, tawny, tigrine, Titian, topazine, vermilion, Votyak, xanthosiderite—

'Shit shit shit.' David's voice again right by my ear. It was in time with the peal of the fire alarm. I tripped on the smoke-spuming package as he spoke, seizing Pip's arm to steady myself.

The roar of orange above us took on a sudden new gulping intensity, and all three of us blundered backwards. The whole of the ceiling was suddenly sheeting with a ripple of flame and the heat of it glanced across my scalp.

Pip's hand was on my collar and she was shouting and pulling at David's sleeve. Who knows the instinct that was flushing through her, dictating her movements and willing her onwards, but she heaved both of us spluttering Swansbyites out of the smoke-filled, fire-filling room, threw us down the stairs just as a beam or bressumer or architrave fell to the ground in a hiss and bang of masonry.

We rolled down the steps and staggered to our feet. A wordless choking heap, we grabbed each other's lapels and ran headlong for the front door and out into the evening air.

X is for *x* (v.)

As the photographer dismantled his camera and the lexicographers congratulated one another for standing quite so still for so long in such a good order, Winceworth made his excuses and slipped back inside. Nobody noticed his departure. He took the stairs two at a time, surprising Tits-cats left and right so that flights of them had to dash out of his way. He hastened up the steps and looped around the corners of landings. Panting slightly, he made a mental calculation of the layout of the building, trying to match its structure onto the snatched glimpse of Sophia's face at the upper-storey window. Would it mean turning left or right? When he reached the second floor, he hovered for a moment and leaned against the banisters, catching his breath.

'Helloa?'

Sophia stood in the middle of a corridor, a brightness of orange skirts and a white shirtwaist. Winceworth approached, checking his step so he did not seem too eager. Bookshelves ran the length of the passage on both sides thick and stodgy with monographs by linguists and dons, these passages seemed far darker than the Scrivenery below. She was standing with one gloved hand resting upon one of the books' spines. She smiled at him as he stepped forward. A small toque hat was pushed back amongst her hair. Its design featured snapdragon embroidery and a feather on a pin.

Out of sheer habit the lisp wormed its way between his lips. 'Miss Slivkovna,' Winceworth said. He took her hand and gave a little bow in what must have seemed like a frenzied jolt. '*Swansby's New Encyclopaedic Dictionary* is not worthy.'

Sophia looked *glowing*, *radiant*, whatever the most beautiful synonym for *flushed* might be.

'You are here to see Frasham,' Winceworth continued, apparently not able to bear a silence between them. The statement cooled in the air as clutter.

'No, no.' Her tone was light, vague, a touch vacant despite the warmth in her smile. As Winceworth drew closer there was a faint sting of alcohol in the inches between them. This was unexpected – for a wild second he wondered whether he might be smelling it upon himself.

She turned shining eyes upon him and blinked a little as if waking up. 'A delight to see you again! How is the new pen?' She flicked invisible dust from his shoulder, admiring him. He was pleased at the change of her manner and at her attentiveness. 'My sincere apologies to disturb you from your podium down there,' she went on. '*Didn't* you look smart? You are quite the picture when you are not waylaying pelicans.'

'I take that as a compliment from one who stabs them in the neck.'

'For surgical purposes.'

'Just so.' He cocked a thumb downstairs. 'And I was glad to get away. Have you been here all morning?' The idea seemed absurd, like not knowing God or the Devil was keenly watching you oblivious at work.

'I arrived some ten minutes ago – everyone seemed occupied so I thought I'd sate my curiosity about the place.' She gestured to the corridor. 'Terence told me about the cats, but I had not imagined quite so many herds of them.'

'*Clowder*. A clowder of cats.'

'But you do herd them, do you not?'

'That is not yet my job and I am not the expert. I am sorry if no one was there to meet you at the door—' but Sophia was not listening, instead making her way down the bookshelves and inattentively touching the books. She trailed her finger along the spines as she went. She did not notice, but as she passed she caught one of the dustjackets at a slight angle and the paper tore.

Winceworth caught up and fell into step with her. He did not know these hallways on the second storey of Swansby House. He presumed they were used by Prof. Swansby for the business side of the dictionary – reference books and source material swapped for ledgers and accounting, the professor's desks used for drafting appeals for the public to submit words and definitions for the greater good.

Sophia said, 'I do hope no one will mind that I took myself on a small tour while you were all down there.'

'May I ask what you made of the place?'

'That central hall is really very extraordinary. I was quite taken aback! Quite the factory.'

Winceworth felt a fleeting twinge of jealousy that he could

not have fresh eyes for the place. He imagined Sophia walking between the desks – by *his* desk! – in the abandoned hall as if a tourist, required neither to be busy nor to appear to be busy as a worker might with the pressure of a job. He imagined walking through that room and being occupied only by leisure and delight. For him, the hall was now too strongly associated with the work done within it, synonymous with a cricked neck and hardened callouses on his middle finger from years of writing. No *pons pons pons* headaches from double-checking references seemed to crowd Sophia's mind as she walked through the heart of Swansby House, and no attendant thoughts of paper cuts, Appleton sniffs. *She* could walk as she pleased and treat the Scrivenery as if she had entered a cloister or a gallery depending on her mood, a grotto or an ossuary rather than hard-won glossary. He imagined Sophia reaching out a finger to one of the pigeonholed shelves on the Scrivenery wall, touching their pale blue index cards, impressed by their enterprise and prowess.

Even in the daydream this could not work as an image – he imagined her withdrawing her hand as if scalded.

Sophia said, 'Terence and I took a turn around a museum yesterday after our recuperative tête-à-tête in the café. He felt awful sending you away like that, you know. Terence cares so much about the blessed dictionary, and I do think it makes him a little inhumane. But he also said that he happened upon you back in the Scrivenery in the evening and I do hope he apologised – they have you working all hours of the day here, I must say.'

'He mentioned meeting me?'

'He did.'

'He did.' Frasham in the dark of the basement yesterday, the sweat on his brow, Miss Cottingham hiding behind the unused presses, their giggles in the dark. Winceworth examined his sleeve.

'Shall we return to the stairwell?' Sophia asked. 'I'm not sure this leads anywhere interesting.'

Winceworth let her take his arm and they doubled back on themselves. 'Perhaps Frasham mentioned to you how my trip in Barking panned out?'

'He did not. Anything of interest?'

The strange terrible colour that defied definition.

'No.'

'Language never sleeps, I suppose,' said Sophia, and she laughed. It was a tight, high laugh and one that Winceworth recognised. He could compile a whole dictionary of fake laughs. This one sounded like a feint he used when anxiety greased the mouth and sprained the throat – when he laughed like this it was to mask a voice that might otherwise break with emotion. As they walked, he watched her look up at the ceiling as if to compose herself.

'Miss Slivkovna—'

'That is not my name,' Sophia said, and again her tone was bright. As if this was an inconsequential fact. Winceworth halted. As she continued, however, he was compelled to scurry forward to keep pace at her side.

'I do beg your pardon,' he said.

'The fault is mine.'

Pons pons pons. 'You do not mean – I am addressing Mrs Terence Clovis Frasham?'

Sophia's real laugh flourished in the corridor and it was her turn to stop walking. She laughed in his face openly with guileless, true human joy.

'Not that, no! Strike that from the books!'

Winceworth cluttered.

'Dear God, you poor man, no!' Sophia wiped a mirth-borne tear from the side of her face. 'Ah, you'll excuse me.'

Winceworth waited.

'I am not used to giving my real name to anyone –' She broke off to stroke a Tits-cat sleeping by her feet – 'I'm afraid you caught me at a moment of improvisation when I introduced myself.'

'Unless I am mistaken,' said Winceworth, who was not, 'it was Frasham who introduced you by that name.'

'Is that right?' Sophia's laugh fluted upwards. 'A commendable eye for details, of course. I'm sure you're right. We are a good team, Terence and I – I do well to follow his lead in such things sometimes. Running with the line he has supplied, maybe elaborating on it a little. But I see I have upset you,' she said, frankly and with an apologetic moue, 'and I am sorry to have not told you the truth.' She straightened and smiled, looking easier about the eyes. 'Names after all, little peshka, should not matter so much.'

'I would not trust Frasham as far as I could throw him,' Winceworth said.

'No,' Sophia said, and she withdrew her arm from his.

'And perhaps – you'll forgive me – perhaps I understand more about him, of him, than you might already know.'

'I think I know most things. I know most things about many subjects, or many things about most subjects – whichever sounds better.'

Concision and decisiveness were more necessary than breath. 'I saw him yesterday,' Winceworth said. 'Yesterday, last evening—'

'In particular,' said Sophia, and they turned a corner at the head of the stairs, 'I imagine that you saw him in company?'

A cat head-butted Winceworth's ankle.

'And,' Sophia continued, 'perhaps he was in a state of some unparticular undress? Oh, peshka,' she said and touched his forearm, 'you do look *worried*.'

'I'm sorry,' he said. Then, louder, 'This does not matter to you?'

'Very little matters to me.' She squeezed his arm. She looked concerned only by his concern. 'Indiscretion, infidelity—' The thought seemed to leave her even as she spoke it, as if she found the subject entirely boring. She studied his face. Just five minutes before he would have given anything for such proximity to her, scrutiny from her. 'It doesn't particularly interest me, I suppose,' she said. 'If I may be candid with you, Mr Winceworth.'

'Of course,' he said.

'I am very aware of the way Terence likes to comport himself.' She made a face. 'But, really, will you listen to me – *indiscretion, comport*. So few days on this island and already I am so at home with using your obscure euphemisms.'

'*Comport, consort—*'

'*Cavort, contort.*' She joined in as one enjoying a word game, glad to be egged on. 'You have your secrets too, I think?' Winceworth said nothing and Sophia paused, then raised her gaze to the heavens. 'You think me cruel for saying so. You are hurt.'

'It is not for me to say.' Winceworth let her finish another entirely winning laugh. He set his jaw. 'Frasham is an idiot.'

'The very definition of an idiot,' Sophia said. 'He is a useful idiot, however. And quite sweet: he said he would make sure *Swansby's* puts an emphasis on Russia in the entry on *chess* just for me, which I think as close to a love-gift as an encyclopaedic article can get.'

'Why are you here?'

'In truth,' said Sophia, and she deflated to see any game was not in the offing, 'it was to make sure that you received an invitation to the party this evening. I can promise you it will be a more lively event than the one at which we first met.'

'You know about this evening?'

'You are speaking to the one who organised it.'

Sophia Unslivkovna enjoyed Winceworth's incredulity, gently joshing him with an elbow. 'Terence said that you would be too delicate for it or find it distasteful, but I just know you'll enjoy it. Loosen those limbs. What could a lexicographer enjoy more than the explicit? Now, no need for such a serious determined little face, Peter.'

Peter the prude. Peter the lisping prissy prig. The shock of hearing his name from her lips did not flip the room upside down or cause his heart to explode with a strange new colour. Winceworth moved his arm away. 'I am afraid I have plans this evening.'

'Nonsense,' said Sophia. 'You are a terrible liar and I would like you to come. I command it.'

'*Command?*'

Sophia rolled her eyes. 'I do not just describe the invitation but also prescribe it. Come! Relax! A bit of sport amongst some statues and *whathaveyou*.'

'It is the *whathaveyou* that makes this ghastly,' Winceworth said.

'Ghastly, oh, dear God,' said Sophia. 'I am quite serious that it will be worth your while.'

'It is – unseemly—' Winceworth said, but he muttered it and she did not seem to be brooking his answers.

'I don't mean *worth your while* because of – heavens, whatever it is that frightens you so – muckiness and daubing your fingers with debauchery—'

'Please do not mock me, Sophia,' Winceworth said, and he tried to face her down.

'I would not dare,' Sophia said. 'I am sorry.'

She leaned forward, and kissed him, softly, *x* on the cheek.

'There is a password you have to say this evening, to get in,' she said. 'Terence was laughing earlier at the thought of you being stranded at the door, lisping guesses at shibboleths. Say you will be there,' she said.

Winceworth did not move. She approached as if to whisper in his ear, but he turned his head and stepped back a little. She laughed, then, a full clear laugh and then she took her leave, descending the stairs just as the staff of Swansby House entered. They doffed their hats to her each in turn as they pooled in through the door.

She glanced up the stairs to meet his eye, but Winceworth was no longer to be seen.

Y is for *yes* (exclam.)

I could mention some of the nouns, verbs and adjectives of the aftermath. I could select the best of all of these or select the ones that seem most obvious or most relevant to me, or the ones that are generally agreed upon as the most useful, appreciable, evocative. I could also take the time to arrange an account of what happened there on the Westminster pavement as Swansby House shrouded in smoke in front of us, and express it using an order that is cogent and coherent and concise. That would be a responsible thing to do.

Simply put is best put.

So what happened? Fire engines added their sirens to the yawp of Swansby House's alarm. That's something I remember very clearly, as well as the lines of people gathered outside – *the second time today!* – where they all stood rubbing their faces or covering their mouths and taking photographs of the building. Everyone looked shocked, baffled, curious. They scattered back a few paces and drew aside as Pip, David and I barrelled out of the burning building. We landed together in a spluttering heap at the bottom of the stone steps.

'Give them some air!' I heard. 'Give them some room!'

Maybe it was a firefighter or a member of this crowd that helped the three of us to our feet and away from the shadow of Swansby House. We were scooped and propped up next to some bollards across the road, and I remember someone checking Pip over. Apparently I was repeating her name as if looking for her even though she was close enough for me to look down and see her hand in mine. Someone else was administering to me, a man with a kind voice and a uniform that had lots of holsters and belt loops. I kept my eyes trained over his shoulder, watching Pip.

She caught my eye. She looked pale, with red-rimmed eyes and grey smudges across her forehead.

'Are you OK?' she asked. Her voice was hoarse, and she repeated the question so that it was a little clearer, calling it across to me despite us being so close together.

'I'm fine,' I said. It was an odd wheeze in the crisp and crisping air.

Pip waited a little, then she said, 'I'm fine too,' over the medic's shoulder.

She was. She is. Pip is fine. All the important facts.

So, what happened?

If I piece it together with hindsight, David must have been looked after by another paramedic nearby, someone who probably took the time to ask him questions while pointing up at the building. Pip recalls seeing David nodding to the medic as if in conversation but it struck her he did not seem to be really listening. David had got hold of Tits: the cat was nestled in his arms beneath his woollen jumper and I could tell from the movement beneath the fabric that Tits had set about palpitating David's shirt-front with his paws. If I knew Tits at all, he was probably crooning and purring. This is a detail that will not make the police reports, nor the newspaper columns nor the trivia books that list the evening's events in their pages, but as I watched David Swansby watching his empire burn to the ground, I saw two furry ears and the top of Tits's head appear up his collar. Momentarily *Swansby's* final editor stood there chimerically two-headed, some greasy residue from the fire stamped in a mask of soot across his eyes.

I remember one of my hands was in Pip's and that with the other I was gripping the dossier of false entries close to my chest.

But, what *happened*?

Onlookers stepped up their *ooh*s and *ahh*s as a snicking burst of glass came from above. As a group we all instinctively ducked and looked up: in Swansby House, flames were visible from the window of the room where Pip and I had been working just minutes before. *Dictionary as accelerant.* Red and orange tongues lanced into the evening sky. Two tourists took a picture of it.

'Is there anybody else in there?' someone asked me and surely I shook my head. Pip tells me that at this point she had shifted her eyes to David Swansby. He was watching the blaze with the crowd and absently patting the cat's head at his neck. He had the look of a man embarrassed that he could not go down with his ship, she said.

Later, Pip explained exactly what she saw when she ran into David upstairs in the dusty, smoky rooms above my office. She had noticed at once that there was a mobile phone kicked aside or dropped by his shoes, its screen still bright with use, and as she rounded the threshold of the room she had found David frantically trying to extinguish a small blue fire springing from a parcel in his hands. We now know that this was a bomb with a timer. David had messed up setting this timer – 'I'm a words man, no good with numbers!' he later joked in the stand, getting not one laugh from the galleries – and had ended up igniting the incendiary prematurely. He admitted this fact in court with a sad defeated shrug.

Pip said she recognised the smell at once, the dull sour tang of electrics fusing and melting.

'He looked aghast,' Pip told me, using a word that sat ungainly and uncomfortable in her mouth. On the evening of the fire she recounted to police officers as precisely as possible what she had seen, then repeated this to different officers at the station, and then again months after that she used the same words in court, wearing a blazer she only ever used for weddings, funerals and job interviews. Each time she chose her words carefully and tried not to get emotional as she *imparted*, *divulged*, *disclosed* the truth whole truth and nothing but the etcs of what she had seen, spelling out the scene as best she could remember. Yet even as I heard it, even as she asked me to check her account for errors or slip-ups, doubting herself, somehow I would not fully let myself believe the truth of what had happened for months. It is hard to shift from one way of understanding the world.

It was certainly impossible to ignore aspects of the facts, however, thanks to the frenzy of press reports and online articles. It began the very night of the fire, with editorials speculating what had happened in the Sad Final Days of Erstwhile Great British Institution *Swansby's Dictionary*. There, my quiet, boring days at Swansby's were suddenly transformed into something far more operatic and formidable. I noticed that every picture printed of David Swansby during this time was edited ever-so slightly before it was published, its filters or colour saturation twiddled infinitesimally so that any discernible cragginess of the editor's face, any hint of a scowl or glower, became supremely emphasised. At the time of the fire I remember him standing mildly and blankly by the SW1H kerbside, looking up at Swansby House and cradling his cat. He might have been humming on a promenade, he seemed that calm. The pictures of him that were snapped that evening and appeared in newsprint, however, had an undeniable air of Vincent Price or Christopher Lee to them.

I noticed also that a number of photographs from that evening had been assiduously photoshopped before they were published so that the cat's ears were removed from the neckline of his jumper. The inexplicable streamlined, the not-relevant smoothed away so that it was not too distracting.

But, *what* exactly *happened*?

One could turn to published accounts. The story in the

press ran thus: heir to a depleted, now–derisory and undeserved fortune and with his family name and its legacy in tatters, David Swansby had been driven mad with financial instability and embarrassment at his folly of a dictionary. All of the spurious and gossipy tabloid accounts of what took place that night prove quite a fun read if you lay the pages out and sift through the fictions. Words like *dastardly*, *bungled*, *diddle*, *dodge* and *hoax* crop up with particular prevalence. I remember that one headline even had a spin on some kind of NOT-SO HARMLESS DRUDGERY pun, above a picture of David sitting in a police car looking baffled. The story ran for about a week that *Swansby's Dictionary* – a 'national treasure' (SEE ALSO: *eccentric, laughable, barely tolerated*) – had run into such economic hardship and existed with such a skeleton staff that its final editor had tried to pull off an insurance fraud of epic, combustible proportions.

According to these reports and much like *Swansby's* infamous editorial probity, the plan had been overly complicated and disarmingly, quaintly ludicrous. David Swansby posed as a hoax bomber and made various threats against the dictionary. He wanted the building gutted, razed and useless so that a big insurance cheque could wangle his way – blame being laid at the feet of anonymous misguided fruitcakes. No harm in that, surely!, and the Swansby name would not be left a laughing stock. In complete tatters, yes, but with some bruised and noble honour attached to it. This way, the narrative ran, the dictionary would not simply dwindle away in the public consciousness as was his greatest fear. *Go out with a bang.* It appeared that he hoped to get away with it all. He thought he would be recognised as the presiding, grieving steward who was there to the last when the dictionary's once-bright light was so violently snuffed out.

Can't buy that kind of publicity.

Of course, I was also called in to have my say and put things into my own words and explain what my experiences at Swansby's had been. *Did I ever suspect David was behind the bomb threats? Do you think this was his plan all along, or was it a hoax that backfired? How could he hide in plain sight?* And Pip was asked similar questions too, where the tone was accusatory rather than exploratory – she wasn't supposed to be in the building, had no authority there: what was her story? But the second that David Swansby confessed, these interviews melted away from our lives.

Pip and I read the reports with incredulity, intrigue. People who barely knew us took the time to remind themselves of our numbers. Whereas before the fire, mention of *Swansby's Dictionary* might elicit conversations about unfinished grand projects and the Lost Generation, now they all began with a nod and a wink about insurance. I did my best to dispel this whenever journalists got in contact or I overheard conversations in Pip's café, but it was a new, tasty, excellent fact. It was stated as such in the dictionary's Wikipedia page on the evening of the fire, and that part of the article became the largest section with the most citations. The rest of the dictionary's history has been eclipsed.

★

To my knowledge, no papers ever made any mention of mountweazels, nor *Swansby's Dictionary* as something contaminated by false words. I hope David thinks of that as a triumph or at least some small consolation.

For years later, every time I read about it – what should it be called: the *case*? Episode? What word fits the bill? – I felt myself become a tangle of question marks. I could not help but scour each and every article to see whether I was mentioned. Not once. No one cares about a hired anonymous amanuensis when such a blundering cartoon villain is at the centre of a story. I *could* have been a nice footnote, I suppose, or cast sympathetically as the naïve patsy in a devious, dog's dinner of a plan. My fielding of these 'threats' on the phone was all part of the scheme, of course. My existence meant that David could provide ample evidence to any insurance brokers that there had been foul play.

'You'd make a wonderful patsy,' Pip said when I voiced this thought. 'My favourite stooge.'

We learned to laugh about it, for each other's sakes.

The truth of it is: I liked David Swansby. He was a sweet man who loved words and played chess with ghosts.

The truth of it is: I hate that this story became about David, a man who dedicated his life to neatly tying things up in a way that he could control, condensing and codifying and arranging. The truth of that corridor and that room filled with fire? The truth *there* was the indefinable leap in my blood and the lurch in my heart when I saw Pip wreathed in smoke. I had put her in danger, for a definition – I had smuggled her into danger, and I was at fault. *Fault.* There's a word for you, and what good is language when your faltering mind is racing faster than your hands, when all you are is guilt and scorching sadness and confusion all at once? Every time I remember that day, it's not about the events so much as the twang of the bomb-threat's voice decoder in my ears, the thud of blood in my temples, the taste of acrid smoke and fear. Every time I remember what happened, I'm not recalling reasons or explanations so much as a keening hurting truth that I'd risk everything for a person half-obscured.

I don't know that I have ever felt clarity like this: the anger at what a waste of my time all this was. My job at Swansby's had been meaningless. Or rather, I did not know its meaning. I was a small part of a small part of something over which I had no control, and I was angry that abruptness and confusion had almost brought the end-frame *FIN* about my ears. I hate that high up in an obscure dictionary house I was suffused in and bamboozled and trampled over by language, and then in a second was forced to realise I was finite, and indefinite, disposable. I hate that David Swansby *arbitrarily* chose the guise of a madman or evangelist hell-bent on wishing I was dead, and that this cruelty was not done with any understanding that it was cruel.

If I think back now about the bomb threats, there was a horror in not knowing who wanted to kill me. That was a definable horror – someone did not know me, but thought they knew that I stood for everything that was wrong. The horror now is different. I'm not sure which is worse: that someone anonymous is out there and wants to hurt you in particular, or that your hurt is something by-the-by, easily folded into some grander, spurious project.

I always disliked the expression *sticks and stones may break my bones but words can never hurt me.* It is one of the least useful ways of understanding one another, or how words work.

The truth of it is: I ran out of a building not knowing what was going on, wanting only for my loved one to be safe.

A truth of it is: I changed in a small way that evening. Not particularly profoundly, unless you count the grit that is still embedded in my elbow from where I fell, grit that will probably stay with me for as long as I have skin. The change happened when I watched Pip dust herself off and tell me she was fine. Some new feeling flooded in. I don't know if I had ever *hoped* before like that, indiscriminately.

The truth of it is: here's to tying things up, and to change, and to hell with neatnesses.

I did not go back to the site of Swansby House, and I did not speak to David ever again. I received a letter from him while he was in custody, sent to my home address. In it he said that he was sorry. The letter was spelled well and grammatically perfect. Characteristically, he was also at great pains to reassure me that Tits was being looked after but did not mention who I should contact in order to be paid.

That is by-the-by. So much is. Keep it salient, keep it sprightly, keep it imprecise. *Simply put* is impossible, and not the way for me.

★

So, what happened?

It is true to say that Pip and I huddled together for a moment by the roadside and looked on as Swansby House caught ablaze. There was a small explosion followed by a larger one, and in an instant scraps of burning paper flew from the windows of the building. We stepped back, compelled by the heat.

A police officer asked, pointing at Pip and I, 'Are you two together?'

And I said, simply, 'Yes.'

I tightened my grip on the envelope of false entries. Pip pressed her arm against mine and amongst a group of strangers we watched as loosed paper flew up and out of a building, dispersing on a breeze – words suspended and newly cooling, as paper met ash met star met nothing, and quickly it all meant nothing at all in a quiet night sky.

Z is for *zugzwang* (n.)

A museum at night is full of a strangeness of shadows. Arte-facts loom out of niches and recesses with oddly heavy eyelids, or with mouths that appear to open an inch as you stroll by. Winceworth dressed in an approximation of his finest suit, and waited in a side street outside the British Museum, until an hour where night fused with morning. At three o'clock, a group of men and women passed him and walked towards the building. They were swaddled against the cold but gave occasional glimpses of finery: *chiffon* and *mousseline de soie* twitched beneath their wraps and stoles. A figure appeared in a sudden slice of light, a doorman with a cigarette at his lips. Words were exchanged and Winceworth watched as the party was ushered inside.

He steeled himself, *I'll show her, I'll show her,* and made his move across Montague Street. The doorman looked him up and down.

'Do you know the password?' he asked.

'I do not,' said Winceworth.

And honesty being the best policy, the man shrugged and Winceworth was shown into a bare anteroom. There, a very quiet, polite young man in an acid-yellow waistcoat welcomed him and confirmed that he was indeed here to attend tonight's *revelries*. Winceworth was so tired and felt generally so numb that he did not even roll his eyes at this ridiculous noun.

'I'm here for the fundraiser,' he said.

'So much to raise,' the young man said, and Winceworth saw his eyes brighten with the zest of euphemism. 'This way, sir. And, sir,' the young man said, 'I am sure you understand that the festivities are intended to be a private affair and I ask that upon leaving the grounds, you are not necessarily indiscreet regarding either the proceedings, your fellow attendees, the nature of the artwork—'

Winceworth let the young man run his excited patter, and let his words bounce off the parquet flooring and stuccoed walls as he walked through dark hallways and passageways. He knew these corridors vaguely through incidental trips to the Reading Room, or weekend visits attempting to find interest in a schatzkammer of *things* rather than *words* as a reprieve from Swansby House. They were walking at such a brisk pace, however, that any sense Winceworth might have had of which part of the museum they were passing or which direction they were facing was soon lost. They continued through heavy doors and skipped down side corridors. The only sound was the tap of their footfall until, after what seemed an age, Winceworth heard the clink of glass and strains of music marbling in the air. Around a final corner, and the refined, honeyed light of candles pooled in a splash across the floor. His companion drew back a velvet curtain,

fnuck—

★

What is there to say of the party, when he found it? The decoration of course should take prominence. He had heard of the Secretum and its contents, its Bacchic marbles, tableaux, statues, pieces of masonry, cups, jewellery – all obscene and all on show for the chosen few. These were artefacts that were deemed too contentious or deemed corruptingly erotic for public display, and yet here they all were in their cases and on plinths and on candle-lit vitrines. Winceworth saw a thrusting, bristling, orgy of treasures.

Dr Johnson once remarked 'I hope I have not daubed my fingers' when congratulated on the omission of certain improper words in his *Dictionary*. It's a prevailing notion, Winceworth thought as he passed a glazed fritware vase, expertly rendered to be some monumental ceramic ode to priapism. The idea that vulgarity should not necessarily enter dictionaries unless it can be appreciated on some rarefied, philological level was pretty standard. Some of the objects on display were clearly from antiquity, carefully dusted and polished so that every nook and crevice was shown to greatest effect. Marble figures' textures had been made to look plashy and dewy by masters of their craft, and the curator tasked with writing exhibition catalogues would be hard-pressed to find synonyms for *buxom*, *straining*, *lewd*, *rude* and *crude*.

The artefacts were not limited to sculpture. Winceworth edged about the room, he glimpsed scenes depicted in frescos and on terracotta tiles that would make ivory blush. Here was a sketch of two witches delighting in the lack of laundry bills; there a zoetrope of a man finding a delightful new hobby with the assistance of a shoehorn and a pat of butter. It was a raucous, riotous, preposterous collection of anything and everything that could titillate, shock and arouse.

Winceworth looked upon it all with a remote curiosity. Rather than the things that were thronging and dripping and rearing so abundantly in these rooms, it was the people that compelled him to stand and stare. The space was packed, waiters navigating their trays at dangerous and devious angles in order to cross the space. Clearly the 1,500 Mile Society had been just a taster for potential funders of Swansby House – this was another order entirely. It might have been Winceworth's imagination, but everyone had a predatory gleam in their eye, sly, wild, seeking pleasure and appreciation. The air was heavy with loud laughs and the richest perfumes, and it seemed as if every shoulder he passed was dressed in expensive furs or some filigree or other denoting fashion. Here, under lock and key, the mood was tinged by the spirit of the artefacts and objects in the room.

As Winceworth turned on his axis, vying to take everything in, he saw the partygoers as if in a series of friezes. Here was his colleague Appleton mid-sniff, disporting over a glass of Vin Mariani, here Bielefeld miming something grimly lascivious by a Roman bust in order to impress a ring of young women. He could have been mistaken, so pressed together were their bodies and so doggedly did he have to fight to see over so many jostling shoulders and outstretched arms, but Winceworth thought he even caught sight of

Dr Rochfort-Smith across the room. If indeed it was he, the elocutionist's finger was at another member of the faction's lips, cooing and guffawing above the sound of the – what, the lute? Mandolin? Oud? Winceworth looked to see the source of the music and recognised the band from the 1,500 Mile Society, their sombre black suits swapped for rich silks and satins.

Everyone's faces were flushed and their mouths were wet and open. Their heat was set in stark contrast to the cool of the marble and silver artefacts around.

An arm snaked through his.

'Not quite your scene, perhaps?' said Sophia, close to his ear.

Winceworth glanced at her. He noted her finery, that she had never looked better and more awful, then looked back at the crowd.

'You think me prudish.'

'No,' she said. She looked a little bored. 'But I do wonder if you have any words for it all. Not too debauched? Just a hint of bauch? I was speaking to Glossop earlier, about one of your great rivals. He told me that the *Encyclopædia Britannica* defines "nudities" in painting and sculpture as "denoting those parts of a human figure which are not covered by any drapery, or those parts where the carnation appears".'

'I did not think to bring flowers,' Winceworth said. 'And you shouldn't believe everything you read in encyclopaedias.'

'That being so,' and Sophia plucked some imagined fluff

from Winceworth's lapel, 'all of this should bring in a pretty penny for old Gerolf, so we can't be too picky.' Sophia moved her head to indicate her fiancé over by the velvet curtain. Frasham was miming the stance of the Laocoön sculpture with a feather boa. 'Terence has already got a couple of politicians to stump up over a good couple of hundred pounds, and I'm working on an opera director—'

'You must be very proud.'

'We make a good team,' she said.

'You have said so before.' Winceworth adjusted his glasses. 'You also called him a useful idiot.'

'He moves in such circles here in London, quite charms a whole host of prospective buyers. Excellent for securing money for Frasham, and all the better for making sure I secure some safe ground for myself.'

Winceworth translated, after a pause, 'You need him for the money.'

She made a dismissive noise. 'No, no – although, it is not so terrible an addition to his charms.' Sophia drummed her fingers against her skirts. 'It is useful to establish a suitable and reputable base for oneself, however, in order to allow various indiscretions and eccentricities to be overlooked. Even if they happen in plain sight!' She seemed keen to change the subject, not so much out of embarrassment but out of tedium, looking to change the pace or stakes of their conversation. She steered his elbow slightly, repositioning him. 'Have you heard of the painter Zichy?' she said, blurting as if on impulse and not wanting to wait for his response. 'He was a court artist for

Tsar Alexander – and on the side did some quite extraordinary sketches of the human form! You understand. Here, look, they're up on this wall—'

'I thank you, no.' Winceworth stood his ground. 'No.' She appeared crestfallen. He looked in the direction she had motioned: a ring of excited potential funders were pushing their noses right up against whatever was mounted on the walls, roaring with delighted outrage.

'Ah. I posed for him, you know.' Despite himself, Winceworth let out a surprised chirrup, but Sophia went on as if describing the weather. 'The pieces are quite disgusting but quite wonderful. They'll come out one day, maybe, when the man is long dead.'

'I am not quite sure why you have taken me into your confidence on these matters,' Winceworth said. 'Other than you enjoy the thrill of scandalising me.'

She relaxed for the first time that evening, speaking with a new energy. 'That is exactly it! *Scandal* – yes! Repercussions, getting under the skin of something! But more crucially, yes, as you say, *confidence* in one another. That's exactly the word for it – and what I thought when I first met you: here is someone who knows the value of confidences. And I am right, am I not? I sense it on you, smell it on you.'

'You can trust me,' Winceworth said. He was beginning to feel something crumble within him, any last vestiges of sureness and forbearance drain away.

'Terence is no good at that side of things,' Sophia said. They walked together arm in arm, passed a shelf with an array of obscene netsuke. 'We were just today talking about the words in English that might best describe his propensity to gossip or pass on someone else's business. *Tittle-tattle, blabber-mouth. Scandalmonger.* Great fun, of course,' she said, sighing, 'and an enviable swagger to it that I truly do admire, but no notion of *confidences.*'

'You have done very well to be in the position to enjoy such things.'

'You say this because you have not yet found the balance.' Sophia halted their pace and held him at arm's length, regarding him as a physician might an ailing man. 'You keep yourself all tight and closed-up. You are *all* confidences and *no* scandal, all battening down of hatches and no great spuming fray.'

'I hear the lady has taken a turn for the metaphorical!' said Bielefeld, eavesdropping and leering into their path. Winceworth and Sophia stared at him for a beat. Bielefeld hiccoughed an apology and scuttled off into the crowd.

'I have my secrets,' Winceworth said.

'But are they interesting ones?'

'I'm not – not at liberty to—' Winceworth felt the room spin a little as if he was drunk. He wished he was drunk.

'I apologise,' Sophia said curtly. 'I am thrilled to hear you have secrets. Your secret life: the most precious thing. You must define your own terms for that.' She smiled, and a part of Winceworth's heart felt good and sore at her frankness and her strangeness but already she had moved on, sighing at their surroundings with a theatrical tone meant for other people's benefit. 'I must not forget – I am on duty and should be charming for the sake of other's coffers. Fewer the-good-so-and-sos than the party where we first met,' she said, nodding, 'but the vulgar do have deep pockets.'

'I'm afraid I am not among their number.' He felt a little sick and a little giddy.

'But, I say,' Sophia said, catching his sleeve and pretending to look cross, 'about my chess set! The one that belonged to my countrywoman, the Tartuffe in skirts. I mentioned it to you before, I think.'

'I've seen enough.'

She regarded him, smiling. 'I'm sure you have.'

'You are toying with me, or trying to embarrass me,' Winceworth closed his eyes as if shutting out the whirls and juttings of the room might make things clearer to him, might make him seem more in control. 'Which is your right and I hope your pleasure. But I have had a long, long day and I would thank you if you could do me the courtesy of—'

Sophia was not listening. He opened his eyes to find her extending a hand towards him. It was not a grand sweep of arm as had been her usual mode this evening – rather, she brushed her fingers against his as they stood close together. It was a gesture designed to not be seen by anyone around them. She passed him something. He took it like an automaton, and he felt a new heaviness in his hand – small and cold – as her glove touched his fingers. She said, carefully and deliberately, so that he caught every word, 'A shame for you to miss it. Each pawn worth over seven hundred pounds alone.'

Winceworth accepted the gift and slid it into his pocket as

he raised his head to thank her or fully ascertain what she had done.

'You cannot mean—'

But Sophia had stepped away and was lost again in the crush and Winceworth, left wordless, let himself be swallowed by the crowd and their carousing. He cast about for some minutes, not recognising anyone, and not recognising any of the emotions on anyone else's faces. The band struck up once more and suddenly his shirt collar felt too tight and the air winched flat and thin about his lungs. He needed to not be confined, and to be somewhere unseeable. He thought of shrinking to one of the corners of the room, pressing his back against some shadowy part of the hallway where he would not be noticed or get in the way. He thought of the moonlight finding tildes and breves on the cobblestone outside, the stop-and-start kerning of London's early-morning traffic. And in his mind he imagined blending into the facelessness of its streets, and outward, *outward*, beyond the remits of the capital and onto paths and edges of maps where he did not know the names of landmarks or roads, down to the sea, or further—

He felt for the pawn in his pocket once more. He looked around the room at all of the lexicographers losing themselves in the moment. He thought about their pride in working for an encyclopaedic dictionary, gathering as many words and facts as possible under their jackets and stuffed into their pockets. He thought about their ambition, their hunger for it all to be set down *just so, just so.*

Setting his shoulders and with a fresh resolve and firmness

to his stride, Winceworth made for the door. Nobody noticed him slip out or challenged him as he traced his way back to the exit. Unimpeded, he began to make his way out of the corridors and dim passages to find the world beyond, its undefined futures, its waiting [SEE ALSO]s.

auroflorous (adj.), to escape at night, usually with a renewed sense of purpose(s). Obsolete

Acknowledgements and thanks

Small book, prolonged expressions of gratitude.

Thank you to the people who made this novel possible: my agent Lucy Luck, and the patient and tenacious editors Jason Arthur and Lee Boudreaux with their teams.

I am indebted to Royal Holloway, University of London for the research scholarship that allowed me time to fall over/into/between dictionaries. Sincere thanks to Judith Hawley and Kristen Kreider for their insights and candour throughout my studies: thank you for your confidence. Thanks also to Patricia Duncker and Richard Hamblyn for their invaluable critiques, comments and kind words, and to Andrew Motion and Robert Hampson for their early encouragement and conversation. Thank you to my colleagues and students in the English department for animating me.

I could not have written any of this without the aid of a number of institutions and organisations. Thanks to the Society of Authors for a Writers Grant in 2017. Thank you to the University of Greenwich for having me as writer-in-residence in 2018, and to Jonathan Gibbs at St Mary's University for support at a crucial time. Thank you for the boost, space and thoughtfulness of the MacDowell Colony: thanks to all that work and worked there, galvanising so much. Thanks, Clare Sole.

I am much obliged to Beverley McCulloch for her assistance in the OUP archives and to curator Davey Moor for helping me see Mountweazel-related exhibition images from the Monster Gallery in Dublin. In terms of the history of lexicography, two books I always kept close at hand were Jonathan Green's *Chasing the Sun: Dictionary-Makers and the Dictionaries They Made* and Simon Winchester's *The Meaning of Everything: The Story of the Oxford English Dictionary*. Fiction only knows and can tell the half of it.

Some elements of this book first appeared in small press publications and online journals: thanks, Jo and Sam Walton at Sad Press! Thanks Soma Ghosh at 'The Demented Goddess'! Thanks Suze Olbrich at *Somesuch Stories*!

Thank you to all long-suffering friends for their zhushing and guidance (witting or otherwise). Specifically, thank you Špela Drnovšek Zorko, Prudence Bussey-Chamberlain, Nisha Ramayya, Matt Lomas, Timothy Thornton, Joanna Walsh, Robert Weedon, Copy Press, Oli Raglan & Jenny Selvakumaran & Rachel Lambert & Victoria Schindler, A & A & E & E & I & M & S & S & X, and the good people of Twitter who clarified words' sillinesses and strangenesses. Thanks for your company.

Nell Stevens   *superlative*, adj. and n.

To my family: thank you.

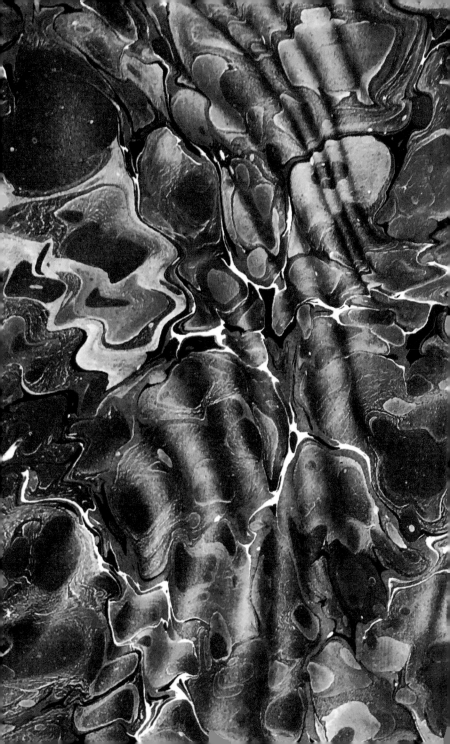